TARTARUS FALLS

TARTARUS FALLS

Titan Bound, Book One

Brian Bychek

TARTARUS FALLS

© 2025 Bychek Creative LLC

Published by Bychek Creative LLC
ISBN: 979-8-9943065-0-5

Interior design by Brian Bychek

Printed in the United States of America

First Edition

For my wife and children—

the reason I fight for every impossible thing.

CHAPTER 1

The backyard felt like a pressure cooker ready to blow.

String lights trembled overhead, trembling not from wind but from vibration — the chanting, stomping, roaring energy of a crowd packed shoulder-to-shoulder around a folding table and a half-dead Bluetooth speaker blasting Drake on distortion. Chlorine dried tight on Jack Callahan's skin. Sweat, hops, cheap beer, and heat clung to everything. Plastic cups crushed underfoot.

Someone had passed out in a hammock that belonged to no one here. Jack clocked faces automatically — old teammates, coworkers-of-coworkers, strangers who already felt like they'd forget his name by next weekend.

Baseball-rules pong. Final cup.

Patch — thick-necked, forearms knotted, a man whose entire worldview revolved around the sanctity of push-ups — tossed Jack the last ball like it was some relic salvaged from a tomb.

"Finish it, LEGEND!" Patch bellowed. "FIELD OF GLORY POINT!"

The crowd fell silent with exaggerated intensity, hips swaying, breaths held. Jack exhaled through his nose, arm loose, wrist steady — a familiar flick from college nights wrapped in smoke and bragging rights. There was a muscle memory to it now; his hand knew what to do even if the rest of him had no idea where his life was going.

The ball arced.
Perfect.
Dead center.

The lawn erupted.

1

They were on him instantly. Hands under arms, palms gripping shoulders, lifting him like a trophy. The chant detonated:

"JACK! JACK! JACK! JACK!"

Patch locked him onto his shoulders and spun once, nearly tipping over the keg. Confetti tubes popped. Someone launched a beach ball into orbit. A cannonball hit the pool and exploded water all over the grass like a baptism by chaos.

Jack grinned, shirt half-untucked, hair flattened by dried chlorine. Lean, athletic, the kind of build that only looked impressive in flickering yard lights after a win. People slapped his back hard enough to bruise, shoved cups into his hands. For a moment he felt suspended above his own life — weightless, triumphant, young in a way that already felt temporary. Some small, quieter version of him watched from the back of his own skull, taking notes like, *Remember this. This is the part they'll swear was the good old days.*

But the thought slid in anyway.
Like a razor under the ribs:

Is this as good as it ever gets?

The question didn't arrive as self-pity so much as inventory, a quick audit of every almost he'd been collecting. He'd won a lot of nights like this and somehow still felt like he was losing the long game.

He forced the smile bigger, pretending the doubt wasn't there. The night air warmed his face. And then a breeze slid through the yard — cold, precise, strangely contained, rattling the hanging bulbs above.

No one else noticed.
He did.

"MAKE THE NAME BIGGER ON THE T-SHIRTS!" Patch yelled from somewhere below. "I'M BOOKING THE TATTOO TUESDAY!"

Jack laughed because it was easier than asking why that moment felt like a goodbye to someone he didn't realize he'd already been.

The chant rose again—

"JACK! JACK! JACK—"

—and then the sound warped.

Not his name.
Not cheers.
Just fluorescent humming.

He jerked awake at his desk, cheek stuck to his keyboard, spacebar imprinted on his skin. His collar smelled faintly of stale hops and chlorine even as office air stung it sterile. For a heartbeat he didn't know which version of himself was the dream — the backyard legend or the guy drooling on a Dell.

"Jesus, man."
Alan leaned over the cubicle wall, eyes bright from too much caffeine. "I thought you flatlined. Was about to start drafting your eulogy. Something tasteful. Maybe with a slideshow."

Jack pushed upright, wiping drool away. "Closed my eyes for a minute."

"Looked longer." Alan pointed at the glossy patch on the keyboard. "You branded the hardware."

Jack blinked the office back into focus — grayscale mock-ups, faceless corporate headshots, bios for partners who'd never learn his name. A four-year degree in marketing, once dreaming of campaigns that stirred people, and here he was tightening jawlines on Chads. There'd been a time he'd imagined pitching work that made people argue in bars; now his biggest fight was over which shade of blue read "trustworthy but disruptive."

The HR fern in the corner had gnats again.
The kitchenette's Italian Sweet Cream bottle was empty. Always empty.
The faint tang of toner in the air felt like ink aging into dust.

He saw himself in the blackened monitor — tired eyes, dulled expression, the small erosion of drive that didn't happen in a day, but over a thousand small surrenders. The kid who'd once stayed up all night

3

rewriting ad copy for a pretend brand in college was now resizing logos for clients who skimmed decks on their phones.

Not miserable.
Just sedated.

Pay was fine. Benefits decent. Job stable. But somewhere between "entry-level" and "replaceable," he'd misplaced the hunger in his gut.

I want to matter — and I'm resizing Chads.

The thought hit cleaner, sharper this time.
No flinch.

He checked the clock: 5:04 p.m.

If he moved, he could still catch the PATH to Hoboken, then the 5:28 NJ Transit up to Mahwah. His usual commuter chain. Comfortable. Reliable. Colorless. There was safety in the ritual of it — the same stops, the same faces, the same two-second nods — but lately the predictability felt less like stability and more like track marks on a life he hadn't actually chosen.

He zipped his bag, slung it over his shoulder.

The building groaned.

A long, cavernous sound — like distant metal being bent by invisible hands.

Jack froze. "Did you hear that?"

The floor trembled. Monitors squeaked on their stands. Pens rolled off desks.

Alan leaned back in, voice suddenly tiny. "Please tell me that's construction."

"Hoboken doesn't get earthquakes," Jack said, steadying himself against the desk.

Lights flickered.
Once.
Twice.

4

The vibration thickened — not shaking, but pulsing. Something pressing outward rather than rattling.

Coffee mugs toppled.
Keyboard trays slid open.
The HR fern shivered like it knew the building was lying.

"DUDE," Alan gasped, clinging to the wall. "If this is the big one, I CALLED IT! SAN ANDREAS IS—"

"Alan—"

Ceiling tiles dropped.
Red strobes ignited.
Alarms shrieked, the sound shredding the air.

Jack shoved past bodies, lungs burning with dust. The stairwell became a crush of elbows and panic — stampeding strangers unified only by the identical shape of fear. Somebody started crying into a phone that had already lost service. Someone else laughed too loudly, the hysterical kind that breaks as soon as it runs out of momentum.

Halfway down, it hit.

Pressure.

Like altitude shift behind the eyes.
Ears popping.
Hair lifting along his arms as if charged.

Then sound — not rising from floor beams or ventilation — but emerging from everywhere at once.

A horn.

Deep.
Ancient.
Resonant enough to vibrate bone.

It didn't howl. It exhaled. A long, mournful note that didn't feel heard so much as embedded into the body. Something not human, not industrial, not emergency protocol. Older than the city. Older than architecture. It reminded him, absurdly, of the church organ his parents

5

dragged him to as a kid — that first heavy chord that made his sternum buzz — except this felt like the *sky* had decided to play him instead.

People screamed.
Prayed.
Filmed in frantic shock.

The horn rolled under the alarms, swallowed them, spoke over the building with a tone that felt like mass, like weight, like knowledge.

It resonated in Jack's ribs until his heartbeat nearly matched its rhythm.

He burst onto the street.

Glass glittered like ice across the pavement.
Cars sat skewed and sideways, alarms blaring in broken patterns.
A traffic light dangled from torn cables like a marionette with its strings cut.

And the Hudson… twisted.
Light refracted wrong.
Ripples moved against the current.
Shapes bent where they shouldn't.

People pointed skyward.
Others covered their ears.
One man just held his hand to his chest, gasping like the horn was speaking to his pulse.

Jack ran for Hoboken Terminal.

Inside, panic had hollowed into reverence.
Phone screens glowed "No Service."
Dust drifted like settling ash.
A baby's cry echoed sharp and lonely.

He dropped to a bench, chest still hammering. The aftershocks felt less like tremors now and more like the world adjusting into new geometry. Every time he thought the sound had faded, he caught the ghost of it again — in the buzz of the lights, in the rattle of the tracks, inside his own skull.

He checked his phone.

No bars.

Nothing.

The departure board flickered, scrambled, then steadied on a message that looked like defiance against the impossible:

5:28 NJ TRANSIT — MAHWAH — ON TIME

That shouldn't have offered comfort, but it did. Routine suddenly felt like oxygen.

The train eased in — half-occupied, passengers drifting on like sleepwalkers. No talking. No complaints. Just stunned silent bodies moving in patterns they didn't understand anymore. There was a strange politeness in the air, the way people get in hospitals and waiting rooms: careful, gentle, as if any sharp movement might shatter whatever was left of normal.

Jack followed, doors sealing behind him with a hiss that sounded final.

The carriage hummed — the fragile sound of motion. Not confidence. Not certainty. Just momentum.

Jack leaned his head to the window. The tunnel outside was black — not absence-of-light black, but origin-black, like the color before existence learned contrast.

His breath fogged the glass.

"What the hell was that horn?"

Lights flickered overhead.

And for a single impossible heartbeat — a split second so razor-thin it could've been imagination —

his reflection smiled first.

Then the lights stabilized.

Just Jack staring back.

But the chill lingered — not fear, not recognition — something in-between.

Something that felt like pressure.
Echo.
Memory.

He had the absurd feeling of being *noticed*, like the sound had taken roll and put a checkmark next to his name. The same part of him that had questioned the pong table victory now whispered that this, whatever *this* was, would not let him stay small.

And he knew, without knowing why, that whatever that horn was…

it wasn't over.

CHAPTER 2

The plan was simple in the group chat.
It always was.

Every year, the older brothers of Omega Chi trekked north to the woods of Mahwah — a cabin fading into its last useful decade, too much beer, a grill that survived purely out of spite, and three days pretending they weren't salaried men with health insurance and lower back pain. The invite always read like a joke, but everyone knew it wasn't; this was the one weekend a year they collectively agreed to still be idiots on purpose.

This year, the ritual overlapped with the Yahweh Music Fest — a sprawling EDM pilgrimage set up on the far fields past the tree line. Ten sober minutes through the woods. Thirty if you'd been playing shotgun beers with Lucas. Close enough that the bass rippled through your drink. Far enough no one could ever prove the noise violation. Jack had seen clips on social: light shows like alien invasions, kids in neon, the kind of weekend people pretended changed their lives and then went right back to spreadsheets.

Jack Callahan stepped off the train and stretched, vertebrae cracking after the Hoboken ride. The last amber of daylight caught in the branches overhead. The air smelled like wet cedar and old smoke — the cabin's signature scent, burned into memory. Every time he came back, it felt like stepping sideways into a version of himself that hadn't signed an employee handbook yet.

The smell always hit him the same way: nostalgia with teeth.

A horn shrieked up the road — long, deranged, continuous.

Aaron Whitlock's battered Tacoma rolled into view, wobbling like the shocks had given up on meaning. Horn still blaring.

Jack lifted a brow.
Aaron shouted through the open window, "Help me before the cops think I'm protesting democracy!"

Jack took his time crossing the parking lot. Aaron didn't lift his hand off the horn until Jack grabbed the passenger door. The blare drilled straight through his skull, too close to the memory of the morning's impossible sound.

"You're an idiot."

"Tradition," Aaron said proudly. Then lowered his voice. "Also yeah…it's stuck."

The moment Jack's seatbelt clicked, Aaron peeled out. The truck shuddered like a dying generator. Dashboard lights blinked cryptically.

Neither of them said it out loud, but the air still felt wrong from that morning — the tremors, the horn that seemed to come from inside the bones, the warped shimmer over the Hudson. Conspiracies were online before noon. Gas main collapse, covert military test, tectonic shift, biblical omen — nothing stuck. Every theory felt too small for what he'd felt in his ribs.

Aaron cranked the volume: The Killers, too loud not to be intentional.

"You good?" he asked without looking.

Jack stared out the window, trees blurring. "Just a weird day."

"My mom texted me to pray. I told her I recycle."

"Hero."

They laughed, but it didn't quite connect. The chuckle died too quickly, trailing off into the kind of quiet where both men decide not to say what they're actually thinking.

The deeper they drove, the quieter everything grew.
City hum fell away.
Even the air felt like it was holding back sound.

Not peaceful.
More like waiting.

By the time the Tacoma crawled up the final dirt path, the sun had vanished behind the ridge. The cabin appeared exactly as Jack remembered: porch sagging, railing crooked, and the same chipped WELCOME sign swinging by a single nail. The air thickened with wet cedar and smoke, more concentrated here, settling under the ribs. For a second he could almost believe the world outside the tree line hadn't changed at all.

Inside, Lucas Raines was mid-rant across the living room, beer in hand.
"If you draft two tight ends early, it's a mathematically sealed championship. Numbers don't lie."

Ryan Cho didn't look up from his phone. "You've been mathematically losing since sophomore year."

"Strategy," Lucas declared, "is a vision problem. Most people lack scope."

Aaron dumped his duffel near the crooked couch. "Gentlemen! Your heroes have arrived."

"Heroes?" Ryan muttered. "Still waiting on the twelve dollars you owe me for propane."

It was like walking back into a preserved version of himself.
Same faces.
Same bickering.
Same feeling that life could be simple.

For a while, that was enough. The rhythm of their nonsense settled over him like an old hoodie — frayed at the cuffs, still weirdly comforting. Part of him clung to it harder than usual, like if he laughed at the same jokes, the universe might roll back whatever it had started this morning.

The next hours blurred: headlights approaching through trees, subwoofer setup, music climbing into the treetops, laughter spilling across the porch. Younger brothers unloaded piles of beer they definitely weren't carded for. Someone tested the grill like it was defusing a bomb.

And beneath it all, Yahweh Fest's bass rolled through the ground.

A low-frequency thump that vibrated in the ribcage.

But for Jack, that vibration didn't feel like music.
It felt like the morning horn echoing inside him — deep, ancient, familiar in a way that scraped at instinct. It was like standing too close to train tracks and realizing the rumble you heard wasn't on the schedule.

He didn't tell anyone.
He just adjusted his jaw whenever the bass dropped, waiting for the pressure behind his ears to settle.

When most of the crowd headed for the festival lights through the trees, Jack stayed.

Lucas paused in the doorway. "You're not coming?"

"Crowds make me itch," Jack said. "And my ears won't stop ringing."

Lucas smirked. "You sound eighty."

Jack lifted a hand. "Enjoy the lasers, Grandpa."

And then he was alone with the "old guys" —
Aaron, Ryan, Lucas — all seated around the fire pit while the cabin emptied.

They lit the wood.
Smoke tangled upward, carrying that scent deeper:
wet cedar and old smoke.

They talked trash about fantasy drafts.
They roasted crooked burgers.
They let the beer loosen the stiffness adulthood left in the spine. The conversation slid easily from stupid college stories to mortgage rates and back again, a reminder of how much and how little had changed.

For a stretch of time, it almost felt like the world outside Mahwah didn't exist.

Except that hum.

It threaded under the bass whenever it pulsed from the festival — a tone too low to call sound. It vibrated through Jack's sternum like the after-image of the Hudson blast.

And every time he caught it, the pressure flared in his ears. He kept telling himself it was stress, or the beer, or some subwoofer trick, but the lie never fully landed.

Ryan tipped another log. Sparks drifted upward — but hung there a beat too long, suspended, before gravity remembered its job.

Jack blinked, shook his head.
No one else reacted.

"Tell me this isn't perfect," Lucas said, leaning back. "No bosses. No deadlines. No thirty-person Zoom where we pretend the world didn't shake this morning."

"Temporary perfection," Ryan said quietly.

Jack stood to clean up — more escape than duty. The others wandered inside for another round, leaving him in the clearing with the wind, the smoke, and the dying flame. For the first time all day, he realized he was actually afraid, not of earthquakes or collapsing buildings, but of the feeling that something had specifically *noticed* him.

The woods were unnervingly still.
Even insects had gone silent.

The hum climbed up through his shoes.

He poured what he assumed was water from the metal canister onto the coals.

WHOOSH.

Blue fire punched six feet high, roaring like pure accelerant.

Jack stumbled back. Heat blistered his skin. "Holy—"

Aaron appeared in the doorway, wide-eyed. "Bro. That's lighter fluid."

Jack forced a laugh, like that explained anything. "Guess I'm a scientist now." His heart was still sprinting, though, and the part of him that loved patterns filed this under *weird in exactly the same way the horn was weird.*

The wind shifted.

Hard.

Every tree bowed once — unified, synchronized, like something massive exhaled. Ash spiraled upward. The smoke didn't drift — it gathered, forming a column dead straight into the sky.

Jack's stomach clenched.

The bass from Yahweh Fest cut out mid-beat.

Silence dropped.
Not quiet.

Absence.

The hum surged — crawling up his spine.

Then the horn.

Faint, buried under distance, but unmistakable.
That same ancient tone he'd heard during the quake, rolling through the castle of his bones.

The flames paled, burning white.
The air thickened, heavy enough he had to fight for a breath.

"What... the hell..." he whispered.

Stars flickered overhead — like a few blinked.

The pressure behind his ears burst.

Sound died completely.

For one full second, the universe went mute.

No fire crackle.
No breath.
Not even the drum of his own pulse.

Just a vacuum.

Then impact.

A pressure wave slammed outward — no noise, just force, shoving him backward, rattling his teeth. The trees shuddered. Sparks shot skyward like meteors from a crater.

White light swallowed the clearing — blinding, violent, unfiltered. Jack hit the ground hard. Vision smeared. Shadows dissolved.

And through the glare he thought he saw something:
a figure, massive, carved from shape rather than light.
Not moving fast.
Moving deliberate.

It looked at him. Or through him.

He reached out a hand, grasping nothing, but air that felt newly alive. For a heartbeat, he had the insane certainty that whatever stood there knew his name without being told.

The light collapsed.
The fire went out.

So did he.

CHAPTER 3

Morning came with the soft hiss of wind through trees and the sizzle of bacon in a pan.

The cabin felt different. Not hangover-different—the cottonmouth, the bruised brain, the quiet promise to never drink again—but alive. The air hummed faintly, like the world had been plugged in overnight and was now purring on standby.

Jack blinked awake on the couch, still in last night's jeans, one shoe on, the other vanished into the pit of blankets and beer boxes. His head should've been pounding. His stomach should've been staging a coup. Instead, he felt... fine. Too fine. Vision clicked into focus fast, colors oversaturated, edges a touch too crisp, like someone had turned up the contrast on reality.

"Morning, Sleeping Beauty." Aaron hummed tunelessly while flipping bacon in a cast-iron pan. "You want your eggs runny or condemned?"

"Surprise me." Jack rubbed his face and squinted. "How are you functional right now?"

Aaron shrugged. "Beats me. I was ready to write my will at three a.m. Woke up feeling like I could outrun his Prius. Not gonna try it, but the confidence is there."

Across the living room, a body groaned and rolled off the couch, landing with a loud thud on the floor. Cocooned in a blanket, Lucas rolled onto his back and glared at the ceiling like it owed him money.

"Speak for yourselves. My mouth tastes like a chemistry experiment."

"You always smell like a chemistry experiment, so that checks out," Ryan said, seated at the dining table with his phone, thumbs moving, eyes not leaving the screen.

Lucas lifted a middle finger from the blanket. "No, seriously—how are you not dying? We crushed two cases. My liver drafted a strongly worded letter."

"Maybe you got old," Aaron said.

"I'm twenty-eight."

"Exactly."

The smell of breakfast spread—eggs, singed toast, and the cabin's permanent perfume of wet cedar and old smoke. Outside, birds argued like this was any other Saturday. Inside, something vibrated in the air, faint and steady, somewhere between sound and sensation—like standing too close to high-tension wires.

Jack noticed it when he rested his palm on the dining table. The wood grain ticked under his skin. Not a heartbeat. Not movement. Resonance. A low frequency you didn't hear so much as feel.

He pulled his hand back as if the table had shocked him.

"You good?" Aaron asked, sliding bacon onto a plate.

"Yeah. Static or whatever."

Jack drifted to the window. Morning light pushed through the trees in thick white shafts. Far off, the faint bass of the Yahweh Music Fest thumped through the ground—low, steady. But beneath it, there was something else. Deeper. Older. The same frequency that had plucked the world like a string last night.

Aaron thumped a plate onto the table. "Eat before you puke on that window."

Lucas's phone buzzed. He glanced down, then sat up straighter. "Uh... guys?"

"What," Aaron said without turning.

"Look."

He held the screen out. The corner TV was off, but the headline on Lucas's phone burned bright:

BREAKING: UNIDENTIFIED BEINGS DESCEND IN ROCKAWAY TOWNSHIP

A shaky livestream thumbnail showed a suburban parking lot: STOP & SHOP—AMC 12 behind the crowd. Rockaway, NJ.

"That's the one off 46," Aaron said. "Twenty-five minutes from here."

"Keep watching," Lucas said.

The feed stuttered and then caught. Panic in motion. Shoppers running. Carts veering in the parking lot. A kid crying. The camera jolted as something invisible hit the ground hard enough to rattle the mic. Screams spiked.

Then a voice—clear, measured, terrifyingly calm.

"Humans, do not fear. We come not as conquerors, but as guardians."

The words didn't come from the phone's tiny speakers. They bloomed behind Jack's eyes, as if someone had spoken directly to the thin place between thought and sound. His ears pressurized like a plane taking off. The air tasted faintly of ozone.

Aaron flinched, hand to his temple. "Did you hear that in your… head?"

Lucas's phone shook. "It says—Hermes. He's saying he's Hermes."

The shot steadied just enough to catch a figure hovering inches above the pavement: winged sandals, white-and-gold armor, hair like sunlight, a smile that didn't need a megaphone. The voice came again, resonant and painless this time, like he'd adjusted the dial.

"The Pantheon has returned. Your Pantheon has returned. We will protect this world from what stirs beneath it."

19

Car alarms staggered out of sync. The camera whipped sideways. The air rippled—and then they were there: Zeus—massive, regal, lightning crawling his forearms like living wire. Hephaestus—broad-shouldered, scarred, one hand glowing molten red as he pressed it to the grocery store's outer wall.

The building moved.

Brick buckled in a slow wave. Metal sighed and flowed. The AMC widened, stretched, rose. Cinderblock softened into polished stone, the roof peeling back into a gilded dome. The blocky red letters liquefied, ran, then reformed as carved characters older than the parking lot, older than the town, older than the country. People rushed out of the store, fleeing as fast as they could in any direction.

"That's not CGI," Aaron breathed.

Ground-level now: a shopping cart bumping a curb, tipping, skating before stopping dead. Wheels spun. One wheel squeaked. A stray kernel of popcorn popped under Hephaestus' heel with a tiny, absurd snap. Someone's bag of groceries burst—apples rolled like marbles, bottles clinked, a loaf of bread exhaled into flatness.

The chyron stamped across the bottom:

LIVE: ROCKAWAY TOWNSHIP — 9:42 AM, SATURDAY

"What are they turning it into?" Lucas whispered.

Hephaestus leaned back. A hammer formed in his palm from nothing but glowing metal and will. He lifted it once. Brought it down. The sound hit through the phone like a bass drop. The asphalt buckled. Stairs rose from the cracked lot, broad and clean and white, each step shedding gravel like old skin. Stone swept outward, swallowing spaces and oil stains. An amphitheater unfurled around the new entrance, seats carving themselves from the earth as if the hill had always been waiting.

Cars lifted and rolled, moving aside like toys in a bathtub wave. One sedan turned neatly ninety degrees and set itself down without a scratch. A minivan bounced, skidded, and came to rest with a sorrowful honk.

Zeus raised his hand.

Lightning dropped from a clear sky, spearing the lot in a perfect broken ring. No one was hit. Everyone understood. People stumbled backward, hands over ears. A woman's sunglasses flew off her head from the shock and skittered under a pickup, which promptly started honking as if offended.

Sirens wailed. Two cruisers fishtailed to a stop at the perimeter. Officers ducked behind doors, shouted orders nobody followed. A bullhorn crackled and died. Gunfire—reflex, not tactic—cracked the edge of the feed: sharp, panicked.

Bullets struck Zeus's chest and fell dull to the pavement. A few flattened against plates and dropped with small metallic sighs. He didn't flinch.

Hermes rose higher, so everyone could see, and everyone did. The next words slid in cleanly—no ear-pop, just a cool ribbon of sound threading thought.

"Your weapons are nothing. Leave now. You are under our protection," his voice said. Then, colder: "But not our mercy."

The feed hiccuped, pixelated, returned. The temple was taller now. Banners unfurled from nowhere. Marble columns grew like trees erupting from seed. In the distance, a drone drifted sideways as if pushed by a hand.

The cabin didn't move. The bacon hissed on a burner nobody remembered to turn off. Jack's lungs grabbed for air and found too much of it.

Aaron reached without looking and shut the stove. "So... we're not hungover."

"No," Jack said. "Definitely not that."

Lucas scrolled as headlines sprinted ahead of the anchors. "They're calling it 'The Return.' Officials telling people to stay home and indoors and to avoid gridlock on forty-six, Governor's office is—yeah— 'monitoring the situation.'"

21

"Classic monitoring," Aaron said, but the humor had been bled out of his voice.

Jack's palm drifted back to the window. The glass vibrated. Not much. Just enough to halo the edge of his fingers.

"You feel that?" he asked.

Aaron joined him, hand to the pane. "Dude... no."

Jack stared through the trees, toward Route 46. The hum in his chest deepened, found its twin in the air, and settled into it like a key in a lock.

Suddenly, silence stepped into the room like a person.

The TV coughed to life by itself. Volume spiked, then leveled. Aerial drone footage of the temple filled the screen—white stone, gold flashes, the crowd ringed back by barriers and common sense. Reporters chattered over each other. The anchor's voice wobbled.

"Authorities are warning residents to remain indoors. Multiple entities believed to be of... mythological origin... have been confirmed at the site. Witnesses report the name 'Zeus' shouted by onlookers just before—"

Static swallowed her. The picture stuttered. Then Hermes' voice wasn't on the TV anymore. It was everywhere. In the wood. In the glass. In their breath.

"Mortals," it said, calm and intimate, the words slipping directly into the part of the ear that had no name. "Do not be afraid. The Titans have stirred, and Olympus has returned to safeguard what is ours."

Jack's plate slid from his hand and shattered. Egg crawled over his shoelace. He didn't move.

The cabin seemed to tremble at the edges. The behind-the-eyes tingle sharpened into a gentle pressure that was almost... pleasant, if being softly pinned by a hurricane could be pleasant. He tasted ozone. The air smelled briefly like summer rain and power stations.

"They are in New Jersey," Aaron murmured, as if the specificity were worse than the god.

The windowpanes rattled hard enough to chatter. The hum peaked. For a breathless instant, Jack felt the line that separated inside from outside go thin. He felt the space his body took up in the room and the space between molecules in the air around him—felt them both, like a coin flipped to show its other side.

And then it ended. Not gradually. Like a switch. The TV died. The forest exhaled. A late bird scolded the silence back into motion.

Jack couldn't step away from the glass. The pulse on the other side had faded, but it wasn't gone. It wasn't random either. It had rhythm. It was focusing. Not in the sky. Not in the trees.

On him.

Jack jerked back and away from the window.

"Everything okay?" Aaron asked, half-turning.

Jack swallowed. "Yeah. Thought I saw… nothing."

He couldn't say it out loud. The wind shifting like it waved at him to come outside. The sentence sounded like he had a concussion.

Lucas had turned the TV back on with the remote like technology still meant something. News anchors tag-teamed disbelief. A lower-third ran out of ways to say LIVE.

"Do we call somebody?" Lucas asked, quieter now. "Who do you even call? You don't dial 911 and say, 'Hi, Zeus parked on the AMC.'"

"Your mom," Aaron said automatically.

"She'd tell me to bring a sweater," Lucas said, managing a thin grin.

Ryan joined them at the window. "If they can speak into our heads, they can probably hear us too?"

"I don't love that," Jack said.

"Me neither."

They stood like that—four guys in a cramped living room that smelled like breakfast and last night's fire, trying to measure a world that

23

had decided to be mythic before coffee. The rest of the partiers who came back after the music fest ended were scattered around the living room in various sleeping bags with pillows, book bags lining the halls half-open and lazily left there.

A helicopter thudded somewhere distant. Car alarms—plural—picked up again, a staggered chorus. A dog down the hill barked, reconsidered, barked once more because dogs respect no pantheon.

"What now?" Lucas asked. The question was too big for the room.

"Now we don't do anything dumb," Aaron said, surprising himself with the steadiness in his voice. "We wait. See if the roads even move. Pack up, and head home?"

"Pack for what?" Lucas shot back. "For the Return of the Gods? Shorts and a light jacket?"

"For being not here," Aaron said. He nodded toward the trees. "I don't think being near anything loud is smart."

Jack felt the wind tease the doorframe, press under it, taste the room. It circled the ceiling once, slow, affectionate, like a dog that considered the house partly its own.

"Okay," he said. "We do the boring smart thing. We pack up and head out, and stop doomscrolling like it's cardio."

Lucas muttered, "You sound like my therapist." He locked his phone, shoved it face-down, then picked it up again, because why not.

Aaron moved to the sink to rinse a mug. He turned the faucet. The stream hit porcelain and flared—just slightly—like a flame catching a hidden breath. He blinked, turned it off, then on. Normal again. He set the mug down carefully, like it might complain.

"Anyone else feel... better than they should?" Jack asked, finally naming it. "Not just rested. Like the air is helping."

Aaron opened his mouth to laugh it off and didn't. "Yeah," he admitted. "Like my lungs got a software update."

Lucas rolled his eyes, but only because habits die slow. "Cool, cool. Love that for us. Meanwhile: gods at the grocery store."

Ryan leaned against the counter, eyes on nothing. "Whatever last night was—it wasn't just a light show. Something touched the world. The horn. The wind. Then the gods show up the next morning, already talking Titans. Like they knew what to call it."

Jack concentrated on the space between his ribs. The hum answered —quiet, steady. Not words. Not even emotion. A… presence. Loyal. Attentive. The way a thousand invisible hands might hold you up without mentioning the effort.

A light rap on the door made all four of them jump. They stared at each other, nobody moving.

"It's probably one of the guys," Lucas whispered, not believing it.

A second, softer rap. "Hello?" a voice called. Not a god voice. Human. Tentative. "Hey—it's Jess. We're back from the store? We got bagels and saw the update on the way back. Figured you might not want to be out on the road right now."

Jack turned to the window again because it had become a habit in a single morning. The glass answered his palm—quieter now, but certain. The hum in his chest matched it, nested there like a tenant who'd signed a lease in silence.

Outside, a breeze slipped across the clearing. Ash stirred in the fire pit, lifted, fell. The treetops tilted their heads as if listening for the next line in a song.

"Okay," he said, more to the air than to his friends. "We eat. We pack. We head out later."

"And if Hermes does the voice-in-our-skull thing again?" Lucas asked.

"Then we don't answer," Ryan said. "Let Olympus talk to its own echo."

The kettle on the stove shrieked at a normal, human volume. Aaron lifted it, poured water over grounds, and for a fragile minute the cabin smelled like coffee and bacon and a Saturday they could have had.

Jack closed his eyes. The air pressed the back of his neck, steady as a hand. He let it. When he opened them, the day had not gotten smaller, but it had gotten clearer.

He was not hungover. He was not fine. He was... connected. And whatever had touched the world last night had left a print on him.

A headline scrolled mutely on the TV: **GOVERNOR: "STAY INDOORS. STAY CALM."** Another: **IS THIS THE PANTHEON? SCHOLARS WEIGH IN.** Another: **TRAFFIC CLOSED ON 46.**

Jack picked up a fork. It shook less than he expected. He took a bite of eggs. They tasted like eggs.

"Hey," Aaron said, quietly.

"Yeah?"

"If they can speak to you whenever they want, can they listen to us and, more importantly... how do we make sure they can't?"

Jack looked at the window, at his handprint smudged there, at the woods that had learned a new language overnight.

"By not being the loudest thing in the room," he said. "At least until we know when, who, and how they are listening," acting as if he was the wise man in the room.

The wind slipped under the door again and curled at his feet, cool as a cat.

Something ancient had woken up.

And it was paying attention to him.

CHAPTER 4

Ryan Cho dropped him at the curb with the engine idling like it was debating whether to stall or soldier on. They sat there for a few seconds longer than either of them meant to. It wasn't awkward—just heavy, like the air had weight and was sitting in both their laps.

"You good?" Ryan asked, one hand loose on the wheel. He looked tired in the way people do when their brain hasn't finished downloading the day yet.

"I'm… here," Jack said.

Ryan huffed a laugh. "Same." He nodded once toward the house. "Text me if anything gets weird."

Jack lifted his brows. "You're gonna have to define 'weird' in this new reality."

"Fair." Ryan reached for the shifter, then hesitated. "That horn thing this morning—you felt it too, right? Not just… the quake. The… other part."

Jack didn't have to fake the swallow. "Yeah. I felt it."

Another short nod, like a box checked. "Okay. At least we're equally screwed."

"Comforting," Jack said.

Ryan gave him half a salute and eased the Tacoma away, the engine grumbling like it had complaints about the gods as well.

Jack stood at the curb a moment longer, backpack hanging from one hand. The air felt thicker than it should, like he was standing in the shallow end of something invisible. Every tiny breeze carried that low hum now, the new background note of the world—like the planet had picked up a second heartbeat overnight and hadn't bothered to clear it with anybody.

His parents' house sat exactly where it always had. White siding that needed a proper power wash. Black shutters fading toward sunburned gray. The flag wrapped halfway around the pole like it'd given up mid-flap. Two pink flamingos guarded the flowerbed, bright plastic beaks oblivious to pantheons and omens.

Normal. Relentlessly, almost offensively normal.

He walked up the path, opened the door, and stepped into a wall of lemon cleaner and air conditioning.

"Look who finally decides to grace us with his presence!" his dad called from the kitchen. "We thought the gods got you. Your mother was about to call Zeus's manager."

"Don't," Jack said, kicking off his shoes. "He's got terrible customer service."

His mom turned from the stove with a glass of iced tea and that half-smile that had been calming him down since he was five. "You hungry? I made pasta. Technically leftover, but I reheated it, so it's legally fresh. I refuse to believe you 'already ate.'"

He took the glass and the quick kiss on the cheek. "You could definitely convince me."

The kitchen TV was on, of course. It was always on now. Footage looped of things that still looked like CGI to Jack's gut even though his brain knew better. Zeus framed by sunlight and storm, lightning crawling his forearms like pet snakes. Hephaestus reshaping cinderblock into marble with bare glowing hands. Hermes hovering like brand-friendly divinity, voice in people's heads instead of through a mic.

The chyron at the bottom had given up on subtlety:

LIVE • ROCKAWAY TOWNSHIP • THE PANTHEON RETURNS

28

His dad pointed a fork at the screen, eyes wide. "Can you believe this? Real gods! And they pick Route 46. Not Mount Olympus. Not the Parthenon. Rockaway."

"They wanted decent parking," his mom said.

"Exactly!" His dad gestured with the fork, nearly flinging a noodle. "And then the blacksmith guy—what's his name again?"

"Hephaestus," Jack said automatically.

"Right. He stomps his foot, flips the pavement like a pancake, and suddenly grass is popping up through the cracks like the world remembered it was supposed to be pretty."

Jack twirled pasta he didn't taste. His leg bounced hard under the table. There was too much energy in his muscles, too much air in his lungs, too much something humming under his skin. The ceiling felt lower, like the house itself was trying to keep him from floating away.

"I'm gonna go for a run," he heard himself say.

Both parents blinked.

"You hate running," his mom said.

"Today I don't." He was already half up. "I feel like I could sprint to Newark and back."

His dad snorted. "Hydrate, track star."

Jack flashed a quick grin. "Hydrating," he promised, grabbing his earbuds from the counter.

He stepped outside before he could talk himself out of it.

The air hit him like a greeting—cooler than it should be in the late-day sun, sliding into his lungs like it had been custom-filtered. He popped the earbuds in; an old playlist kicked on, full of songs from college that had convinced him he could bench-press bad decisions.

He started down Maple Avenue at a jog. Two strides later, it wasn't a jog. His body found a rhythm immediately. The sound of his footfalls collapsed into a single beat, background to the main track of his breathing.

Except… his breathing never struggled to keep up.

No burn in the lungs.
No protest in his thighs.
Just motion.

He turned onto Longview, letting his body choose the pace. The houses thinned. Lawns blurred. Sweat started on his skin and then vanished as a cool slipstream formed around him, drying it too fast. The sensation was bizarre—like running with a portable fan glued to his chest.

The air didn't resist him. It parted. Welcomed. Guided.

His laugh came out without permission. The sound carried farther than it should have, pulled along by the breeze.

He pushed harder. The world narrowed to pavement and pulse. His shoes struck asphalt with less and less weight, like someone was quietly dialing down his gravity. Every inhalation came flooded not just with oxygen but information: eddies between houses, warm pockets by parked cars, the distant crosswind off the main road. He could feel all of it in his ribs.

A car horn snapped the moment like a twig.

He looked up just as a sedan shot across the intersection, way too fast for a residential street.

Reflex took over. Or maybe it was something deeper than reflex.

The air shoved him upward.

His entire body went light. His ears popped, a quick little pressure shift, like a plane taking off in miniature. His feet left the ground.

He cleared the hood by inches, body twisting in the air as if something invisible had grabbed and placed him. He saw the driver's eyes go wide—Ethan, two doors down. Then the curb rushed up to meet him.

Jack landed on the far sidewalk in a stumble that turned into a jog, then an awkward standstill. His heart hammered—not from effort, but from the yawning "What the hell" of almost becoming hood art.

The sedan squealed to a stop. Ethan leaned out the window, face pale, hair wild.

"Dude," Ethan gasped. "You just… jumped over my car."

"Adrenaline," Jack said, because his brain had nothing better.

Ethan stared. "That's not how adrenaline works."

"It's how mine works now," Jack said before he could stop himself.

Ethan barked a shaky laugh, because the alternative was panic. "Be careful, man. People are crazy today."

"Working on it," Jack muttered.

When the car rolled away, the street went quiet again. Too quiet.

Jack sat down on the curb.

Except he didn't quite sit. His weight felt delayed—like gravity filed his paperwork and got distracted. A thin cushion of air gathered under him, not enough to levitate, just enough to make contact feel… negotiable.

He pressed his hand into the strip of grass beside the sidewalk. The blades bowed in a perfect circle, flattening outward from his palm in a smooth wave.

He pulled his hand back. The grass took a breath, then stood up again, one blade at a time.

He did it again. Press. Flatten. Release.

"Okay," he whispered. "That's not nothing."

He pushed his hand down harder, this time exhaling with it. "Down," he thought—not as a word, but as intent.

Air pushed back.

A tiny gust puffed outward from his fingers, ruffling the grass in the opposite direction. He felt it on his wrist, then his forearm, then in the hollow of his chest—like something inside his ribs was answering a question he hadn't realized he'd asked.

Jack stood, slowly.

He looked up at the oak trees lining the street and felt every gap between their leaves. Every little slip of atmosphere, every quiet current. It was like seeing the skeleton of the wind.

"Test phase," he said, because saying it out loud made it feel less like he was losing his mind.

He bent his knees and pushed down.

The air caught him.

He rose, not in a leap, but in a held breath. Three feet. Then four. His stomach did that little drop like the end of an elevator ride, but his body stayed weirdly calm. The world shrank just enough for the roofs to look almost toy-like.

Ear pressure fluttered as the air adjusted around him, tightening one second, easing the next. Sweat cooled instantly, a chill running across the back of his neck. He could feel the flow sliding beneath his feet, sluggish when he wasn't asking much of it, eager when he did.

He laughed—quiet, incredulous.

"I'm actually—"

His weight shifted. The current supporting him stuttered.

The air's grip loosened for a fraction of a heartbeat.

He dropped.

He crashed through the lower branches of a nearby maple, snapping twigs, smearing bark down one shoulder. His forearms scraped rough against wood. His nose clipped a limb. His face smashed into the trunk.

The smell hit him first: resin and sap and sun-warmed bark, sharp and earthy, jammed up his nostrils. His palms burned. A rough patch of lichen rasped across his cheek like sandpaper.

Gravity cheered, satisfied, as he slid the rest of the way down and hit the ground hard enough to rattle his teeth.

He lay there, staring up at the canopy, breath coming in quick half-laughs.

"Ow," he said to nobody, then, "Okay. That one's on me. But I'm…. Fine?" Shocked that he was barely injured from the fall.

The breeze tumbled through the leaves overhead and across his chest, cool and almost apologetic.

He sat up slowly, flexing his fingers. They stung, but the pain was surface-level, already fading. No deep bruise. No broken anything. His heart pounded with adrenaline now, but under it was something else—excitement, bright and childish.

"So," he told the tree. "I can fly. Kind of."

The tree declined to comment.

He checked his hands. No blood. Just raw skin and a faint tingle under the surface that matched the thrum in the air. Like both systems were booting up together.

"Okay," he said again, softer. "Maybe we don't climb over traffic yet."

He headed toward the park two streets over, keeping to the sidewalks, trying not to look like a man who was reasonably sure he could bench-press a breeze.

The little municipal park was mostly empty—a playground, a loop path, a sad baseball field. The sky had tilted toward late-afternoon gold. The air smelled like freshly cut grass and charcoal from someone's grill a few houses away.

He cut across to the open field and stopped in the middle, listening.

Cars, distant.
A lawnmower, droning.
Kids shrieking on the slide.
Wind.

Always the wind.

He could feel it wrapping around the posts of the backstop, sliding through the worn chain-link, curling under the bleachers.

He closed his eyes.

"Okay," he thought. "Talk to me."

He didn't hear anything, but the breeze shifted—like a dog tilting its head.

He bent his knees and gave a smaller push this time. Not a leap, not a demand. More like asking permission.

Air gathered under his feet, thickening, cool. His shoes left the grass by inches. A slow, careful rise—six inches... a foot... eighteen inches. His balance wobbled. Currents tugged at his calves, correcting.

His ears popped lightly, pressure equalizing.

He opened his eyes and nearly laughed again. He was hovering a foot and a half off the ground like a glitch in gravity.

He leaned forward just a little. The air flowed with him, catching his center of mass, letting him drift. Small, slow, a controlled slide over the field.

It felt like surfing, he realized. Not like flying in a cape, not like superhero punch-through-the-sky nonsense. More like catching the perfect wave—finding the point where force and surrender met and holding it for as long as balance allowed.

He shifted his weight left. The current curled around his ankles, nudging him that way. He inhaled deeply, picturing lift, and felt the wind respond, cool hands on the bottom of his feet.

When he exhaled, he imagined "down," and the air eased him toward the ground, resetting to zero.

He touched grass as lightly as if he'd only hopped.

Jack grinned, helpless.

"Again," he told no one.

He spent the next twenty minutes in trial and error. More error than trial, but he didn't care.

Short lifts.
Sideways drifts.
Discovering that inhaling sharply while thinking "up" gave him an extra jolt, while exhaling through pursed lips while thinking "slow down" bled momentum off. At one point he spun himself in a lazy circle, wind scarfing around his waist, nearly dumping him on his side until he threw his hands out and felt the air grab his wrists.

He took one bigger risk—pushing hard, harder than before, wanting to see what his ceiling was.

The ground dropped away fast. Ten feet. Fifteen. His stomach lurched. His ears popped harder this time. The wind roared past his ears, then flattened to a steady pressure as the slipstream formed. His sweat turned freezing in a heartbeat, cooling his back and neck as if he'd stepped into a walk-in freezer.

Panic finally caught up.

He'd meant to see what was possible. His body, apparently, had heard "takeoff."

"I'm actually—" he started.

The realization hit fully formed: **I'm actually flying.**

Right on the heels of it came a spike of fear.

What if it stopped?
What if he couldn't get back down?

What if the wind changed its mind and dropped him from thirty feet instead of ten?

His breath stuttered. The currents around him wobbled.

The air answered his fear with turbulence.

He tilted, losing his center. The world angled. Instinct screamed.

"Down," he thought, not calmly this time but with full, animal urgency.

He exhaled hard, imagining every part of him getting heavier, denser, anchoring.

The wind compressed under him like a spring, then released.

He dropped. Not like a stone—more like a badly executed landing—but it was enough. He crashed down in a tangle, rolled once, slid on the grass, and ended up on his back staring at the clouds.

He lay there, heart racing, lungs pumping, vision strobing with afterimages.

The sky above looked exactly the same as it had that morning. That was the worst part.

He laughed—short, breathless. "Okay," he told the sky. "Noted. Respect the ceiling."

Grass tickled his neck. The air moved over him, gentle again, like it was smoothing his hair back into place.

He sat up after a minute or two, legs shaking now that the adrenaline had somewhere to go. His palms smelled faintly like crushed grass and bark, with a resin ghost underneath from the tree.

His phone buzzed in his pocket.

Mom:
Dinner's in an hour. You coming home or did the gods draft you?

He smiled despite himself and the very corny joke and texted back:

Coming. Just catching my breath.

As he slid the phone away, his whole body prickled.

Not goosebumps from exertion. Something else.

The breeze went still mid-movement, like a song pausing mid-note.

"Okay," he said to himself. "We're done for today."

He walked home.

Not running. Not floating. Just walking.

Hands jammed deep in his pockets, shoulders slightly hunched, like that would make him smaller on whatever cosmic map he'd just lit up.

As he turned onto his parents' street, the late afternoon light had gone soft. Someone was grilling; the smell drifted over asphalt and freshly watered lawns. A kid rode a bike past him with streamers on the handlebars, oblivious to thunder gods and radar sweeps.

Normal tried very hard to reassert itself.

The air wasn't buying it.

A small breeze slid down the block to meet him, threading between parked cars, slipping around his ankles, then climbing him—up his legs, his back, curling around his neck.

It combed through his hair once, slow and deliberate.

Not playful. Not random.

A warning.
A promise.

He didn't have to translate it. He already knew.

The wind threaded his hair like a warning.

He'd been noticed.

CHAPTER 5

Jack sat in his cubicle breathing recycled air and burnt-coffee fumes, surrounded by beige partitions that had learned the weight of small dreams. Outside the strip windows, cranes picked at half-wrapped buildings—plywood, blue tarps, orange fencing. Three days of emergency repairs; three days of everyone pretending the crack in the sky had just been weather.

His monitor glared rows of CSS and a spreadsheet of alt text a client would ignore except to ask if the font felt "more premium."

Click. Copy. Paste. Refresh. Save. Repeat.

He spun a quarter on the laminate. It whirled into a bright circle, faltered, collapsed with a tired clack. He spun it again. Again. The coin wobbled once as if insulted, then settled into a cleaner spin, like something under the desk had nudged it. Jack pretended he hadn't noticed.

In the lower-right corner of his screen, he'd carved out a rectangle of reality. A muted livestream from Rockaway sat between a dev build and a Slack thread about button radius. **GOD WATCH** glowed in the corner like the world had decided to schedule the apocalypse.

Three days since lightning put a temple in a parking lot. Three days since Hermes' voice had walked in through the side door of Jack's skull and made itself at home.

The chyron crawl tried to keep score: **VANDALISM AT HOUSES OF WORSHIP UP 600%. CHURCHES REQUEST POLICE DETAILS. INTERFAITH COALITION CALLS FOR "CALM, CLARITY."** Someone had spray-painted **JUPITER SUCKS** across a Catholic church in Newark. Someone else had tagged **ZEUS IS BACK** over a mosque's side door. Livestreamed prayer circles and rage rants ping-ponged down the screen.

The internet metabolized wonder without chewing.

On the feed, cameras panned across the barricade that ringed what used to be the AMC. Concrete barriers, cruisers, black SUVs, armored vans. Local PD, state troopers, SWAT, a dark blue FBI tac team with **FEDERAL** printed across their chests like a dare. Helmets, visors, rifles at low ready. Behind them, the white marble geometry that had been an eleven-screen multiplex shone like it resented the asphalt.

"They've maintained this perimeter for seventy-two hours," the reporter was saying under the captions. "Authorities insist the complex was fully evacuated before the structure... changed. Since then, witnesses report hammering, grinding stone—what sounds like interior construction—from inside the so-called 'New Temple.' Law enforcement sources tell us today is the day they intend to go in."

Jack nudged the volume up a notch.

"Conference room. Now."

His manager, a man shaped like a stress ball that had learned to walk, speed-walked past, then backed up when Jack didn't move fast enough. "Come on."

Heads were already popping up over cubicle walls, people drifting toward the glass box. Jack spun the coin one more time. It jumped to its edge with a little eager twitch, like a dog seeing a leash, and spun harder.

"Stay," he whispered at the air before he could stop himself.

The vent above him puffed against his cheek in what sure as hell felt like wounded dignity.

He palmed his phone, left the quarter spinning, and followed the herd.

Twelve people ringed the big TV, breath fogging the glass where someone had leaned too close. The room smelled like dry-erase marker and the second day of donuts. Someone had killed the overhead lights; blue from the screen washed everyone into one tired color.

Live feed. Barricades, black SUVs, floodlights even though it was midday. Heat shimmered over marble. State troopers formed a black line. The FBI team jogged into frame, stacking up, red dots shaking across white stone.

"Authorities confirm," the reporter said, voice steady and failing at it, "a joint task force of local law enforcement, state police, and federal units is preparing to enter the structure now being called the New Temple —"

A gunshot cracked off-screen. Then another. Then a ragged volley.

A scream cut the feed in half.

The picture smashed to asphalt. The camera lurched back up through a forest of legs and riot shields and a streak of gold.

He resolved as he rose.

Hermes climbed out of the gun smoke as if reality had remembered it owed him an entrance. Winged sandals. White-and-gold armor that wasn't costume, wasn't CGI. His mouth wore the tight, clean line of someone who'd been patient for several millennia and had finally run out.

Bullets found him and failed. They pinged off his chest like coins thrown into a fountain and fell dull at his feet. One round ricocheted sideways toward the officers—bright, lethal. Hermes flicked two fingers without looking.

Air snapped.

The slug veered like it had thought better of its life choices and kissed a cruiser's light bar with a tink. A shard of red plastic skittered under the bumper and died.

"STOP."

The word wasn't loud. It was big. In the conference room, Jack's molars vibrated in his jaw. Plastic chairs creaked under people who'd forgotten how to sit.

"HOLD YOUR USELESS FIRE."

41

The All-Speak slid behind Jack's eyes, cool as a coin melting. The fine hairs along his forearms leaned toward the screen like grass toward sun. The ventilation system hiccupped and shifted pitch, an obedient dog deciding which human to stand behind.

Guns lowered in a shamefaced wave.

Hermes hovered twenty feet up now, directly over the first ring of vehicles, exactly in the center of their circle. Anger cooled to something older—judgment with a long memory.

"You misunderstand our purpose," he said. "We did not come to wage war. We came because you are in danger."

The camera found his face and clung to it.

"The horn you heard," Hermes went on. "The tremors that shook your cities. Those were not storms. Those were the walls of Tartarus collapsing. The prison of the Titans has eroded. Its gates have fallen. What was locked away now walks."

He said *Titans* and the audio threw in a tiny crackle, like the mic had flinched.

"The Titans are not stories," he said. "They are not your movies. They are older than your nations. They bend sea and sky, stone and flame. They pull at minds and hearts until brother kills brother and calls it righteousness. They interfere in your lives not to guide, but to gratify destruction."

Someone in the room swore under their breath. Someone else whispered, "Jesus," out of habit.

"They will tear this world apart," Hermes said, "if left alone. We will not allow that."

He dropped his chin a fraction, eyes sweeping the barricades, the cameras, the distant rooftops.

"We did not return to rule your laws or choose your kings," he said. "We will stand apart from your governments and let your empires pretend to be eternal. But this place—"

He gestured back at the transformed multiplex.

"—this hall is now our throne room. Our New Temple. Your AMC has become our new Athens. These walls are Our Residence upon the earth."

The word **Residence** hit with capital letters even without captions.

"We will not harm you," Hermes said. "If you cherish your lives, you will not storm our doors. You will not aim your toys at Olympus. You will give this ground wide berth and remember that when the Titans come, we stand between them and you."

Radios crackled. On screen, cops and troopers did the same choreography: heads tilted, shoulders listening. The feed caught it: **COMMAND: ALL UNITS—STAND DOWN. REPEAT—STAND DOWN. HOLD PERIMETER. FALL BACK TEN METERS.**

Rifles sank. The front line of troopers began stepping back, boots scuffing, faces trying to remember how to be blank on national television.

The camera operator, either brave or bored of living, pushed closer as Hermes drifted backward up the marble steps.

"Since your third day of watching," the reporter said over the image, "authorities have heard constant hammering, grinding, what they describe as 'massive interior construction' from within the New Temple. No human has entered. No god has emerged—"

"Until now," someone in Jack's conference room murmured.

Hermes turned once more before the threshold. From inside, now that gunfire had shut up, the feed picked up faint sounds: rhythmic impacts, stone meeting metal, a low, continuous ringing like a blacksmith had convinced an earthquake to keep time.

Then: a human voice from outside the frame, distant but insistent.

"Lord Hermes! Messenger of the gods! I am a fellow messenger—a storyteller! Help me tell the whole story!"

The shot swung. A man in a rumpled shirt and loosened tie had climbed onto a jersey barrier, one hand white-knuckled on the rail, the other waving a press badge and a tiny digital recorder like they were shields.

Air cracked.

Hermes was there, floating inches from the man's nose, wind clenched around him like a flexing muscle. The blast flattened the reporter's hair and shirt. The crowd nearest him went abruptly very quiet.

"I go by many titles," Hermes said. "Messenger of the gods. Protector of travelers. Lord of language. Patron of shepherds. Herald of Mount Olympus." His mouth bent into something that was not quite a smile. "What story do you intend to tell?"

"The world's," the man said. His voice shook, but the words came out right. "People need to know what's happening. They... they need the full story. Please."

Hermes' eyes narrowed, interest sharpening. Opportunity, recognized.

"Walk with me," he said.

He didn't so much grab the reporter as rearrange him. One fist in the collar, a flex of the sandals, and they rose together, clearing the barrier, weaving through the air above the murmur and the phones and the guns. The camera scrambled to follow, bouncing off helmets and shoulders, then caught them again at the top of the marble steps.

"May I record this?" the reporter asked, breath loud in the mic. "For the... the history?"

Hermes inclined his head. "You may."

They crossed what had been the sticky, popcorn-salted lobby of an AMC three days ago. Popcorn had been exorcised. Something older had moved in: iron, clean stone, crushed leaf, incense that wasn't any church Jack had ever suffered through.

"Do you know why we left?" Hermes asked, conversational. His sandals whispered across marble no human poured. "Humans like to imagine we faded when you stopped saying our names. That is... imprecise."

They passed a theater whose walls had been erased—three screens joined into one massive amphitheater, seats torn and re-tiered into marble benches. Balconies that had been mezzanines now arced with carved laurels. Where a concession stand had stood, a colonnade rose, capitals still half-finished, reliefs climbing themselves into stories.

Hephaestus worked beneath the largest arch.

He brought his hammer down. Sparks fountained like migrating fireflies, then remembered they were gold and ran obediently into the waiting stone. Each strike sent a subtle shiver through the columns, arrested lightning chasing the veins. The hammer's tone rang clear as a struck bell.

"We stepped back from the lives of men when your empires changed the script," Hermes said. "When Rome ground Greece beneath its heel at Corinth—one hundred forty-six years before you started counting everything from The Carpenter in Judea—we watched your conquerors loot temples and libraries and thought, ah. The play goes on without us."

"The Battle of Corinth," the reporter blurted, like a student desperate to show he'd done the reading.

"Good," Hermes said. "Yes. Your Romans took our stories and scraped the names off. Zeus became Jupiter. His brothers—Poseidon and Hades—became Neptune and Pluto. I was made into Mercury, courier for your coins. Athena became Minerva. Ares, Mars. You preserved the shapes and pretended they were yours."

He smiled, sharp and bright.

"We are not jerseys you can change," he said. "We tolerated the translation. For a while. But humans always chase novelty. New gods, new creeds, new revelations. We watched altars go quiet at Delos and Olympia while mosques rose, and basilicas, and temples beyond number

45

on lands you had not mapped. We saw that worship would never be one thing again."

They turned down what had been the long corridor to Theaters 8–11. The walls now bore frescoes wet and drying at the same time—Titans chained, Titans falling, Titans burning. In each, the gods stood above them, victorious, smug, terrified in tiny, telling details.

"So we left," Hermes said simply. "We stepped fully onto Olympus. Out of your world. We watched from afar while you renamed us in your books and comics and films. It was... occasionally flattering. Often tedious."

"Mount Olympus," the reporter said. "Is it— is it in Greece? Is it on Earth? Is it... heaven?"

Hermes huffed.

"It is not the heaven your Bibles speak of," he said. "And it is not one of your comic-book 'dimensions.' It is a plane of existence. Adjacent to your world, touching it at peaks and storms and certain doors. Less geography. More... address."

"So, like, a different dimension," the reporter muttered.

Hermes stopped and looked at him.

"If it helps you to think so, you may," he said. "But words shape thought, and thought shapes belief. Choose carefully which cheap metaphors you staple to the sky, little messenger."

He resumed walking. The reporter hurried to keep up.

"We return now not because you remembered us," Hermes said, "but because Tartarus forgot how to hold. The Titans strain against walls that cracked long before your skyscrapers. The horn you heard? That was stone giving way. The quake you felt? That was a gate unhinging."

They reached the main amphitheater, carved from three former screens and half a food court. The ceiling had been opened into a dome that showed no roof, only blue—too deep, too high, a sky that belonged on another world. Statues were moving themselves into place: Hera's brows forming, Artemis' bow finishing its curve.

"We are here for them," Hermes said, voice dropping into steel. "To keep Titans and their pets from tearing this little experiment of yours to pieces. To ensure that, this time, mankind remembers: we are what we have always been. The true power upon the earth. We protect. We are worshiped. That is the natural order."

He turned the reporter gently toward the doors again.

"Tell them this," Hermes said. "We will not police your petty wars. We will not answer your elections. We will not sit in your parliaments. We will stand on our hill of stone and hold back the things that would end you. If you are wise, you will thank us. If you are foolish, you will shoot at us and learn futility in one serious lesson."

They reached the threshold. Hermes paused on the marble lip, back in view of the world and its cameras.

"Now we return," he said, for the microphones and the men with guns, "before Titans write you a story you cannot live inside."

Air cracked—absence as punctuation—and the doors began to close. Not slammed. Sealed. A slow, irrevocable meeting of stone against stone. The last image before they kissed shut was Hephaestus, profile limned in molten gold, raising his hammer again.

Static ate the feed.

The TV threw them back to a desk and an anchor whose throat had forgotten how to be a throat. The chyron crawled: **PENTAGON SOURCES: UNPRECEDENTED SHIFT IN GLOBAL STABILITY.**

Nobody in the conference room exhaled until the building's air system reminded them oxygen was a thing. Someone laughed wrong; it came out like a hiccup. Someone else said, "Well, shit," in a whisper that wanted to be a prayer.

Jack stood still. The cool of the temple stuck to him like a second shirt. The hammer's ring hung in his bones.

He put his palm on the conference table. Nothing happened. He took it away and wanted the living grain of the cabin under his hand so badly he felt stupid with it.

He walked back to his desk because that's what you do when history steps on your neck in an office—you go sit down.

His chair sighed. His editor blinked. The spreadsheet waited, polite and pointless.

He stared at code he'd written yesterday in a world that had just admitted it wasn't made of code.

Three thoughts lined up behind his eyes like planes on approach.

I have powers. The gods are real. I'm copying code.

He put his hand on a paper stack. The top sheet budged—a whisper, a nod. The air underneath it felt like a dog's head pressing into his palm, eager, pleased he'd finally decided to play.

He snatched his hand back. The air settled, but the sense of attention didn't go anywhere.

The quarter he'd abandoned earlier ticked. Rolled a degree. Then, without his finger anywhere near it, it rose onto its edge and began to spin. Not showy. A clean, steady rotation, like a very patient animal nudging a toy closer and saying, *well?*

Jack watched it turn. The low vibration in the room came back—not from the vents, but through them—like a bass note the HVAC had started to imitate. The plastic blind slats rattled softly and then aligned themselves on their own with a little embarrassed click, slanting just right to cut glare off his screen.

"Okay," he whispered. "I see you."

The breeze that leaked from the ceiling vent brushed his face in a quick, happy swirl. Tail wag.

He wasn't short of breath. He was full of something that wasn't oxygen and had no intention of leaving.

Jack turned his phone over. The New Temple filled the lock screen thumbnail again, thumbnail gods in a thumbnail world. The light lit the underside of his hand with the cool color of commitment.

"Everything okay?" his manager asked, hovering with the energy of a man who wants every problem to be a spreadsheet.

"PTO," Jack said. The decision arrived in his mouth already formed. "Family thing. Taking the rest of the day. Probably tomorrow."

The man's mouth opened and closed like a small fish in a big aquarium. "Of course. Yes. Family is—absolutely. Send me an email so HR can—"

"On it."

Jack packed like leaving was a class he'd taken and passed. Laptop. Charger. The blue notebook no one else knew was a map. When he stood, the chair rolled back a neat four inches without catching on the carpet tile.

Helpful, the air said, in the universal language of objects doing what you meant instead of what you asked.

He cut past the conference room. The TV held the New Temple in a two-inch box while a financial expert speculated what gods would do to interest rates. Someone had scrawled **Q3 Goals** on a whiteboard in a handwriting that had looked optimistic when written and tired now.

The elevator was a mirror. He didn't look at his face. He watched the red LED numbers tick down and listened to his own breath find a rhythm that felt less like coping and more like arrival. The air in the car pressed close, attentive, like a big dog in the backseat waiting for the window to go down.

In the lobby, a security guard watched the feed on his phone with his mouth open. A delivery guy signed for three cases of paper. Life kept trying to be Tuesday.

The door sighed open and the outside hit him full in the face: heat, asphalt, the smell of hot metal and a city pretending today was normal.

49

Wind coming down the block paused, seemed to take stock of him, and then fell into step.

It took him by the collar the way a friend does when the bar gets weird. Not force. Invitation.

He walked.

At the corner he caught himself in a black SUV's glass—him, yes, but with a faint shimmer at the edges, the way things look on hot days when the world forgets how to hold still. The shadows at his shoulders wobbled like the air itself was wagging.

He blinked and it was gone and not gone at all.

On the sidewalk, a kid dragged a backpack the size of a small moon. He glanced up at Jack with the beatific stare of children and drunks and asked, "Are you a superhero?" like he was asking if it might rain.

"I'm late for something," Jack said.

The kid nodded like that checked out.

He cut east toward the river, crossing with a herd of people who had their eyes on their phones and their ears on the sky. When he stepped off the curb, the cross-breeze surged, looping around his calves, his waist, his ribs in a figure eight that felt suspiciously like a dog doing zoomies around its person.

"Easy," he muttered.

The gust eased, still pressed close, content to match his stride.

At home, he opened drawers quietly so they wouldn't remember this as a leaving. Jeans, hoodie, the compression shirt that held him together when breath tried to be too much. He set his blue notebook on the table, flipped it open, and wrote a single word under the page full of names.

Move.

His mother texted **Are you eating.** He sent a photo of a sandwich he hadn't made yet and then made it so the universe wouldn't call him a liar. He fired off the PTO email—Subject: **PTO**, sent from his phone, please excuse brevity—and let corporate language do its limp little dance without him.

Dusk elbowed the window. The house got that summer-night hollowness that makes sound travel differently. He thought about it — wind farm, horizon, less to break — and felt something in him lean toward it with relief and a little hunger.

He closed his eyes and found the presence in his chest because it had never left. Now it felt less like abstract pressure and more like a big, excited animal sitting on his sternum, tail thumping, waiting for him to say the magic word.

A thought rose, simple and clean: *Be brave now, while you can afford it.*

Tonight, he was going to the coast.

He slipped the notebook into his bag. The lighthouse card with the cramped names rode under the cover like a compass pretending to be junk mail. He stuck a note on the fridge—**Back late — love you**—and hoped the magnet would hold it.

He stepped onto the porch. The neighborhood had the hush of people pretending to watch TV while they refreshed their feeds. Somewhere, a dog barked twice and decided not to pursue it. A flag scraped its pole like a zipper.

The air pressed a cool palm under his ribs, familiar now, then whooshed happily around his legs, circling once, twice, like it had spotted the leash.

"Okay," he told it. "Let's go learn what I am without breaking anything."

It didn't understand the words. It understood the direction.

He walked to the curb and the breeze came with him—loyal, a little too eager, like an air-made German shepherd at heel, ready to run as soon as he said *go.*

CHAPTER 6

Jack woke up hungry enough to fight a bear and considerate enough to make a breakfast wrap instead. Two eggs, bacon, a heroic amount of hot sauce, folded like he was auditioning for a New Jersey diner. He ate on the back deck while the morning wind combed the oak leaves and pressed cool fingers along his face like a golden retriever asking, *Ready?*

He washed the last bite down with a Red Bull. "Nothing like air drills on a full—okay, semi-full—stomach."

Gym bag over his shoulder—really a water bottle, a hoodie, some athletic tape for… ankles? Spirit?—he cut through the side gate into the trees. The sun slanted between trunks, turning spiderwebs into strings of glass. The trail he'd run since he was twelve forked into Ringwood State Park after a mile; his feet knew every root and stone.

The air knew him too.

It moved when he moved, breath syncing to his breath, that low hum that had threaded the world since Rockaway became Olympus' annex. Over the last week he'd learned a dangerous truth: the more he used the thing in him, the more instinct took the wheel. Half the time he didn't decide. His body made a choice and the wind agreed.

He stepped into a small clearing he'd started treating like a personal gym. Logs as barbells. Boulders as cones. A fallen birch for balance. It smelled like dirt and sap and that faint metallic buzz that came whenever he pushed too hard too long.

He rolled his shoulders until they clicked, exhaled, and set his feet. "Warmup. Ten easy bursts."

He thrust both palms forward. The air punched the clearing like a silent cannon. Leaves rippled in a perfect O, dust fanning in a low ring. He grinned despite himself.

"Two." Tighter—enough to ruffle the nearest fern without disturbing the moss behind it.

"Three." A precise shot that flicked a pebble off the birch without moving the branch.

"Four." A wide cone, a gentle hand that pressed grasses flat and let them spring back.

He counted until his shoulders loosened and his thoughts lined up. Then he bent his knees, drew a breath, and pushed the air downward. The ground slid away. One foot. Two. Three. He hovered there, ankles wobbling, arms out at awkward angles—a man-shaped drone with social anxiety. Around thirty seconds, a tremor fluttered in his deltoids and the wobble deepened: limit noted. He sank, reset, tried again.

"Try not to eat a tree today," he told the leaves.

He tipped forward. The wind caught him like an unseen harness, skimming him at knee height around the logs. He shot up, floated down, pivoted in place. Control was better now—less falling-with-style, more piloting. If he didn't psych himself out, it was almost easy.

He drifted over a fallen log, thick as a thigh, and curled his fingers, picturing the air as threads he could grab. The log trembled, lifted, hovered to his height.

"Up." It rose another foot, slow and smooth.

"Rotate." It turned like a rotisserie. He laughed—delighted and a little afraid of how natural it felt.

A pinpoint ache woke at the base of his skull: the headache that came if he threaded the wind too fine for too long. He set the log down. The thump ran up his calves like a satisfied heartbeat.

He walked to the edge of the clearing, palms open, feeling the currents talk: a squirrel slapping its tail against a trunk to his left; a crow's wingbeat chopping air high overhead; something smaller tickling through the ferns at shin level—

A spark of blue zipped across his path and stopped at eye level, bobbing like a firefly with a to-do list. Not a bug. A tiny woman, except "woman" was a costume she wore to be polite. Six inches tall, wings like etched glass, a hard little face that could flip from joy to murder between blinks. Her wingbeats threw a cool micro-breeze on his cheeks. When she spoke—if that's what the braid of bell-tone syllables was—the sound tasted like copper on his tongue.

"Uh," Jack said. "Hi?"

Three more lights winked in—pink, green, and an indignant lemon yellow. They circled his head with precise little arcs, leaving ribbon-tails of glitter. The blue jabbed a finger at his hair, sang something extremely opinionated, and belly-laughed until she toppled backward. The yellow caught her and scolded in tiny operatic fury. The pink peered close at his eye like she was checking the finish on a marble. The green hovered near his ear, listening to his breath like a mechanic listens to a misfire.

"Right," he murmured. "So… fairies."

They weren't the only new neighbors.

The past week had felt like a decade smashed into five days. After Hermes' "we're here to keep you alive" speech, North Jersey had turned into a map of myth with municipal overlaid.

Rockaway sprouted a six-foot concrete wall first—government fast, which meant it looked half-permanent and entirely annoyed. Floodlights. Checkpoints. A ring of pop-up tents and satellite trucks outside it, a modern pilgrimage in hoodies and portable chargers. Hellenist groups built folding-table shrines and burned olive branches; people who hadn't prayed since their cousin's wedding were now leaving figs by marble barricades.

Elsewhere, faith fought back with batons and caution tape. Some churches organized guard details. A statue of the Virgin in Clifton got a toga and a laurel wreath overnight and then got re-wreathed with police tape by morning. A pastor in Paramus spray-painted THOU SHALT NOT GRIFT across his own doors to keep both protestors and opportunists off. The American habit of worshipping anything with merch pivoted awkwardly; you could buy laurel headbands at the mall kiosk next to vape juice. Less "Team Zeus," more a run on votive candles and olives.

The news ticked off mythic calls like a dispatcher:

— Lake Hopatcong: two drownings after witnesses saw "beautiful women" waving from the water. Sirens. State police launched quadcopters over the coves; the feed showed drone-eye ripples and then a pale arm sliding under the surface. New signs went up: NO SWIMMING UNTIL FURTHER NOTICE, QR codes linking to a state bulletin on "aquatic entities." The hotline's recorded menu added a deadpan: "For deer, press 1. For bears, press 2. For… harpy? Say 'operator.'"

— High Point: harpy sightings, not cute. A hiker's clip caught a shadow shredding a deer in a tree, then the camera flailed and the audio devolved into breath and shoe-slaps. Rangers closed trails with laminated notices that tried to be calm and failed: RESPECT AVIAN CREATURES OF UNUSUAL SIZE.

— Ringwood: centaurs. Not rumors—video. Three, maybe four, horse bodies butter-smooth with muscle under summer coats, human torsos like somebody's best statue walked off its pedestal. They herded hikers out without touching them. One threw a chain between two trees and hooked it like a gate, pointed to the ground with a don't-test-me stare, and melted back into green.

Olympus learned PR. Dionysus hosted a "public symposium" under the temple steps—a ramble about wine and community that was half community-building, half liability nightmare. Hera moved through crowds palm to palm, greeting women like she was sorting petitions with her bones. Pundits called it recruitment. The comment sections burned with a hundred kinds of awe.

Jack wasn't sure what to call any of it. He only knew the air felt busier every day, full of names that hadn't been said aloud in a long time.

He popped a second Red Bull. "Alright. Drills are cute. Let's see the neighbors."

He kicked off and skimmed the canopy. Branches brushed his shoulders. Sunlight strobed. He kept low—ten, twenty feet—riding the invisible slope of the currents like a kid who'd finally learned to keep the bike upright. Forty-five seconds in the hover when he paused to test a tight turn and his shoulders whispered a burn; he sank briefly, shook it off, rose again with smaller corrections. Limits were real. So was the part of him that wanted to test them.

Hoofbeats rolled ahead—heavy, rhythmic, the ground ringing like a drum. He angled toward the sound.

They appeared at once: a rush of bodies through green. A lead centaur—broad chest, hair braided tight—two flanking, a young one lagging and too aware of it. They clocked him immediately. Eyes flicked up. A hiss in a language that tasted like sage smoke. He rose a touch, hands open, not a threat.

The earth snapped.

A whipcrack of coiled cable. The young one went down screaming, a snare cinched tight around his rear leg. Instinct detonated. The herd split —three vanished right, two left—and four skidded into a circle around the trapped one, human torsos twisted, weapons up.

The hunters stepped out of the trees like a bad idea that had been waiting. Five of them. Camo. Rifles. Eyes too bright.

Jack's stomach went cold. The hunters moved in slow—not cautious. Hungry. The front man smiled without warmth. "Easy, boys," he said to the air, and that's when Jack stopped thinking.

He dropped.

He hit the ground between men and herd and threw his hands wide. The air he'd been skimming kicked back hard, a shockwave rolling in a circle from his boots. It hit the men first—silent, brutal—picked them up and pitched them into trees. Bark cracked. A rifle pinwheeled into ferns. Another discharged into the canopy and scared three crows into inventing new words.

Five bodies crumpled. Groans. A curse that ended in a cough.

Jack didn't look at them.

He spun, palms carving spirals, and pulled a column of wind up around himself and the centaurs, a spinning wall that churned leaves and dust into a pale green cylinder. Not wild—tight, controlled. Breath in, pressure up. The woman with the bow shouldered in, eyes cutting between him and the cable.

"Hey! Hey, it's okay!" he shouted, voice thinned by wind. She drew on him anyway, arrow steady at his eye. He held both hands up, palms open. "I'm here to help."

Her gaze flicked to the snare, back to him, down to his feet hovering an inch off the ground, then to the spinning wall. She barked a word that might have meant *Do it.*

He nodded, set his feet, and threaded the air into a narrow lance. He lined the blast along the cable's tension, pictured the weak point, and pushed.

The steel snapped like rotten twine. The recoil whipped back and dented the trunk. The young centaur collapsed, panting, leg shaking, then heaved himself upright and found balance with furious dignity.

Jack opened a seam in the cyclone, wide enough for a doorway. "Go!" He gestured.

They didn't thank him, not verbally. The archer met his eyes and held them for a beat that said *You're not ours, but your choice counted,* then she spun and signaled low. The herd barreled through the gap and vanished so fast the forest swallowed the noise. The young one limped last, tossed him a look that was almost human in its complicated pride, and was gone.

Jack let the wind unwind. Leaves helicoptered down. A hunter tried to roll to his knees and failed. Another glared up through grit. "What the hell are you?"

Jack hovered three inches and drifted backward into the trees without answering.

He didn't feel guilty.

He also didn't feel the tug he expected: *Are they okay? Did I overdo it?* What rose instead was a cold, clean certainty: *If they come back with more, I'll throw them farther.*

The ease of that thought unnerved him enough to land. He walked until the burn in his shoulders became an ache and the headache at the base of his skull faded. Hunger returned like a practical friend.

He found a knoll above the highway—good view, bad place to get nostalgic. Trucks whispered south like migrating whales.

He sat cross-legged under a maple and unwrapped an Italian sub—extra vinegar, hot peppers for dignity. He ate and watched the day slide by.

"Day eight," he said to the air, like a diary entry delivered to a very specific, judgmental cloud. "Saturday: horn, light, ground trying to breathe. Sunday: gods retrofit a movie theater. Monday through Friday: the world argues with itself." He took a bite, chewed, swallowed. "Today: fairies, harpies, sirens, centaurs… and me running air traffic control."

It sounded like a joke. It wasn't.

He wiped oil off his wrist and leaned back on his hands. "I keep thinking—maybe this is the Titans. Whatever woke them up woke up everything else. Maybe it woke up whatever I am."

The wind curled against his shoulder, sympathetic. He tried not to assign intention to air and failed.

His brain did math uninvited. Powers meant capability. Capability meant choices. Not leaping to spandex and speeches—no cape, no soundtrack—just the small, human math of bills, debt, and *what if.* All week he'd been practicing lifts. He knew how much force he could hold steady with one hand, with two, with a full-body brace. He could cradle something fragile in a slipstream and set it down gentler than gravity. He could knock a locked door off its hinges without scratching paint.

A white armored truck hummed along the highway below, heavy and oblivious, splitting the air into two neat wakes that tickled the hairs on his forearm. He could feel its mass, the pressure it carved. He could picture it stopping. He could picture it lifting.

He took another bite like chewing could drown temptation. It didn't.

"Don't be an idiot," he told himself. "You saved a herd. Take the win."

He finished the peppers and sat until the wind cooled the back of his neck. He packed up, stood, and skimmed the treeline toward home, keeping it slow to keep the headache away.

The family barbecue smelled like charcoal, cumin, and sixteen competing debates. His dad tended the grill with a beer in one hand and tongs in the other, turning chicken like a priest turning pages. His mom moved between patio and kitchen like a field general with love as doctrine. Uncles clustered at the cooler. A cousin fished a Frisbee out of the azaleas like he'd rescued a child from a well.

"Jack!" his dad called. "Grab a plate before your uncle invents a second stomach."

Jack hugged his mom, dodged two sticky children, and let himself get shepherded toward protein.

"What a week," an aunt said, shaking her head at the porch TV. It held a panel of people pretending to understand gods for money. "We're living in Revelations."

"We're living in Homer," his dad said, tapping the tongs in time with the host's nonsense. "And if Zeus wants a burger, he can get in line."

Laughter—relief disguised as jokes. The kind of laugh people use when the horizon's different and they still have to take out the trash.

Jack met Uncle Frank at the cooler. Frank had the eyes of a man who loved you and knew exactly how to make you tell on yourself.

"You good, kid?" Frank asked, popping a beer and handing it over.

"I'm good," Jack said, meaning *I'm something*.

Frank clinked bottles. "Wild times. If I had... you know, something? I'd do anything." He leaned in, conspirator quiet. "Who's gonna stop them?"

Tossed lightly, like a bit. The words slid under Jack's ribs and hooked. *Anything.* The wind at his back seemed to stiffen, paying attention.

After burgers and the inevitable sidebar on whether Hermes would cheat at fantasy football ("He'd invent a scoring category called 'steals'" got the loudest groan), Jack drifted to the fence line with a paper plate and watched the trees.

He could still feel that rattling bank truck in his bones—the way its mass pressed the air, the way the wake feathered out and died. He could feel the line between *could* and *should* like a wire pulled tight between his fingers.

His phone buzzed: protest flare at the Rockaway wall; Dionysus announced a "community tasting," hospitals quietly called in extra staff. He swiped it away without reading the think pieces.

Beyond the yard, the woods held their breath the way woods do at dusk, everything awake and pretending it wasn't. The breeze braided itself through high branches and came down softer, more intimate, like breath over glass.

"You're not that guy," he told himself.

The air didn't argue. It also didn't agree. It threaded his hair like a warning and a dare.

Headlights slid through the trees on the road beyond, rising and falling with the contour. Heavy. Slow. Familiar in the clean slice they cut through the air.

He closed his eyes and listened with his whole body.

When he opened them, the wind was already lifting the hair at his temples, waiting.

He took a long drink of beer to cool a heat that wasn't from August. Somewhere to the south, a siren wound up—thin, distant, unimportant. He didn't register it. Somewhere even farther, thunder rolled. Or maybe that was just the highway telling its old story.

He set the empty bottle on the fence post and smiled without humor. "Tomorrow," he said to no one. "We'll see."

The breeze stroked his cheek like a deal.

And far down the road, unseen from the yard, another armored truck eased past a green mile marker and kept going, steady as a heartbeat. The distant siren rose, fell, and resolved into silence Jack didn't notice at all.

CHAPTER 7

Jack spent the start of the week trying not to vibrate out of his own skin.

He told himself it was just work. Working from home always felt like being trapped in a box made of emails, and today the box smelled like reheated coffee and anxious mouse clicks. But it wasn't just work. It was everything under his skin tuning itself to a faster station, some constant invisible metronome tapping his ribs and whispering: *more.*

His home office looked normal if you didn't know him. Laptop, second monitor, USB dock, a houseplant that had given up on photosynthesis and was now purely decorative. If you knew him, you'd notice the new additions: the black balaclava draped over the corner of a bookshelf like a bat waiting for night; the ski goggles set face-up on the desk; the black leather gloves tucked under the keyboard like a secret.

He had his company Slack on Do Not Disturb and his calendar on Out of Office—doctor's appointment, back later—which was true, if "doctor" meant wind and "appointment" meant five thousand feet over North Jersey.

On his second screen, a spreadsheet populated in hypnotic gray boxes. He typed three formulas, checked a cell reference, and minimized it like he was closing a window on a smaller life. His right leg bounced under the desk—fast, tight, like a rocket warming on the pad.

He tried to breathe slow. He failed.

Sunday afternoon at the barbecue kept replaying behind his eyes like a preview he hadn't asked to see. Uncle Frank squinting down a cigar, beer in his other hand, the exact smile of a man who had made peace with his vices decades ago.

"If I could do anything?" Frank had said, already grinning. "Shit. I'd do anything I wanted. I'd probably go to a museum and take a bunch of shit for my house just 'cause. Imagine a friggin' T-rex skull in my living room? Mona Lisa above the toilet? You ever use the Stanley Cup as a pitcher for a regular-ass Sunday football afternoon? Anything is possible."

Everyone laughed. Jack laughed too. Later he'd stood at the fence line and told himself he wasn't that guy.

Days later, that line still hummed between his teeth like a loose filling. *Anything is possible.*

He spun in his chair, looked at the balaclava, then at the window. The August light was bright enough to feel physical. The world outside waited the way a wave waits—apparently calm, but full of force you could ride if you had the nerve.

He stood. "Okay," he said to the empty room. "Let's go."

He slid the balaclava down over his face. The fabric smelled faintly of laundry soap and choices. Ski goggles to the forehead. Black hoodie, black sweats. Gloves. He looked like a Halloween store's idea of *wind robber,* and the absurdity almost made him laugh.

"'No major harm, no major foul,'" he said, trying the words out loud. They didn't sound evil in his mouth. They sounded like a rationalization wearing a friendly shirt. "One time. Maybe two. Three at most. In, out. Easy cash. Lay low. Don't be stupid."

The worst part was how reasonable it felt.

He cracked his bedroom window. The air pressed a cool palm to his face like it was checking his temperature. He stepped onto the sill, crouched, and kicked into the sky.

Two houses away he stopped and swore, spun back, and slid his window shut. "Right. That would've been a fun police report."

Then he was up again, the cul-de-sac falling away, roofs flattening, yards shrinking to Monopoly pieces. He rose above the town's patchwork—Wayne's big boxes, Lincoln Park's strip of small businesses, Pequannock's curving neighborhoods like puzzle pieces that didn't quite fit.

He skimmed at speed along Route 23, passed close enough over a personal injury lawyer billboard that he could've read the fine print if he cared about numbers that small. He didn't. He cared about the heavy, steady signatures of armored trucks. You could feel them without eyes if you knew how to listen—their mass pushed a particular trench through the air, a blunt, snub-nosed pressure that lingered in its wake.

He played first. He had to. The joy was part of the fuel.

He buzzed a Cessna—not close enough to be dangerous, but close enough to see the pilot's hat and the "are you kidding me?" hands he threw up when a human shape arrowed past his left window and saluted like a lunatic. Jack laughed into the balaclava, peeled off, and climbed until the plane shrunk to a toy on blue velvet.

He made himself small, then big, pulling air tight around his body until the wind noise cut out. In the hush he could hear his own heartbeat and, weirdly, someone mowing a backyard two towns over. Then he let the slipstream go and the world screamed past him again, volume back to eleven.

He skimmed low over a reservoir and flicked his wrist; the water surface bulged in a ring that chased him like a happy dog. He pulled it behind him until he remembered sirens and drowned men and scolded himself like a parent catching a kid roughhousing at the pool.

"Be smart," he said. "Be smarter than your own fun."

He saw the truck near lunchtime.

White cab, armored body, the kind of vehicle that always looked like it belonged in grayscale. It cruised south out of Pompton Plains, turned toward Lincoln Park, and Jack felt it like a riff under the song of the day. He rose and circled, watched it from two blocks up as it did something he already knew by heart from a week of scouting: hit the bank loop, idle by the fire zone, blink the hazards, wait for the two guards to go in with an empty cart, come back with full bags.

He landed across the street on the McDonald's roof, crouched at the edge like a gargoyle with poor nutritional choices.

A car rolled into the drive-thru below. The worker handed a paper bag out the window.

Jack made a small grabbing motion with his left hand and sucked the bag up into his palm like the world was a claw machine and he'd finally learned how to beat it. Fry perfume hit his mask—a cruel, perfect joke.

"Sorry!" he stage-whispered to no one. "Wind tax!"

He set the food behind the rooftop HVAC and peeked back at the bank. The guards were exiting—two men in dark uniforms, heavy vests, the bored walk of people who did risk for a living and had inured themselves to it. The cart rattled, heavy with bags.

Jack pushed his hood over the balaclava, goggles down, and breathed deep the way swimmers do when they're about to do something dumb and beautiful.

"Accidents," he told the air. "Little ones."

He focused on the intersection and nudged the bumper of a sedan into the SUV ahead—just a tap. The SUV jolted, honked, and stopped diagonal. The fender-bender blocked the lane in front of the bank's entrance. Horns chorused immediately, because New Jersey.

He reached down the block with his other hand and flicked a newspaper box hard. The metal cabinet tipped and clanged on the sidewalk. He blew a clipped gust and the papers exploded into the street like a flock of startled pigeons, pages tumbling and slapping at windshield glass.

A banner hung across Main—a cheerful LINCOLN PARK DAY sign strung between two poles like the town was trying to remember its normal life. He let it be.

The guards swapped glances. The driver looked at the clogged lane, looked at the cart, decided to unload fast and move. He keyed the back door, swung it, and pulled the ramp out. Money bags made that specific dead-weight sound on aluminum. The driver stood in the doorway, the other man still maneuvering the cart.

Jack measured the air.

He didn't want noise. He wanted force.

He dropped off the McDonald's roof and slipped behind the banner's shadow, ten feet up, invisible to anyone not actively looking straight up while dealing with traffic and newspapers. The wind wrapped his limbs like a suit that fit because it was built from him.

He exhaled and sent the first shockwave.

It wasn't a big one. It didn't have to be. A targeted punch of compressed air slammed the ramp. The cart jumped. One bag toppled, landed on the asphalt, split a seam. Straps flashed.

The driver swore, bent. The second guy turned, saw papers everywhere, shouted something about "secure the—" and that's when Jack dropped hard and fast into the lane.

The impact concentric-ringed the litter at his feet. He shoved the nearest guard with a flat palm and the air carried the man three yards into a parked car—back-first, a thud and a wheeze, alive. The other guard reached for his holster and Jack cut it with a lateral gust that spun the guy against the open door; the door slammed the man, the man cursed.

"Sorry!" Jack said reflexively, which was stupid and also, somehow, perfectly him.

He scooped two bags, hooked another with his forearm, squeezed a fourth against his ribs. The weight surprised him—money had a way of being heavier than it looked—but the air adjusted, lifting with him, his muscles just the suggestion and the wind the actual work.

Someone screamed, "Oh my God!" Another voice—"Is he—what is —" A phone lifted. Another phone lifted. Two shadows crouched behind a Corolla, screens up, eyes wide.

A minivan tried to inch around the fender-bender. Its tire rolled over a tangle of newspapers and spun like an ice move, bumping a parked truck. The truck honked by reflex; the air filled with horns as if chaos had its own soundtrack.

Jack rose.

This was the moment where he could have stopped—dropped the bags, said sorry again, left the scene, gone home and told himself the trial run had been trial enough.

He didn't stop.

He pushed higher and yanked the banner by accident. The LINCOLN PARK DAY fabric snagged his shoulder, tore down the middle, and snapped around his waist like a sash that read BAD DECISIONS.

"Come on," he hissed, trying to shake it free with one knee while keeping four bags clamped and the wind steady. He pulled sideways and the banner's wire twanged, whipped, and ripped down the pole. It flapped behind him like a bright blue fish on a line.

He could hear his heart roaring in his ears and knew, dimly, that it wasn't just his heart. The power had a sound when he pushed it too hard —like pressure in an airplane cabin, like a storm far away getting closer. It did something in his head that felt good and wrong in equal measure, a rush that lifted his face into a grin he didn't recognize on himself.

"Let's go, let's go, let's go—" he told the air, and the air said yes like a lover.

The two men behind the Corolla kept filming. One whispered, "Dude. Dude."

The other said, with the exact weight of prophecy and gossip combined, "We gotta tell the Pantheon."

The words hit Jack like a thrown rock to the shoulder—small pain, big meaning. He shot a look down without meaning to, and for a fraction of a second his eyes met the camera lens. His own reflection looked back: black mask, ski goggles, town banner trailing, four fat bags hugging his ribs.

This is a mistake, he thought—

—and the thought slid off him like rain on oiled glass.

He angled up and out, cutting between buildings, the wind wrapping tighter as he increased speed. He tried to pull the banner free mid-flight; it fought, then tore loud enough to make a dog bark three blocks away.

Behind him, traffic was a wrecked line of startled choreography. No one was dead. The guards were hurt, not broken. One sat up, clutching his ribs. The other pushed to a knee, dazed, breath whistling. A woman in a sundress shouted at someone to call 911 and then realized everyone was already calling 911.

No major harm, no major foul, Jack told himself, and the words hit the inside of his skull and didn't echo. They just settled. Nice. Reasonable.

He cleared Main and banked north. The bags dug into his forearms, straps biting through glove leather. He shaped the air to carry them— tethers of pressure that took some weight and stabilized the load. It felt like learning how to ride a bike while carrying groceries and also being the bike.

He swung over rooftops he recognized—the laundromat with the mural; the vape shop with the sign that tried too hard; the deli where the owner always called him "boss" and never sounded sarcastic. The world looked the same and would not ever be again.

His arms burned now. Not pain—effort. He hadn't trained to carry weight at speed for this long. The current wobbled. The bags threatened to swing. He overcorrected, and the overcorrection turned the swing into a sway, and the sway became a wild flail he choked off with a sharp, panicked *Stop* that the wind, bless it, obeyed immediately.

He landed hard in a stand of pines two miles out, knees bending, bags thumping into the needles with the muffled, expensive sound of someone else's future. He crouched, breathing through a grin he couldn't wipe and a tremor he couldn't hide.

"Okay," he panted, and then laughed because there was nothing okay about any of this. "Okay."

He yanked the balaclava up to get air. His face felt hot, wired, alive. The trees were shock-still in the absence of wind, like even the woods were holding their breath to see who he was now.

He cracked one bag's zipper an inch—saw stacks, banded, the pale green of so many choices. He zipped it shut again fast, like looking too long might make it disappear.

He listened.

Sirens far off, Doppler-warped. Voices somewhere close—kids, maybe, or no, teens; he heard the chaotic pitch of a story being told. "I'm serious, he flew, like flew—" "You got it?" "Yeah, dude, it's on my phone."

He licked his lips, tasted salt and something like metal and something like guilt trying to be born.

He pushed it away. Not forever—just for now. He cinched the bags tighter and lifted again, low and careful, hugging the treeline back toward home in a jagged pattern he hoped wouldn't make any immediate sense on a map.

He slipped in through the side gate and landed in the narrow strip of shade between the house and the garage. The air here was quiet, domestic, trustworthy. Someone on the next block over was frying onions. A dog barked, bored. The normal world always pretended to be stronger than the weird until the weird put on boots.

He carried the bags to the basement bulkhead, eased them down the stairs, and stashed them behind a stack of plastic bins labeled HALLOWEEN and OLD TAX STUFF and CABLES?? He covered the haul with an old blue tarp that smelled like camping and mildew, then stood there looking at the tarp like it might start glowing.

"Temporary," he told it. "We're smart. We're careful. No major harm, no major foul."

He heard his mom upstairs, humming with the radio, and his name in her mouth at a distance that made him feel both six and invisible. "Jack? You home?"

He closed the bulkhead door, climbed the stairs, peeled the balaclava up to his hairline, and walked into the kitchen like he'd just come in from the yard. "Hey," he said, and kissed his mom's cheek because that's what good sons do.

"You look flushed," she said, opening a cabinet. "You run again?"

"Yeah," he said, which wasn't exactly a lie. "Hot out."

"Drink water," she said, the eternal line of every mother in every world, and handed him a glass like a benediction.

He drank. It helped. A little.

His phone buzzed on the counter—news alert. He looked without meaning to. A thumbnail showed an image paused mid-frame: a masked figure in a black hoodie, goggles, bags clutched, banner trailing like a tail. The chyron read: LINCOLN PARK: 'FLYING THIEF' HITS ARMORED TRUCK.

He clicked the volume down with his thumb until the words were only moving mouths.

They'd gotten him. Not him him. But the idea of him. Two bystanders from behind a car had filmed the takeoff, shaky but unmistakable.

He watched his own outline rise on the tiny screen and felt his heart bang once, hard, like it wanted to break something on the way out.

A caption under the upload said: "We're sending this to the Pantheon."

He put the phone face down and smiled at his mom like nothing in the world had shifted half an inch toward a cliff. "Mind if I hop on a quick call?" he asked, and didn't wait for an answer.

Back in his room, he shut the door, leaned his head against it, and counted to ten. Then he pulled the balaclava off, dropped it on the chair, and sat on the edge of the bed with his hands braced on his knees.

The rush was still in him. It wanted to be his friend forever. It said things in his ear that were mostly flattery and a little bit murder. He breathed in, out, in, out, trying to find the part of himself that was still anchored to the old rules.

You crossed a line.
No one died.
You hurt people.
They'll be fine.
You stole money.
From a truck.
That makes it better?
No major harm, no major foul.

He stared at the floor until the pattern in the wood grain turned into a map he couldn't read.

Outside, somewhere to the east, thunder rolled. Or maybe it was a plane. Or maybe, faint and patient as tide, Zeus was testing the air again like radar, and the air was deciding how candid to be.

Jack stood.

He walked to the window and cracked it, and the wind came in as if it had a key. It pressed its cool mouth to his cheek the way it had when he jumped the first time—gentle, familiar, his first and worst co-conspirator.

"Okay," he said softly to the room, to the tarp downstairs, to the people who would watch the video and draw their lines in their own sand. "Okay."

He didn't add *I'll stop.*
He didn't add *I promise.*

He didn't add anything that felt like closing a door, because the door, once open, liked the way it looked on its hinges.

He pulled the goggles from his forehead, set them carefully on the desk, and watched the news thumbnail loop silently on his phone until he hated the look of himself and loved it in equal measure.

In Lincoln Park, a torn banner flapped from a streetlight in a puzzled wind.

And two miles above, where he couldn't see it yet but would soon, a quiet seam in the sky opened and tasted the shape of a man who thought he could steal from the world without the world noticing.

CHAPTER 8

Morning at the New Temple began with thunder that wasn't weather.

The marble steps of the former AMC still gleamed with that too-clean brightness of something recently born. The concrete wall the government built to keep people out now corralled them in—pilgrims and gawkers pressed shoulder to shoulder at the barricades, a tide of faces held back by plastic barriers and officers who tried not to look upward too often. The air around the Temple held a metallic taste, like a storm that had learned patience.

Inside, the lobby had been flayed and rebuilt—carpet gone, seats gone, echoes sharpened. Hephaestus had skinned the building down to bone and then given it new bones: vaulting arches, fretwork ribs, a coffered ceiling with constellations carved into its squares. Where theaters had once divided crowds into assigned silences, a single circular space now drew them inward like a throat.

At its center, they were constructing an arena.

It rose from the floor like a white bloom—tiered rows of stone benches around a ring of sand where concession stands used to be. Hephaestus hammered, and with each strike stone oozed and hardened into perfect fit. The smell of hot metal and crushed lime made the air vibrate. Athena walked the circumferential stairs barefoot; where she stepped, olive branches sprouted from cracks and unfurled silver leaves that threw cool shade.

"Colosseum," Hermes said, drifting backward as he watched the tiers grow. "Miniature. Portable. Unignorable."

"Training ground," Athena corrected without looking at him. "And theater. They learn better when they are watched."

Apollo stood in the gallery above, hands resting on the rail, eyes hooded. He didn't smile, but his face had the preoccupied joy of a man listening to a song only he could hear. In the shadows near him, Hera spoke in low tones to a half-dozen women with notebooks and clear eyes. They were not attendants. Not worshippers. Interviewees. Recruits.

Zeus moved like he had no weight. Every time he passed beneath the ceiling, the constellations in the coffers changed, as if the sky above wanted to please him.

He stopped in the circular sand, turned, and held out a hand without speaking. Hephaestus handed him a spear that hadn't existed five seconds ago. Zeus tested the balance, nodded once, and let the weapon dissolve back into air.

"Where are they?" he asked, not loudly. His voice didn't need size to go far.

Hermes tilted his head toward the doors. "Outside. Two mortals. Claim to have news about the Titans. Loud claims."

Zeus looked toward the entrance, the muscle in his jaw bunching once. "Bring them."

Hermes didn't leave so much as vanish forward and rematerialize at the threshold in one smooth shrug of reality. The doors parted. The noise of the crowd knifed in—shouts, phones, someone crying like a prayer, someone hawking a t-shirt. Hermes stepped into the crush with a smile and it parted around him like oil around a stone.

Two young men were trying to shove their way past the barricade—not brave so much as compelled. One clutched his phone like a talisman; the other had the look of someone who'd discovered the worst kind of lottery ticket: the kind you can't cash in without consequences.

"Zeus needs to know!" the first one cried over the wall of bodies. "We saw a Titan!"

One of Hera's attendants—already in the habit of command—lifted a hand to the guard at the door. Hermes took it from there.

"Inside," Hermes said lightly. "Don't make me say please."

They stumbled in, breathless, suddenly very aware that marble floors echo panic. The doors sealed behind them with a bass note. Inside was cooler; inside was eyes. Athena's calm attention. Apollo's clean, unblinking gaze. Ares leaning on a balustrade like a wolf who'd eaten well but could make room. Hera with that patient, terrible stillness of a judge who already knows the verdict.

Zeus descended the last step into the ring and did not have to ask a question for the questions to answer themselves.

He took each mortal by the back of the neck—his hands enormous, gentle only by intention—and lifted them a fraction off the ground. Their feet were still on stone, but their bodies understood who carried the weight.

"You claim sighting of a Titan," Zeus said.

The phone-shaker gulped. "We—y-yes. We saw—he was made of air, or something. Like the sky had—"

"A Titan," the other interrupted, desperate to be useful. "He stole money from a truck. He flew. We got him on video."

Ares snorted. Hermes's grin took on a razor's edge. Hera's face didn't move.

Zeus didn't look at Hermes. "Explain."

"Their story has done laps outside the wall," Hermes said, as if he were reciting stock prices. "They slipped the checkpoint with religious fervor. The phrase *'for the Pantheon'* was used twice, *'for clout'* maybe three times. But they do carry a recording."

"Show me," Zeus said.

The mortal's hands shook so violently the phone pinballed across options. He found the clip, pressed play, turned the screen toward a god.

The video was chaos stabilized by certainty. A street. A bank. A man-shaped blur in black with ski goggles and a banner flapping from his waist like a conquered flag. Guards knocked aside. Bags lifted. A body rising on air no one else could see.

Zeus watched it once. Then again.

He reached out and took the phone between thumb and forefinger.

For a heartbeat he simply held it. Then his hand tightened and the device collapsed inward with a crunchy, wet-sounding crackle, glass spitting out like grit. Powdered pixels fell to the sand.

The mortals flinched as if bones had broken in their wrists.

"This is not theft," Zeus said, almost gently. "This is noise."

Hermes tilted his head. "A Titan, then?"

"Not of the First," Zeus said. Lightning hummed along his shoulders like impatience. "But wind answers him. That matters."

The men stared, eyes flicking between dust and divinity. When two of Hera's attendants moved to guide them away, one man panicked at the thought of being dismissed.

"Please," he blurted, voice cracking. "We came through everything to tell you. We… we thought you should know. We want to help."

Zeus turned his head the way a storm looks at a tree before deciding whether to spare it.

He stepped forward until the mortals had to tilt backward to take him in. For one irrational instant it felt like he was going to put his hands through their chests and pull out something glowing.

Instead he took their faces in his palms and measured them like tools.

"What are your names?" he asked softly.

"Alex," said the first. "James," said the other, and only afterward did he remember to add, "My lord."

Zeus lowered his hands to their shoulders. "You will be my first chosen."

Hera's chin lifted a degree. Hermes's smile widened by exactly the amount calculation does. Ares stretched his neck and cracked it. Apollo watched.

Zeus spoke, and the Temple answered. Air tightened. Stone thrummed. Alex and James arched as if a wire threaded through their spines had been pulled. The whites of their eyes went bright as fire. Light moved under their skin like a second circulation.

When it finished, they were still themselves—just more of it. Broader. Taller. Tendons like cables. Vision swimming for a moment as their pupils learned new rules.

Hephaestus tossed a pair of gold-plated cuirasses from a palette that hadn't existed a minute ago. They landed at the men's feet with a ringing that went directly into their bones.

"Armor," Hephaestus said, not unkindly. "Learn the gift you just accepted before it kills you."

Zeus rested a hand on each man's head. "You are my **Bishops**," he said, picking a mortal word and making it his. "You will be sent among men to call them to order. You will find those who think they are Titans, and you will bring them to me." He smiled, and it was inexplicably worse than anger. "Tell your families your names have just become bigger than your bodies."

Alex swallowed. James swallowed. They both whispered something that might have been thanks and might have been survival.

Hermes clapped them on the shoulders, translated their panic into movement, and walked them toward the far corridor. "We'll fit you," he said. "Introduce you to the concept of not breaking your own doorframes. Do not hit anything that looks load-bearing."

In the stands that had begun to fill with the boldest of the faithful, a low mutter ran like current: **heroes.** Another voice, nastier, chuckled **zeros** with the particular delight of those who hate the chosen. The words stuck and began breeding outside like graffiti.

The arena continued to rise. The first of Zeus's many power structures had a stage now.

"Station them at each gate," Athena said, watching the new Bishops go. "Mortals taking orders from mortals keeps other mortals calm. They'll hate you less for the same directive."

"They will still hate," Ares said, amused. "Hate sharpens. I like it."

Hera's voice was a string pulled taut. "They will learn love. Or they will remember fear."

Apollo's fingertips drummed once on the rail. "Either way, they will look up when you speak," he murmured. It wasn't praise. It wasn't not.

From outside the Temple, a ripple of attention turned their heads at the same time. It wasn't a noise. It was a *change*. The air shifted as if it remembered a different owner.

Hermes cocked his head, listening with his whole body. "Incoming," he said lightly. "And not a mortal."

The doors blew inward—not shattered, just suddenly a foot farther from their hinges than anyone had designed them to be. Heat licked across the floor like an invisible dog's tongue. The mortals closest to the threshold squealed and skittered back. A couple of guards raised their rifles and then thought better of it; recently, anyone who looked like they were about to shoot inside the Temple had stopped being a guard.

She walked in carrying her own weather.

Sarah looked exactly like someone who had been ordinary until Friday and had spent the week trying very hard to remain that way. Her hair was still pinned like a shift manager's. Her shirt was a festival tee under a denim jacket. She had slept badly, then decided to do something brave.

She stopped at the edge of the sand and lifted both hands, palms open to show there were no weapons. Her mouth trembled. She fought it steady.

"Lord Zeus," she said, and her voice was both tiny and clear. "I—my name is Sarah. I... I am told I am a Titan."

80

A murmur rolled the tiers. The newly minted Bishops, halfway to the corridor, slowed and glanced back with faces that already assumed they belonged here.

Zeus didn't move. His eyes were the kind a camera tries not to look at directly.

"We have house rules," Hermes said, mild. "Announce from the gate. Submit to counsel. Do not bring your storm indoors."

"My storm is me," Sarah said, and to her credit, she didn't apologize for the sentence. "I came to show you I am not your enemy."

Athena, at Zeus's shoulder now, shifted her spear and did not soften.

Sarah took a breath that fogged the air in front of her even as heat rolled off her skin. "I can raise heat," she said. She glanced toward the barricade outside, where the street still owned a few cars that hadn't been towed. "Or remove it."

She turned her hand palm-down. Heat thickened—a sauna moment. A sedan across the barricade shimmered, paint bubbling in a sigh. The windshield crazed, then sagged. Someone outside screamed *car!* like the word could stop chemistry.

Sarah flipped her other palm and the temperature fell like an elevator. Frost flashed across the ruins of the car. The rearview mirror cracked clean off. A man in a Mets hat laughed once in that way people laugh at funerals, because they've run out of better reactions.

Inside, the air around Sarah went white with cold. The marble under her feet steamed.

"I don't want to hurt people," she said, small and loud at once. "I just want you to know—if you are here to protect humankind from what's… from what's coming—" her throat fought— "I am here to help."

Hera rotated one wrist and a coil of gold rope slid down from nowhere into her palm. Artemis swung into the ring from the opposite side atop a white horse that had never been inside the building and didn't care; she dismounted in one liquid movement and the horse evaporated like breath on glass. In her hand: another rope, bristling with hooked barbs like stars.

"You are not a god," Artemis said, voice like flint. "You are an accident we buried once. We are here to re-bury you."

Sarah flinched, then set her jaw. "I'm trying to talk to you."

"Talk faster," Ares suggested pleasantly, picking dirt from under a nail.

Zeus still hadn't moved. He didn't need to. Power dripped from him in tiny lightning filaments that skittered along his forearms and vanished in little forked sighs.

Sarah raised both hands again, and the heat twitched up reflexively. "Please," she said. "Let me prove—"

Hera's rope snapped out, pure gold answer, wrapping Sarah's left wrist and shoulder with a hiss that seared and then cooled. Artemis's rope followed, barbs sinking into denim and skin with surgical joy, locking Sarah's right arm to her ribs. The ropes pulled opposite, cruciform.

Sarah cried out without permission from pride. Frost and steam leapt and fought along her cheeks where the tears tried to choose a state.

The crowd outside went quiet. Inside, it was already quiet. The new arena was very, very good at teaching listening.

"Do not," Athena said, almost motherly, and the word was worse than a shout.

"Please," Sarah said again, shaking now with the insult of being held more than pain. "I came to your house to say I am not your enemy."

Zeus lifted his eyes to the constellations carved in the ceiling and found they had arranged themselves into a pattern he liked. He looked back down.

"We tolerate no risks," he said.

The lightning didn't come down. It came out—from his skin, from his teeth, from the idea of him. It crossed the space between them with no theatrics and all the finality. Sarah tried to pull heat into her hands to meet it; the ropes sang tighter against her bones. For an instant her skin lit from under like paper lanterns. The smell hit the first row and made two people retch.

Then she was a body in ropes, and then a body on sand, and then something brighter than a body lifted from the meat and went up into the rafters, where carved constellations did not deform to make room. It found its own door and left.

The mortals did not cheer. Someone in the cheap seats sobbed. The bishops-in-progress stood a little straighter, because there are only so many ways to stand when you've just learned what your employer means by **order**.

Artemis coiled her rope without comment. Hera wiped one fleck of black from the edge of her gold with a thumb and looked mildly irritated that it had tried to stick.

Outside the wall, a thousand phones had tried to record and a hundred had succeeded and not one would capture what it felt like to be there.

Hermes tapped the toe of his sandal against the stone, wings fidgeting. "The press will call it necessary. Or monstrous. Or both," he said brightly. "Either way, they'll spell our names correctly."

Athena turned her face toward Zeus. "The Titans will not come to talk again."

"They never were going to talk," Ares said, delighted. "Now they will run. Running makes better sport."

Zeus looked toward the doorway where mortals queued in their daily devotions, then past it to where the world continued its small rotations of commerce and panic.

"Station the Bishops at each gate," he said. "Build more." To Hephaestus: "Finish the arena. I want the floor to remember the weight of what falls on it." To Hera: "Find me ten more with steady hands and no tremble." To Apollo: "Make them sing about the order we bring. And if they do not, make them quieter."

Apollo's mouth curved—not a smile, exactly. "As you wish."

Hermes was already moving, overflow-charmed, a publicist for apocalypse. "Shall I tell them," he said, glancing back, "that Olympus is accepting applications for *Heroes*?"

A breath later, from the outer ring of the crowd, came the first hissed response: "Zeros." It caught and spread, a parasite riding the same sound wave as praise.

"Call them what they like," Zeus said, bored by nomenclature. "They will be seen doing what I tell them to do. That is the point."

He stepped into the ring where Sarah had fallen, and the sand there darkened a fraction under his naked foot, then returned to its original color as if even evidence wanted to make him happy.

He looked up. The constellations in the coffers of the ceiling chose a different shape to please him: a hunter, a lightning bolt, a bound figure.

Outside, the wall rattled with a chant that couldn't decide whether it loved him or hated him but that made his name anyway. Inside, the arena took another row, and another, becoming a bowl for events that people would pretend they hadn't wanted and then complain about the scarcity of tickets.

Somewhere not very far away, a man who had told himself *no major harm, no major foul* stared at a tarp in his basement and tried to decide which word in that sentence had the lie inside it.

Zeus didn't know his name yet.

He would.

CHAPTER 9

Guilt, Jack discovered, didn't sit like a rock in your stomach. It fizzed. It lived in the radio static between stations, the tiny buzz under your tongue, the urge to hum so you didn't have to hear yourself think.

The Garden State Parkway unspooled like a long exhale, and he tried to make his breathing match it. His Subaru purred at seventy-one with the air just cracked, salt sneaking in though the ocean was still miles away. Spotify shuffle chose violence and served "MMMBop," and Jack barked a laugh he didn't know he needed.

"Okay," he told the dashboard, turning the volume up instead of down. "We're doing this."

No flying. No shortcuts. No... whatever you call air-assisted lane changes. He white-knuckled his self-control and let minivans pass on the left like they had earned it. Every so often, muscle memory tugged at his wrist—just a nudge, the way he'd learned to shape the breeze inside the cabin—and he'd yank his hand back to keep himself honest.

"Normal," he said out loud, like it was a spell. "Be normal."

Atlantic City rose out of the flat light like a promise made by someone who owed you money. Neon before sky. The billboards here had always been loud; now they were shameless. A liquor ad had a laurel wreath. A sportsbook flashed a lightning bolt that looked suspiciously licensed.

He self-parked at Harrah's because that's what normal people did. No valet for the guy who'd decided the last thing he needed was to be remembered by one more person. Up the escalator, across the carpet that turned feet into whispers, check-in behind a couple in matching "Bride/ Groom" shirts who took a selfie with the clerk and yelled "Zeus bless!" after getting their keys.

His room looked across a pool deck where three guys already slept like question marks on blue floats. He tossed his backpack onto the bed, splashed water on his face at the bathroom sink, and held his own gaze in the mirror. Still him. Same eyes. More static.

"Vacation," he told his reflection. "We're on a normal person vacation."

He lasted ten minutes before the itch sent him out the door.

The Tropicana felt like stepping into a circuit board made for human ants. Everything blinked. Everything chimed. It smelled like smoke politely pretending to be nostalgia and perfume pretending to be luck. Jack slid into the current and let it carry him past the blackjack islands and the craps crowd, past a slot machine that meowed when someone won, until the roulette pit pulled on his attention like a magnet.

He picked a table under a chandelier that looked like a frozen fireworks bloom and bought in for way too much in five-dollar chips. The dealer was impossibly calm, the way good dealers were. The name tag said Theron, and when Theron turned to grab the extra rack of reds, Jack's brain short-circuited for a second.

Hooves. Not costume hooves, not cheap silicone. Glossy, thick, bronze-dark. Calves furred to the knee in a color that was more gold than brown. The faintest shimmer moved through the hair when he stepped, like sunlight under ripples. And—Jack inhaled—a ghost of grapes, like someone had opened a jar of jam across the room.

"First time?" Theron said without looking up, voice light as a flute line.

"At a table run by... uh," Jack gestured vaguely under the felt lip, "—that."

Theron's smile made the corner of his eyes crinkle. "You're looking at Local 121, Satyr Division."

"You unionized?"

"We didn't, then we did," Theron said, dropping the ball with that little flick that made pros look like magicians. "Management had a crisis over whether we counted as exotic dancers or wildlife. Lawyers got rich. We landed a floor of rooms, food, water, and the kind of wine that makes the gods nostalgic. We don't need much."

"Do you—" Jack pitched his voice low. "Do you remember where you were, before?"

Theron's hand paused over the payouts for a fraction, then resumed as if time had hiccuped and moved on. "Woke up in the pines outside Brigantine with a hangover that felt prehistoric. Some of my cousins came out of statues. One uncle came out of a painting, blinked at the ocean, and asked for a pan flute and a sandwich. We all adjusted."

A woman in a sparkly jacket two seats over tossed a stack on 17 and said, "Hon, I adjusted twelve times this week, and that was just my bangs." She winked at Theron. "Do you do birthday parties?"

Theron laughed. "Only if the cake's good."

The ball clattered home. Winners cheered; losers shrugged like they'd paid for a ride. Jack started with outside bets, the way sensible people did when they were pretending sensibility. Red hit. Even hit. He sipped a drink that tasted cold and sweet and distant.

He wasn't going to push anything. He had told himself that. No nudges. No "help." Just let the world do what the world does and be one more bobbing head in the current.

The problem with promises was how quiet they got when adrenaline started humming.

He felt the spin like music. Not just heard it—felt the tiny pressure ripples the ball sent out as it ran the track and stuttered in, how the air carved around each pocket. Without thinking, his shoulders matched the rhythm. His fingers, idle on the felt, rolled a chip. Floated it a millimeter. Spun it in place.

"What the hell was that?"

The voice came soft from across the wheel. Guy in a clean navy suit, not flashy, not cheap. Banker, lawyer, something professionalized into calm. Early forties. His face had the kind of neutrality you learn in meetings—a face that asks for clarification without giving anything away.

Jack fumbled theatrically and let the chip clack onto the felt. "Static," he said, and grinned like he knew it was a stupid joke and leaned into it anyway. "Air's dry."

Theron's eyes flicked up and away in a move that said I saw, I won't make it a thing, don't make me have to make it a thing. The banker didn't push. He just watched with that same tidy curiosity, like he'd filed something away and was thinking about where it might fit.

Jack hovered a hair too long before he remembered to breathe.

The ball dropped. He won again. He won more than again. He won enough that the stack of reds started to look like it needed a seatbelt.

He told himself it was luck. He told himself he hadn't touched anything but feelings, and feelings weren't illegal. He told himself this was what casinos were built for—risk translated into lights and sound.

He also felt his blood get a little louder in his ears. The room crisped at the edges, colors sharpening the way they did when he leaned into wind and let it hold him. He forgot, for a few spins, how to be guilty.

"Color me up?" he said after a while, voice a notch too bright, because smart people quit while it all still felt like a joke.

Theron nodded, swept the mound of reds into a glittering waterfall, and pushed back bacon-thick plaques that suddenly felt too heavy for the size of them.

"Good run," Theron said. "You keep a soul that knows how to leave the table, you'll survive longer than most."

"Trying to cut back," Jack said, cleared his throat, and wished the joke didn't sound like a confession.

He slid the plaques into his jacket. When he stood, the banker stood too—slow, as if his joints were thinking about it. Not a block. Not a creep. Just... movement timed to Jack's.

Theron lifted a hand. "Hey—Jack, right? You left your card."

Jack didn't hear. Or pretended not to. His feet had already decided the direction his head would call bravery later.

The pit boss arrived with that quiet pressure of someone who could eject you and make you say thank you for the exercise. She tapped the card on the rail, squinting at the name. "Comp points, honey."

The banker smiled politely. "I know him. We're at Harrah's too. I'll run it up."

Theron's gaze dipped to the man's shoes—soft leather, the color of expensive coffee—and then back to his face. Satyr eyes were good at reading posture.

"Harrah's is a lot of rooms," he said, tone easy. "You want me to call him back?"

"I jog," the banker said, a little dry humor bending the words. "I'll get the steps."

The pit boss, whose job was to keep friction off the floor without calling security every ten minutes, shrugged and handed over the card. "All yours, cardio man."

"Your karma," Theron murmured, more to the chips than the man.

The banker tucked the plastic into his breast pocket like a business card he'd decided to actually save.

Jack drifted into the casino's bloodstream and tried to look like he belonged to no one. Bass thumped through the carpet; notes from two different songs fought in the air until one won by force of proximity. He slid past the $25 blackjack into the safer anonymity of quarter slots, then hooked toward the long hallway where the ocean sneaked into sight through glass.

He didn't feel followed.

He felt observed.

That was new. Or maybe that was now.

A trio of bachelorettes in matching pink sashes spilled out of a nightclub entrance like glitter had evolved into mammals. One had a tiara. One was crying because she loved everyone. One held a shoe in her hand like a weapon.

"Picture!" Tiara yelled at no one in particular, then at Jack in particular because his face made the mistake of having eyes. She thrust a phone at him.

"Absolutely," Jack said, stepped into the hurricane, held the phone high, and turned his shoulder so that whoever might be watching got a faceful of BRIDE SQUAD instead of Jack's jawline.

The picture took.

Then six more.

The banker's navy suit paused three beats away, did the math on whether following through a cluster of squealing thirty-somethings would either get him killed or married, and opted for a detour.

Jack laughed with his new best friends, hugged a stranger who smelled like champagne and victory, handed back the phone with a "Happy almost!" and slipped into the side door that led to the escalators.

He didn't run. He didn't float.

He just moved the way a person moves when he needs to leave without being a story and decided to head to his room that he didn't need to get if he'd be driving home anyway.

Elevators.

Hallway.

Key card.

Door.

The room smelled like recycled air and ambition.

He set the chips on the dresser and stared at them like they might climb down and explain themselves. He turned on the TV and surfed past the channel with the wall of sports and the channel with the buffet ad until he landed on news.

The anchor had the voice people use when they're excited to be calm.

Footage from Rockaway—again.

The New Temple glowing like bone under stadium lights. The new "Bishops" standing at the gates in gold chest plates, perfect posture, expressions stuck somewhere between pride and what happened to pride when it tried to be obedience.

Public opinion graphs.

A clip of Hera shaking someone's hand and their face breaking into relieved tears.

A replay of Sarah—not by name, because no one on TV said Titan names like they were people—raising her palms to show surrender and becoming a warning instead.

The lower third read:

ORDER RETURNS TO OLYMPUS HQ

Jack clicked the volume down until the words moved lips only.

He stood at the window.

The pool glowed sorbet-blue. The sleeping men on the floats had rotated in the wind; now they formed a constellation only their chiropractor could name.

He went to the desk to drop his player's card in the drawer with the little paper pad and realized his wallet had a phantom ache where it lived.

He flipped it open.

No card.

For a second, panic flared stupid and bright.

Then he exhaled and replayed the last hour.

Theron calling after him.

The pit boss.

The banker in the navy suit, polite, professional, saying, I'll take it.

Not weird.

Not creepy.

Just... practical.

He'd probably give it to the front desk at Harrah's and feel good about himself for doing a good deed, and Jack could pick it up tomorrow with a sheepish smile and a thanks he would mean.

"Normal," Jack said again, softer. "We're doing normal."

He showered long and too hot, like heat could scrub out humming. After showering, deciding he was alone anyway, he stepped out of the shower and onto the bath mat. Jack wraps his towel around his waist and then pauses. Thinking to himself, he takes a deep breath in , and then a short quick exhale and focuses air away from his body expelling every drop of water drying him instantly.

He lay on the bed with the AC clicking on, off, on, off.

He told himself not to check the news.

He checked the news.

A trending video from Lincoln Park climbed another hundred thousand views. Comments divided into cheering, fear, and conspiracy math. Someone had slowed the footage to try to catch the exact angle of his face in the goggles.

He dropped the phone face-down. He turned off the TV.

The dark room hummed. The air moved under the blackout curtains the way tide moves under boats.

He laid back and didn't sleep for a while and then slept all at once, like someone had flipped a breaker.

CHAPTER 10

The Garden State Parkway at this hour was a graveyard of headlights and bad decisions. Jack had made this drive more times than he could count —post-parties, post-hookups, post-regrets—but this one hummed different. The guilt still lingered from Atlantic City, but it had shifted flavor. Less sour, more… static. His body was restless, electric. He rolled down the window just to hear the air move and let it calm him. It didn't.

The Subaru's clock glowed in the dash when he hit Route 23 north. Home stretch. A few more turns and he could collapse into bed, sleep for a day, maybe two. Pretend the world outside wasn't melting into mythology.

Then he saw it—a smear of black across the sky, blooming higher than the treeline. Smoke. Thick, rolling, too dense to be anything small. His first thought was factory fire. His second thought was don't get involved.

The scanner under his passenger seat disagreed.

He'd tossed it there after the heist, a leftover from "planning days" when his bad ideas still felt like strategy. He dug it out and flicked it on.

Static. Crackle. Then:

"—structure fire, Chilton Memorial Hospital, multiple floors affected —"
"—suspected explosion on third level—"
"—patients being evacuated—"

Jack exhaled through his teeth. "Great. Perfect. Sure, why not."

He sat at the red light, staring at the rising column of smoke just a few miles away. Rational thought told him to go home. Every other part of him was already turning the wheel.

Sirens flared up ahead. Two ambulances screamed past him in opposite lanes, followed by a fire engine and a squad car. He slowed, pulled over, watched the flashing reds and blues reflect across his hood like guilt in color form.

He didn't need to be seen here. Not after Lincoln Park.
Especially not if anyone was looking for "a man made of air."

He turned off onto a residential side street, weaving past sleeping houses until the road dead-ended at a patch of woods. He killed the engine, coasted the Subaru just beyond the tree line, and parked in the shadows.

The smoke was visible now—dark, angry plumes rising behind the hospital roofline. The smell reached him a second later: burning plastic, disinfectant, and the faint metallic tang of something worse.

He stepped out, hoodie up. The night wind curled around him, familiar, obedient. He closed his eyes, reached for that rhythm inside him —the pulse of air that was more than breath, the living current that had started answering to his will.

He'd been practicing invisibility. Not literal vanishing—just learning how to make air bend light, distort the edges of him, blur him out like heat waves. He focused now, felt his heartbeat slow, his molecules hum, the edges of his reflection thinning.

When he looked down at his hands, they shimmered. Not gone. But ghosted.

"Alright," he muttered, smirking despite himself. "Let's see if this works."

He crouched, inhaled deep, and launched upward. The air caught him like an old friend.

The world fell away.

He skimmed the rooftops, half-seen, the wind hissing past his ears. Below, firefighters lined up hoses while nurses corralled patients on the lawn. The main blaze was on the upper floors, west wing. Emergency lights flickered through black smoke. He angled toward the back side, where there were fewer eyes and more shadows.

He leveled out and blasted forward—too fast, too confident—and crashed through the third-floor window in a shatter of glass and pressure.

"Shit—!" He hit the floor in a roll, air cushioning him before the shards could cut. Fire danced along the walls, devouring curtains, crawling up IV poles. He coughed, waved away the smoke, and instinctively pushed out with his hands—a heavy gust swept the hallway, snuffing flames along one side.

The temperature dropped fast. He almost smiled.

His first good act in days, and it felt incredible.

He stalked down the corridor, kicking open doors. Some rooms were already cleared—empty beds, wheelchairs abandoned mid-run. But others still screamed. Patients behind closed doors, blocked by flame and collapse.

Jack aimed his palms at the fire choking one doorway. He exhaled sharply—the gust blasted the oxygen out of the flame, smothering it in a swirl of white-hot smoke. He stepped inside.

Two nurses huddled near the wall, one coughing hard, the other dragging an oxygen tank.

"Get out!" Jack yelled, voice half-lost in the roar.

They looked up, eyes wide, seeing only a blur of a man half-swallowed by smoke.

He waved toward the door and wind surged through the hallway, parting fire like curtains. The nurses bolted through, pulling the tank behind them.

Jack stood still, panting. The world slowed. The air shimmered, and through the waves of heat, he saw something move at the far end of the corridor.

A silhouette in the fire.
Broad shoulders. Shirtless. Standing perfectly still while the flames licked around him.

Jack squinted, blinked smoke out of his eyes. The heat made the figure dance, but the longer he looked, the less human it seemed.

"What the hell…" he whispered.

The man stepped forward through the blaze, and the flames bent around him like bowing. Each footfall left the tile glowing. The smoke twisted away instead of choking him.

Not immune to fire.
Connected to it.

Jack's heart stuttered.
No way.

He launched forward, boots skidding on wet tile. "Hey! You need to —"

The man turned. His face flickered in the light, half-hidden behind soot and flame—but the eyes, those unmistakable brown eyes—

"Ryan?"

Jack froze mid-step. "Ryan Cho?"

It couldn't be. His old frat brother, the one who always showed up to parties in too-nice shoes and swore he was allergic to beer pong. They hadn't talked in months. Not since… well, everything went to hell.

The fire pulsed around Ryan's frame like it wanted to claim him but couldn't.

He didn't speak. Didn't even look surprised.

Jack took a slow step forward. "It's me, man. Jack. What are you doing here?"

Ryan blinked, disoriented—or something like it. "I… I don't know." His voice sounded layered, like two people speaking in unison. "It burns, but it doesn't. I can't—" He staggered, gripping his head. "It's inside me."

Jack reached out, reflexes on autopilot, grabbing his shoulder. The instant their skin touched, a shockwave of heat blasted between them. Flames flared, smoke twisted violently, alarms wailed as ceiling tiles dropped like snow.

"Okay, okay—hey!" Jack yelled, forcing wind outward to snuff the spreading fire. "Stay with me!"

He wrapped Ryan in an air bubble, a swirling sphere that pushed oxygen and smoke apart. It shimmered blue-white in the light of the burning ceiling. Ryan gasped as the flames receded from his skin.

Jack could feel it now—power radiating off his old friend. Hot, molten, angry.
Titan energy. He didn't know how he knew that. He just… did.

The air bubble pressed tighter as Jack concentrated. It muffled everything—alarms, sirens, screaming. Only their breathing remained.

"Calm down!" Jack shouted, trying to drown out the instinct rising in his own chest—that same violent pulse that wanted to control the air, to crush instead of calm.

The bubble compressed further, locking Ryan in. He thrashed, gasping.

Jack's pulse spiked.
"Stop struggling! You're gonna—"

He realized what he was doing too late.

The bubble was cutting off more than smoke.

He was choking him.

Jack recoiled in horror, letting the air snap back. Ryan collapsed onto the wet tile, hacking in huge, burning breaths.

Jack stumbled backward, hands shaking. "Jesus Christ…"

He crouched beside him, grabbed his wrist, checked his pulse. Still strong. Hot as a furnace.

For a moment they just breathed—Jack's shallow, Ryan's ragged.

Then the fire alarms screamed to life again. Red strobes painted the hallway in bursts. Shouts echoed from below. More responders were coming up.

Jack looked at the doorway—then at Ryan. He couldn't be found here. Not like this. Not by anyone.

"Alright," Jack muttered. "We're leaving."

He grabbed two hospital gowns off a supply cart, tore the bottom hem, and wrapped one around Ryan's shoulders. Then he hoisted him up —dead weight, heat radiating off him like an engine. The wind answered, lifting them both off the ground.

"Hang on," Jack said, voice tight.

He aimed for the broken window. The night swallowed them.

They landed hard among the trees near the back of the hospital property. Steam rose from the wet grass where Ryan had touched down. Jack staggered, shaking soot from his hair.

He laid Ryan against a fallen log. The man's eyes fluttered open, still glowing faintly, like embers hiding in ash.

"Ryan," Jack said again, forcing calm. "Talk to me."

"It's not... just me," Ryan whispered. "There's something else. I see things. Fire. Walls breaking. Voices calling from... below."

He gripped his temples, grimacing. "They're coming back, Jack. All of them."

Jack's blood went cold. "The Titans?"

Ryan nodded weakly. "The walls of Tartarus are gone. I can feel it— they're... leaking. I don't know how I know, but I do."

Jack looked back at the glowing horizon, where the hospital lights blinked through smoke. The world was unraveling faster than anyone could patch it.

He knelt beside his old friend. "Alright. You need to go back inside. Tell them you escaped out the side stairwell, got knocked out by smoke, whatever. Don't say you saw me. Don't mention... any of this."

Ryan stared at him, dazed. "You saved me."

Jack forced a half-smile. "Let's just call it even for college."

He helped him to his feet, adjusted the gown around his shoulders. "You can walk?"

"Yeah."

"Good. Walk slow. Look confused. You'll blend in."

Jack stepped back, the air already swirling faintly around his boots. "We'll figure this out later, okay?"

Ryan nodded once and turned toward the flashing lights in the distance. He stumbled through the brush, then disappeared into the haze.

Jack stayed behind, hidden in the shadows. Watching. The smoke thinned, the sirens dulled. He finally exhaled—a long, shaky release of everything he hadn't processed yet.

He'd almost killed his friend. He'd just saved him. And somehow, both of those things felt equally impossible.

He looked down at his hands—soot-streaked, trembling—and saw them shimmer again, translucent at the edges. The air pulsed softly, like it was waiting for his next move.

He whispered to no one, "What the hell are we turning into?"

Above him, a faint rumble echoed through the sky. Not thunder. Deeper.
Older.

And for the first time since the gods came back, Jack felt the wind shiver.

CHAPTER 11

The world had a way of going back to pretending.

Even after gods landed in parking lots and men started glowing in fires, the sun still rose, traffic still honked, and the smell of burnt plastic still clung to the morning air like a hangover.

Ryan Cho stood in the crowd outside Chilton Memorial Hospital, wrapped in a borrowed blanket and a haze of disbelief. His hair was damp, his skin slick with dried soot, and the paramedic who'd bandaged his arm kept asking if he'd inhaled smoke. He nodded when it seemed polite. He didn't remember. Not the smoke, not the heat, not the way the walls had folded in like paper.

What he remembered was Jack's voice.
And the wind.

He kept his head down now, eyes on the pavement, trying not to look like someone who had just been reborn through fire. The parking lot was chaos — flashing lights, cameras, civilians holding up phones. Police pushed people back with calm voices that couldn't hide the edge of fear. Everyone here had seen something impossible and was desperate to name it.

"Two figures," a woman nearby was saying into a news mic. "One looked like... like he was on fire. The other — he flew."

"Can you describe him?" the reporter pressed.

"Just... air," she said, voice cracking. "Like heat shimmer. Like nothing."

Ryan's pulse thudded. He tugged the blanket tighter and edged farther into the crowd.

And that's when the air itself seemed to shift.

The first to arrive was Athena.

She rode through the crowd astride a horse the color of moonlight, her bronze armor glinting beneath the pale morning sun. Her presence didn't need sirens. The sound around her dimmed naturally, as if the world decided it was better to listen.

Behind her came Artemis — lean, severe, her stallion black as wet ink — and Hermes, winged sandals whispering against the asphalt as he descended from the sky, late and unbothered as ever.

Gasps rippled through the crowd. Someone whispered, "It's them," and like a contagion, everyone around him dropped to a knee. Even the police at the perimeter hesitated before their training gave way to awe.

Two officers stepped forward, weapons holstered, heads bowed.

"Lord Hermes, Lady Athena, Lord Artemis—" one stammered, voice shaking. "We — uh — we secured the perimeter. Fire's out. Casualties zero, thank the gods." He flinched as soon as he said it.

Hermes smiled like someone who had heard the phrase too many times. "You're welcome," he said smoothly.

Athena ignored him. She swung down from her horse, scanning the charred hospital wing. Smoke still curled lazily from the roof, white and harmless now, but the air felt charged. Residual power hung thick, like ozone before a lightning strike.

"Tell me," she said to the officer. Her voice carried easily, without effort. "What did you see?"

The man swallowed hard. "Witnesses said a man on fire — he was... setting things off, I guess? Then another man, translucent, like... like he wasn't all there, came flying in. They fought the fire. Then both of them disappeared before we could get eyes inside."

"Translucent?" Hermes tilted his head, intrigued. "That's new."

The officer nodded nervously. "We pulled what security footage we could from the hospital, but, uh—" He gestured toward a small TV cart the techs had set up near the ambulances. "—the cameras all shorted out. Electricity fried."

Athena approached the screen, hands behind her back. The grainy footage played: the hospital hall, smoke, static, and then — something flickering. Fire spreading too fast. Then a gust of invisible force knocking it down like it had been scolded by nature itself. A human outline glinting and vanishing in the chaos.

Hermes whistled low. "You humans sure are useful, aren't you? Always catching half the story."

Artemis snorted, dismounting with a metallic clank. "They're lucky they caught any of it. If that was truly a Titan, they should've run."

Athena didn't answer. She leaned closer to the screen, eyes narrowing. "No. Not a Titan. Not yet."

She turned to the nearest officer. "Where were these sightings again?"

"Third floor, west wing."

She nodded. "Fire and air. One consuming, one extinguishing. Opposites in chaos." Her tone shifted — less statement, more calculation. "They weren't enemies."

Hermes smirked. "Teamwork makes the dream work."

She ignored him again. "The Titans' powers have always been elemental at their core. Fire. Air. Earth. Sea. If two vessels have awakened this close together—"

"Then more are coming," Artemis finished grimly.

Apollo arrived silently, like a reflection already in the light. No horse, no announcement — just there, golden and still. His gaze locked on the burned facade of the hospital. His eyes glowed faintly, sunlight refracting where no sunlight reached.

Athena looked at him. "What do you see?"

Apollo didn't blink. "Residue," he said finally. His voice was low, sonorous, dangerous in its calm. "Whatever burned here wasn't human."

He turned toward the crowd — hundreds of people now, some crying, some praying, some livestreaming. His eyes swept across them like radar, each movement calculating. He stopped, briefly, as if catching something invisible in the air. A heartbeat out of place. But then it was gone.

He looked back at Athena. "Nothing remains."

Ryan had felt that stare.

He didn't need to look up to know whose eyes had brushed over him. His skin burned under the blanket, not from heat but from recognition — prey recognition.

He slipped farther into the crowd, careful not to rush, careful not to draw eyes. The gods were busy with the police now, questioning, commanding, existing like the world bent naturally around them. The mortals near them trembled in awe and confusion, but awe won.

Ryan reached the line of news vans, kept walking. A reporter shouted a question at Athena, and her reply rolled like thunder: "We will investigate. We will find them. And when we do — there will be no mercy for what stirs beneath our skies."

He didn't need to hear more. He kept walking, shoulders hunched, the blanket dragging like a cape.

Athena turned back to the officers. "Secure all footage, all witness statements. Send them to Olympus immediately."

The officer nodded so fast his hat nearly fell. "Yes, ma'am — uh — yes, goddess."

Artemis paced near the ambulance line, disgust curling his lip. "Look at them. Obedient little things. They kneel before whoever has the loudest thunder."

Hermes leaned on a paramedic truck, arms folded, casual as ever. "Don't knock it, brother. Obedience saves time."

"Obedience," Artemis muttered, "isn't the same as loyalty."

Athena ignored the bickering. She mounted her horse, eyes still on the smoldering wing. "We're too late here. But this... pattern can't be coincidence."

Hermes tilted his head. "Pattern?"

"First reports of creatures at High Point," she said, reciting like a tactician. "Sirens near Lake Hopatcong. Centaurs in Ringwood. And now this — fire and air awakening within hours of one another."

Apollo finally spoke again, his tone absolute. "The Titans are stirring."

Artemis frowned. "How? We sealed Tartarus."

Athena's gaze hardened. "We thought we did. But even walls built by gods crumble when mortals forget why they were raised."

She pulled the reins. Her horse reared once, smoke curling around its hooves. "They're not attacking yet. They're hiding. Testing. Reclaiming the elements."

Hermes smirked. "Just like old times. You know, minus the smartphones and gun worship."

Athena didn't smile. "If two Titans have found their hosts already, then Olympus must prepare. The mortals can't face what's coming."

"Should we tell Zeus?" Artemis asked, with a tone that made "should we" sound like "do we really have to?"

Athena's eyes flicked upward, toward the faint streak of lightning splitting the clouds miles above. "He already knows."

Hermes glanced sideways, muttering, "He always does."

The gods mounted once more — Hermes lifting effortlessly into the air, wings trailing light, Athena and Artemis side by side, horses trotting past the kneeling police line.

As they passed, the officers lowered their heads, not by command but by instinct. Power was its own gravity.

A young firefighter near the curb looked up at Artemis as they went by. "Are you here to protect us?"

Artemis looked down at him, eyes cold as marble. "We protect what deserves it."

Then he was gone, hooves pounding the pavement like thunderclaps fading into the distance.

When the gods vanished into the horizon, the spell broke. The crowd exhaled collectively, some weeping, some clapping, all unsure which was the appropriate response.

Reporters swarmed the still-smoking hospital entrance. Drones buzzed overhead. A lieutenant shouted orders that nobody really followed.

And in the noise, Ryan slipped back into the hospital with the crowd.

He didn't look back.

Somewhere deep inside, something ancient stirred, whispering in a voice that wasn't his.
Air meets fire. Two awakened. The balance breaks.

He clutched his blanket tighter. "Not yet," he whispered to himself. "They can't know yet."

The wind rustled through the trees, and for just a second, it answered.

CHAPTER 12

Jack's car still smelled like cheap fries and adrenaline.

The morning air was gray and heavy when he pulled up in front of Ryan Cho's place — or what was left of it. The street had been taped off by police, the kind of yellow tape that said "Don't look too close." Two tow trucks idled nearby, one hauling off the scorched frame of what used to be a Honda Civic. The other car involved was already gone, just a stain of oil and black rubber on the asphalt.

Jack parked a few houses down and walked the rest of the way, hood up, keeping his head low. Ryan sat on the curb, hospital wristband still around his arm, wearing clothes that didn't quite fit — somebody's donation from lost and found, probably. His elbows rested on his knees, eyes fixed on the cracked pavement in front of him.

Jack stopped beside him. "You look like shit," he said softly.

Ryan smirked without looking up. "Thanks, doc." He hopped in Jack's car and closed his eyes as he pressed his head against the cool passenger window.

They sat in silence for a while. Sirens wailed somewhere far away, just white noise now. The smell of burned plastic lingered in the air like bad memory.

***

Coffee solves lots of problems. Pour over in the kitchen can't solve everything though. Finally, Ryan spoke. "You saw the hospital."

Jack nodded.

"I didn't mean to—" He exhaled sharply. "I didn't even know what was happening."

Jack sat beside him. "Tell me."

Ryan rubbed his palms together, watching his fingers flex as if they belonged to someone else. "Friday night. August seventeenth. I was driving home from my cousin's place in Paramus. I stopped at a red light by that Sunoco on Valley Road. I remember the song that was playing — 'Electric Feel.' Fitting, right?"

Jack cracked a small grin. "Always knew you'd go out dramatic."

"Yeah, well, I didn't go out." He paused, his expression darkening. "Light turned green. I hit the gas. Then—"

He mimed a crash, hands jerking. "Drunk driver blew the red light. Must've been doing eighty. Hit me square on the driver's side. I spun. I remember the sound more than anything — metal folding, glass everywhere, this bright flash that didn't make sense. Then… fire."

Jack leaned forward, elbows on knees. "You were conscious?"

"Barely. Everything was upside down. I smelled gas, and I remember thinking, this is it. But the explosion—" He hesitated. "It didn't start outside. It started inside the car. Like… something blew up from the middle out. Cameras caught it, too. Gas station, traffic light — all showed the same thing. It wasn't a spark. It was a pulse."

He flexed his fingers again, staring at them. "They said I should've died. No broken bones. No burns. Just — heat."

Jack waited, letting the silence do the asking.

"They took me to Chilton," Ryan continued. "I was out most of the night. My parents came, saw I was fine, went to the waiting room to fill out the release paperwork. I was sitting there, waiting for discharge, and my hands started to feel… warm. Not tingly. Alive. Like my blood was turning into fire."

He glanced up, eyes glowing faintly in the light — maybe reflection, maybe not. "Next thing I know, the gloves they gave me to keep warm caught fire. I waved my hands to put it out — and the flames moved with me."

Jack stayed quiet. Every word lined up too perfectly with his own memories. The same night. The same impossible awakening. The same why me question with no answer.

"Then everything went to hell," Ryan said quietly. "The alarms went off. People ran. I tried to stop it, but the more I panicked, the bigger it got. Then—well, you showed up."

Jack exhaled. "Yeah. I did."

They sat in Jack's kitchen now, hours later, both showered and cleaned up. The sound of the fridge humming filled the silence. Jack's mom had made coffee and toast, then gone upstairs after a long talk about how "of course your friend can stay for a few days, that poor boy's been through enough."

She didn't ask many questions.
She'd seen the news. She didn't want answers.

Ryan's hospital bracelet lay on the counter between them. The name was half-burned off. His fingers drummed against the Formica like a slow metronome.

"So," he said finally, "what about you?"

Jack took a sip of his coffee. "What about me?"

"You've been flying around since Saturday. You showed up in a burning building like it was a Tuesday errand. You've got something. What is it?"

Jack hesitated, then exhaled through his nose. "Air."

"Air?"

"Yeah. All of it." He held up his hand, palm open. The napkin on the counter fluttered once, then lifted off the surface, spinning lazily in place. Ryan leaned back, eyebrows up. Jack smirked faintly. "I can feel everything that moves through it — every vibration, every molecule. I can push it, pull it, carry it. I can even…"

109

He leaned back, focused, and slowly lifted himself two inches off the chair, floating weightless for a heartbeat before settling again. "...do that."

Ryan's jaw dropped. "You can fly?"

"Yeah," Jack said, shrugging. "It's as awesome as it sounds. And about as dangerous."

He leaned forward again, the humor fading. "Listen. Whatever this is, it's not just us. You heard the news — gods at the hospital, creatures showing up in the woods, cops kneeling to Zeus like it's Sunday mass. The world's losing its mind. And we—" he gestured between them "—we're in the middle of it."

Ryan nodded slowly. "You think we're connected."

"I don't think. I know." Jack's voice hardened. "That fire last night? It didn't just happen. You're one of them. A Titan. And so am I."

Ryan stared at him. "That's insane."

"Yeah," Jack said. "Tell that to the gods building a temple in Rockaway."

Jack leaned back in his chair, rubbing his temples. "Okay, we need rules. Real ones."

"Rules?" Ryan frowned. "What are we, superheroes now?"

"No," Jack said, "we're the guys they'll kill first if we screw up." He pointed toward the TV, where muted footage from the hospital played on loop. "They're looking for people like us. You saw what happened to that temperature girl on live TV. One wrong move, and Zeus plays executioner again."

Ryan's mouth tightened. "So what, we just hide?"

"For now." Jack's tone left no room for argument. "No powers in public. Not at the store, not in traffic, not even a jog. You use it, you use it here. Quiet. Controlled. Nobody can see you."

He stood, pacing slightly, energy bleeding into the room like static. "I've already been seen once. That heist—" He caught himself, cursed softly. "Never mind. Point is, we can't draw more attention."

Ryan crossed his arms. "You robbing banks now, Robin Hood?"

Jack shot him a look. "Don't. It's handled."

"Uh-huh."

"Focus." Jack jabbed a finger at him. "If we're going to figure this out, we need to be smart. Whatever happened to us wasn't random. We got chosen."

"Chosen by what?"

Jack didn't answer. He didn't know how to.

***

When Jack's mom came downstairs a few minutes later, she found them in the living room, trying their best to look like two normal adults who hadn't almost caused divine panic.

She adjusted her glasses, giving Ryan a kind smile. "You poor thing. I saw the fire on the news this morning. It's a miracle you made it out."

Jack cut in smoothly. "Yeah, Mom. He's waiting to move into his new place, so I told him he could crash here a couple days."

"Oh, that's fine," she said, waving her hand. "Guest room's clean. Just no parties this time, okay?"

"Promise," Jack said, meaning it only mostly.

She gave him a suspicious glance that said she remembered every party he'd ever thrown, then smiled again at Ryan. "I'll make extra pasta tonight."

"Thank you, Mrs. Callahan," Ryan said softly.

When she disappeared back upstairs, Jack exhaled hard. "Okay. Ground rules stay the same, but we'll need supplies. Food, clothes, something to train in—"

Ryan snorted. "Train? You mean like Rocky?"

"I mean like don't set the house on fire."

"Fair."

They both laughed — just once, short and sharp, but it felt good. Human.

The laughter faded, and for a moment, the only sound was the hum of the AC.

Then — a knock at the door.

Three short raps. Firm, deliberate.

Jack froze mid-step. He glanced at Ryan, who raised his eyebrows. "You expecting someone?"

"No," Jack said. "You?"

"Not unless Amazon delivers existential dread now."

Jack sighed, stepped forward, and muttered, "Well, it can't get worse."

He opened the door.

A familiar face stood there — the man from the casino. Clean navy jacket, neat beard, calm eyes. The kind of face that belonged in both a boardroom and a poker table.

"Jack Callahan," the man said, voice smooth as glass. "I believe this belongs to you."

He held up Jack's Harrah's casino card between two fingers.

Ryan was standing in the hall behind him. Jack looked back at Ryan, who raised an eyebrow. "Friend of yours?"

Jack stared at the card in his hand. The casino logo gleamed under the front door light. "Not yet," he said. "But I think he's about to be."

CHAPTER 13

By the time Jack's pulse came down from seeing the casino guy on his front step, he'd decided to call the man not a problem. Optimistic? Sure. But optimism was free, and he was short on other currencies that weren't chips.

Ryan materialized behind him, hospital wristband tucked half under his sleeve. Chris clocked it, glanced at Ryan's eyes, and filed something away behind his own.

"Come in," Jack said, because he had no idea what else to do with this kind of energy.

"Thanks," Chris said, breezing past with the confidence of a man who had RSVP'd months ago.

He stepped into the hallway and—without warning—his face rippled. Cheekbones reshaped, hairline rolled back, jaw sharpened. The navy jacket hung on a different posture. When the shift finished, Jeremy Piven stood in Jack's entryway, radiating Ari Gold's impatient glamour like the carpet should be red and the walls should be holding Emmys.

"Baby!" Chris-as-Ari boomed, pointing both fingers at Jack like a done deal. "Tell me you've got the pages because I haven't got all day."

Jack blinked. "Oh my God."

Footsteps creaked upstairs. Jack's mom leaned over the railing. "Jack, do we have—" She froze. Her eyes went dinner-plate huge. "Oh... my... God."

"Mrs. Callahan?" Jack winced.

She descended three steps like she was onstage. "Is that—? Are you —? Ari Gold is in my house." She clapped a hand to her chest. "You were so mean and so funny and I loved you so much."

Chris flicked to Piven-charm level ten. "You are an icon," he told her, which, scientifically, is the fastest way to Jack's mother's heart. "Your son tells me you run the tightest ship on the eastern seaboard."

Jack made a choking sound. He had told Chris nothing.

His mom shook herself like a dog coming out of water. "Dinner. You're staying. I'm making sauce." She pointed at Jack. "Set another plate. Now." She turned, sprinted kitchen-ward with the speed of a woman for whom celebrity dinner was a lifelong emergency plan.

As soon as she vanished, Chris's face rippled again, and the house exhaled as Jeremy Piven evaporated into Chris—mid-thirties, average height, pleasantly handsome in a way that slid past descriptions, like your brain couldn't hold his exact face long enough to sketch it.

"Okay," Jack said, voice aiming at stern and landing on impressed. "That's a neat trick."

Chris grinned. "Thanks. I can do Clooney, but the eyebrows are a pain."

He stuck out a hand. "House call seemed more efficient than mysterious texts."

Jack shook. Ryan did too, warily.

"Chris Towers," Chris added. "We shared a craps rail earlier when you were making roulette your personal ATM. I grabbed your card off the felt when you bolted. Figured you'd want it back."

"You also grabbed my wallet," Jack said.

Chris shrugged. "Yes, but with panache." He peered past them into the kitchen. "Is that gravy or sauce? Because if we're doing Jersey semantics, I want to be respectful."

"Sauce," Jack and Ryan said in unison. Then they looked at each other and laughed, the sound surprising all three of them.

"Dinner?" Jack said.

"Try and stop me," Chris said.

They ate like people who'd been running all week and didn't realize it until they smelled garlic. Jack's mom did her version of casual—fresh basil like confetti, bread basket "I just threw together," salad "if you want it" that could have fed a softball team, and a pitcher of iced tea that tasted like every summer Jack had ever had.

Halfway through bowls of ziti that glowed in the light, Chris turned into Ari Gold again to compliment the sauce, and Jack's mom made a sound only dogs could hear and disappeared to retrieve more bread. When she returned, Chris had politely reverted to himself.

"So," she said, loading Ryan's plate like an artillery exercise, "Jack tells me you're a celebrity friend."

"Adjacent," Chris said. "Mostly I'm a quick study. Good with faces."

She narrowed her eyes affectionately. "You're staying in the guest room. Sheets are already on. Bathroom's the door with the tiny lighthouse art. Don't use my fancy towels."

Jack coughed. "Thought Ryan had the guest room."

She swatted his arm as if he'd asked whether water was wet. "Ryan's in the room above the garage. He needs quiet. He nearly burned to death."

"Didn't," Ryan said around a mouthful of bread, "but close."

"Exactly." She pointed a wooden spoon at Chris. "You—help me with dishes after. Celebrity hands can touch suds."

"Yes, ma'am," Chris said, and meant it.

She turned for the fridge, pulled out grated cheese, and as she did, her elbow clipped the corner of a postcard tucked under a magnet. Three magnets skittered; the postcard fluttered to the tile.

Jack leaned down to pick it up, then froze.

Cape May. A photograph of the lighthouse. On the back, in block capitals, a list of names—first names only, lined down the card like a grocery list of fate. JACK. AARON. LUCAS. RYAN. And then more…

117

names he didn't recognize. Some crossed out. At the bottom, two words in a different hand:

REMEMBER THIS.

"Mom?" Jack said.

His mother snatched the card with a speed that didn't match her age, slid it under a spray of other magnets: a pizza coupon, a dentist reminder, a photo of Jack and his dad at a Yankees game from a decade ago. "Old mail," she said too fast. "From that day trip we did when you were little."

"Uh-huh," Jack said, not taking his eyes off the corner still poking out.

Chris watched Jack not taking his eyes off the corner and filed away a second folder in his mental cabinet.

"You boys need more bread," Jack's mom declared with battlefield authority. "And less staring at my refrigerator."

"Yes, ma'am," three grown men said.

After dishes (Chris, true to his word, washed with the enthusiasm of a man auditioning for Human Son-In-Law), they migrated to the living room. Jack's mom retreated upstairs with a "don't stay up too late, and if you do, invite me," which had been her line since he was thirteen.

For a moment, the house hushed. The kind of quiet where a new team either forms or fails.

Chris broke it first. "Okay. Everyone powers up at once or do we do it like a talent show?"

Jack and Ryan exchanged a look. Jack nodded at Chris. "You start."

"Sure." Chris leaned back, laced his fingers behind his head. "It was Friday night—same as you two, if I'm reading the energy right. August seventeenth. Drove a buddy home after we pretended to like a bar on 287, too many dudes in button-downs pretending they invented whiskey. On the way back, I realized I had half a beer and the bladder of a squirrel, so I pulled over near a tree line. Took three steps into the brush, and—boom."

He snapped his fingers. His face flickered into an unfamiliar guy in a trucker cap, then back again. "Woke up face-down in gravel. Thought I'd passed out. Cop rolls up, asks for my ID. I go to grab my wallet and—" He shifted into the cop's face, voice and all. "—I hand him his own face. He makes a sound only dolphins understand, I make a sound only cowards make, and I snap back to me. He looks at me, looks at the road, hands me a warning for being alive, and waves me on with a 'get out of here before I have to fill out paperwork.'"

Jack tried not to laugh. Failed. "So your origin story is a roadside pee and identity theft."

"Alleged," Chris said. "Because I don't sign autographs."

He steepled his fingers. "After that? Practice. Mall bathrooms. Stock rooms. I learned faces, voices, heights. Turns out it's easier to steal if the manager is you. I visited Atlantic City to test it out. Dealers are easy if you look like a floor boss. And that's when I saw you in Tropicana—spinning a chip without touching it. Not creepy—curious. Followed you with the bachelorette decoy, lost you, found your card, grabbed your wallet to get your name, paid it forward at your front door."

"You paid it forward by breaking and entering," Jack said.

"Tomato, tomato," Chris said, pronouncing them the same way twice. "Point is, we all got hit that same night. You"—pointing at Ryan—"caught fire. You"—pointing at Jack—"caught the air. Me? Faces. Three for three."

Jack exhaled, gave the room a small, stubborn push with his will. A stack of mail on the coffee table slid three inches to the left like obeying was its favorite thing. He hadn't meant to move it. The air was starting to answer thoughts he didn't ask.

He caught Chris catching the movement with the visual sensitivity of a hawk. "That happen a lot?"

"More," Jack admitted. "It's like… background music now. If I don't concentrate, stuff hums. Moves."

Ryan held up a hand and snapped his fingers. A pinch of heat flared yellow at the tip like a lighter that wanted a promotion. He closed his fist; it died obediently. "I can make it big," he said, uneasy. "I don't want to in here."

"Please don't," Jack said, imagining his mom's face. "She'll make us sleep in the yard."

They traded stories. The cabin in the woods. The party. The horn no one heard but everyone felt. Waking up on Saturday feeling good in a way that felt like cheating.

They compared timelines and realized the overlap was too neat to be coincidence: Friday night, August seventeenth. The same hour the New Temple had dented the sky and the earth had yawned and something behind the world's wall had rubbed its eyes.

"When did you two crash at the cabin?" Chris asked.

"Friday," Jack said. "We stayed overnight. Me, Ryan, Aaron, Lucas."

"Just four?" Chris asked, already making a list in his head. Names had weight. Names closed loops.

"Just four," Jack said. "Everyone else went home."

Chris whistled softly. "So if we're mapping this... air, fire, faces. That leaves water, earth, whatever else the Titan starter pack comes with." He tilted his head. "Your guy Aaron—good swimmer?"

"Aaron's a lifeguard turned real adult," Jack said. "He's from Sparta. Loves the lake. Keeps his head down."

"Okay," Chris said, adding mental underlines. "And Lucas?"

Jack smirked. "Allergic to miracles."

Ryan snorted. "He literally said that."

Chris grinned. "Then he's either the most human of us or the scariest one when it flips."

Silence stretched. Not empty. Just full of possible futures.

"Look," Chris said, tone shifting a degree toward serious, "we're a thing now. Whether we like it or not. I figured I'd roll solo when all this started, because I'm built like a cockroach in a hurricane. But it's dumber to do this alone."

He leaned forward, elbows on knees. "So here's where I'm useful: intel, faces, walking through a door looking like the guy who belongs. You"—to Jack—"are a one-man SWAT fan. You"—to Ryan—"are a space heater that can cut a house in half. Together? We can clear rooms, get out clean, and pick our fights."

Jack raised an eyebrow. "You hear yourself?"

"Loudly," Chris said. "And because I hear myself, I'm going to say the thing you won't: we should hit something bigger. Not sloppy. Not greedy. Clean. Fast. Enough to get ahead of this before the gods put checkpoints on our toothbrushes."

Ryan lifted his palms. "Hard pass on 'bigger' until we know what we are."

Chris held up both hands. "Pitch, not plan. And I'm not married to a bank. There are art couriers who deserve it more."

Jack stared at the rug because it was easier than staring at the idea of momentum. The air in the room danced lightly around his ankles, tugging at his socks like a kid. He realized he was flexing his fingers without meaning to, and each flex made the hallway mirror tilt a degree and settle again, like the house had a breathing problem.

He flattened his hands on his knees. The mirror behaved.

"Rules," he said finally. "Same as today. No powers in public. Not yet. Training, here. We get control before we touch anything that gets our names on Olympus's lunch menu."

Chris nodded, unoffended. "I like not dying. It's one of my better habits."

"And we call Aaron," Jack added. "And Lucas. See if anything's... changed."

"Do we trust them?" Ryan asked.

"We'll find out," Jack said. "But they were there when it happened. That matters."

Chris leaned back, satisfied, like he'd gotten ninety percent of what he'd wanted and planned to root for the last ten. "Good. Team meeting adjourned? Because I promised your mother I'd help put away leftovers, and if I fail her, she will end me."

"You're not wrong," Jack said.

They stood. Movement felt different now—like the room had weight that shifted to let them pass. On the way to the kitchen, Jack brushed the fridge with his shoulder and an avalanche of magnets tried to reenact Pompeii. He grabbed at them, flustered.

The Cape May postcard tumbled again. He reached, but his mom was faster, plucking it up, sliding it back beneath a magnet shaped like a dolphin.

"Old mail," she said lightly, the exact same words. "Wobbly magnet."

"Yeah," Jack said. "Magnet."

Chris's eyes flicked from the postcard to Jack to Ryan. He didn't ask.

They ate cold ziti over the sink because some laws are universal. Chris told a story about once shapeshifting into a mall Santa and getting stuck in the beard glue when a kid pulled too hard. Ryan laughed until tears sat bright in his eyelashes. Jack realized it was the first time he'd seen him look twenty-something since the fire.

When the dishes were stacked and the lights turned low, Jack walked them down the hall like a host whose party had turned into a strategy session.

"Garage room's this way," he said to Ryan. "Guest room for you," to Chris. "Bathroom's the lighthouse. Towels are fair game unless they have lace."

"Noted," Chris said. "Lace equals death."

They paused outside the guest room. Chris stuck out his hand again, different this time—less introduction, more pact.

"Ride or die?" he said, half joke, whole offer.

Jack looked at his hand. At Ryan. At the faint tremble in the hallway air that meant his power wanted to finish the sentence for him.

He shook. "Ride or die."

Ryan piled his hand on top, palm shock-warm. "Try not to die."

"Working on it," Jack said.

They broke. Doors clicked. The house settled.

Jack stood alone in the hallway for a beat, listening to the air breathe through vents and under doors and across picture frames. The Cape May postcard peeped from under magnets like it was eavesdropping.

He touched the corner of it, just once. The paper hummed under his fingertip—nothing magical, just memory doing what memory does when you ask it for a favor.

"Friday night," he said quietly to the empty kitchen. "All roads lead back."

From outside, a breeze nosed the screen and slipped in, familiar as a friend who never knocks. It curled around his wrist, gentle, possessive.

He lifted his hand and it lifted with him.

"Tomorrow," he told it. "We start tomorrow."

The air agreed.

Upstairs, his mom turned in her sleep and dreamed of Cape May lighthouses and names written like warnings. Down the hall, Ryan dreamed in color—orange, red, white—and didn't burn the sheets. In the guest room, Chris slept like a switch, one click and gone, his features softening until you couldn't have picked him out of a lineup of himself.

In the morning, the list would get shorter, the rules would get bent, and the trio would learn how difficult it is to stay hidden when the world has finally remembered what to look for.

For tonight, they were just three guys in a house where the fridge magnets barely held.

CHAPTER 14

The morning hit slower than it should have. Jack woke up before his alarm, stared at the ceiling fan, and tried to ignore how it started turning just a little faster the longer he looked at it.

"Stop," he muttered.

It didn't.

Downstairs, his mom had already left for work. The house smelled like leftover coffee and dishwasher steam. He poured himself a mug, didn't drink it, and scrolled through news headlines that made less sense the longer he read:

OLYMPUS GUARDS MASS-ORDAIN HUMAN "BISHOPS."
PANTHEON TEMPLE REACHES CAPACITY, CONSTRUCTION CONTINUES SKYWARD.
RELIGIOUS TENSIONS ESCALATE — POLICE STAND DOWN ORDER REISSUED.

He set the phone down and looked out the window. The sky above Rockaway had a bruise-colored haze — not smoke, but something heavier. The kind of atmosphere that knew too much.

Ryan and Chris were still asleep. He wanted to let them be — one recovering, one probably dreaming himself into celebrity again. Today was his turn to follow the thread backward. To that night. To see if anyone else had changed.

Lucas lived like he'd won the lottery of avoidance. Jack's knock on the door was met by the sound of a deadbolt turning — once, twice, then a voice muffled through wood.

"Who is it?"

"It's Jack."

Pause. "Jack... Callahan?"

"That's the one."

The door cracked open an inch, and Lucas's face appeared — hair messy, eyes bloodshot, a PlayStation controller in hand like a stress ball. "Jesus, man. Thought you were a missionary."

"Close enough," Jack said. "You got a minute?"

Lucas sighed, opened the door, and motioned him in. "Make it quick. My game doesn't pause."

The living room looked the same — couch cratered in the middle, two empty pizza boxes, and the faint smell of weed trying to be subtle. Jack sat down. Lucas didn't.

"So," Jack started, "how've you been?"

Lucas snorted. "Since the literal gods came back? Great. Really thriving. Thinking of converting."

Jack cracked a smile. "You seen the news?"

"Can't not." Lucas sat, leaned forward, elbows on knees. "Church near my mom's got trashed last night. People painted omega symbols on the walls. The cops just... watched."

"Yeah," Jack said. "It's getting worse."

Lucas looked at him, squinting like he was trying to read a hidden subtitle. "Why are you really here?"

Jack hesitated. "I've been checking in on people. From that weekend."

"That weekend," Lucas repeated. "You mean the one where we all drank enough to ruin our livers and heard some kind of earthquake?"

"Something like that."

Lucas eyed him. "What's this about?"

"Just… weird stuff happening lately. Powers. Abilities. You felt anything off?"

Lucas leaned back, let out a half-laugh. "Oh my God. You're one of those now. What, you found religion?"

"Not exactly."

Lucas raised a hand, mock solemn. "No lightning bolts here, man. No magic. Just bills and anxiety."

Jack smiled politely but couldn't stop noticing the faint flicker of static on the TV — the way the screen rippled every time Lucas gestured. Maybe it was coincidence. Maybe it wasn't. But he didn't press it. The last thing Lucas needed was Jack shoving myth down his throat.

He stood. "All right. I'll leave you to your… spiritual journey."

"Yeah," Lucas said, unpausing his game. "Tell Zeus I'm busy."

Jack chuckled under his breath as he stepped outside. But by the time he reached the side of the house, the smile had faded. He crouched behind the tree line, glanced once around to make sure no one was looking, and shot up into the air.

Flying had stopped feeling like flying. It was instinct now — like running, or breathing, or lying well. The wind knew him, obeyed before he gave it orders. The air slipped under his arms and spine like a current that had been waiting for him to remember it.

Below, New Jersey stretched in squares and veins — towns, rivers, highways. Off in the distance, near Rockaway, the New Temple glimmered in sunlight. A massive, metallic monument that hadn't been there a week ago.

Jack slowed, hovering high enough that the world hummed quieter. From here, he could see movement — hundreds of figures pouring from the temple like ants from a broken nest. Each one wearing the faint golden gleam of the gods' chosen: the Bishops.

They were everywhere now — blocking roads, standing guard on rooftops, patrolling highways. Zeus's new order of humans. Jack felt a chill.

He hadn't even crossed the halfway point of the sky, and the air itself felt… crowded. Like the gods were using it too.

He cut the wind, angled toward Sparta, and dove.

Aaron's backyard still smelled like grill smoke and lake water. The same house. The same wooden deck. The same blue cooler sitting by the porch stairs. But the air felt off — heavier, denser, like humidity before a thunderstorm.

Aaron was already outside when Jack landed at the far edge of the yard. He looked up from his Adirondack chair, beer in hand, wearing the kind of calm that came from either enlightenment or marriage.

"Well," Aaron said, "you could've used the driveway."

Jack grinned. "Driveway's for people without superpowers."

Aaron smirked. "That a confession?"

"Maybe."

They sat across from each other at the patio table. The lake shimmered behind Aaron's house, the kind of blue that only existed in postcards and unedited photos. A gentle breeze ran through the trees. For once, Jack didn't make it.

Aaron took a sip of his beer, studying him. "You came all this way to catch up?"

"Something like that."

Aaron nodded slowly, then tipped his bottle slightly too far. It tumbled off the edge of the table, mid-air. Jack reacted on instinct — hand flicking forward, wrist twisting — and the bottle stopped, hanging in the air between them.

He blinked. The beer hovered perfectly, a small ripple of air distorting its outline. Then it snapped to his hand like it had been magnetized.

Aaron raised his eyebrows, impressed. "So it's true."

Jack froze. "What is?"

Aaron nodded toward the bottle. "You've got the wind."

Jack's heart jumped. "You've seen—?"

"I've seen them," Aaron said quietly. He reached toward Jack's hand, and the beer bottle suddenly jerked. The liquid inside coiled upward in a ribbon, twisting out of the glass in a shimmering spiral before reforming into a floating orb of water above Aaron's palm.

Jack's jaw went slack. "Holy—"

"Yeah," Aaron said. "That's new."

The orb hovered for a second, then collapsed back into the bottle without spilling a drop. He set it down gently.

"You're the water guy," Jack said, still stunned.

"Apparently."

They both laughed — an unspoken, of course it's you laugh. It felt good. Human. Then it faded.

"Since when?" Jack asked.

Aaron leaned back, gaze distant. "That Friday night. Same one you're thinking about."

They moved inside, down to the basement — Aaron's man cave turned makeshift lab. Weights, tools, boxes, and a dozen half-empty cases of water stacked against the wall. Half the bottles were crushed or split open like tiny implosions.

"That night," Aaron said, gesturing, "I thought I was hammered. Every bottle started popping. Caps flying off, water everywhere. I figured I'd gone nuts."

He picked up a stray bottle, turned it upside down, and the water just… stayed. It hung there like syrup until he snapped his fingers and it fell in a clean stream to the floor drain.

"Then the next day, I go down to the pond," Aaron continued. "Couple of the Sparta locals were swimming. I see something big — like big big — moving through the trees behind the waterline. Thought it was a bear."

Jack frowned. "It wasn't a bear, was it?"

Aaron shook his head slowly. "No. Two of them. Maybe fifteen feet tall. Pale, like marble that never saw sunlight. They weren't attacking — just watching. One of the swimmers yelled. They looked over, made this… sound. Deep. Like a horn underwater."

Jack's skin prickled.

"By the time I called the cops, they were gone," Aaron said. "Next day, the park's closed. 'Structural damage' or whatever. But the people who were there moved. Packed up. Said they felt watched. Like the forest didn't want them anymore."

"Giants," Jack murmured.

Aaron nodded. "If the Titans are waking up, their old guard's coming with them. The creatures. The myths. Everything."

Jack exhaled, hands on knees. "This is getting worse."

"Understatement."

They both sat in silence for a minute — just two guys in a basement, the weight of legend hanging between them. Then Aaron took another drink and said, "So what's your plan, Captain Airborne?"

Jack smirked. "Trying to figure out who's on which side before Zeus finds out I exist."

"And then what?"

"Then… I don't know." He glanced at the floating water bottle, still trembling slightly. "I just don't want to be hunted."

Aaron leaned back, sighing. "You're playing soldier. You, Ryan, whoever else. That's not my life anymore."

"Aaron—"

"No." Aaron shook his head. "I've got Claire. Kid on the way. I can't throw myself into some god-war because my college buddy wants to play Avengers."

Jack felt the sting but didn't argue. "You're right."

Aaron blinked. "What?"

"You're right," Jack said simply. "You've got people to protect. If I were you, I'd do the same."

The air between them softened. Aaron looked relieved, then guilty. "You're not mad?"

"I'm a lot of things," Jack said. "Mad's not one of them."

They both smiled — tired, understanding smiles that came from growing up too fast.

Later, on the porch, they stood looking out over the lake. The sun was going down — gold bleeding into purple, reflecting off the water like it was lit from below.

Aaron cracked another beer. "You ever wonder why us?"

"All the time," Jack said.

"You think we're Titans?"

Jack shrugged. "If the shoe fits."

Aaron laughed softly. "I liked it better when you couldn't fly."

"Yeah," Jack said. "Me too."

A comfortable silence stretched between them. The cicadas started up. The wind off the lake smelled like rain.

Jack finally stepped back. "Stay safe, all right?"

"Always."

He took a few steps away from the porch, let the air gather under him, and lifted off. Aaron watched from below, small against the fading sky.

As Jack climbed higher, the world spread out again — the lights of Sparta flickering on, the dark veins of the highways connecting towns, and in the far distance, a faint glow from Rockaway where the New Temple stood like a living mountain.

Even from here, he could see the streams of people — hundreds, maybe thousands — pouring in and out. Bishops in gold armor catching the last light of sunset. It looked like a pilgrimage and an army all at once.

Jack hovered, heart heavy. "They're multiplying."

The wind pushed at his back gently, as if agreeing.

He angled south again, heading home — faster this time, almost too fast, air cracking behind him in invisible thunderclaps.

CHAPTER 15

The Parthenon had not been rebuilt so much as rewilled into the world.

On Thursday mornings the marble woke first. Columns brightened from pearl to sunlit bone, friezes shed their soot and centuries, and the hill itself seemed to breathe—old Athens remembering the weight of worship and shrugging it back onto its shoulders. The wind off the Saronic Gulf climbed the steps carrying olive and salt, and the city below answered with a thousand camera shutters and a million whispered prayers.

Hellenism wasn't back. It was daily now.

Mass at dawn. Mass at mid-day. Mass again at twilight—two on Saturdays, two on Sundays, and an extra Thursday service that had already become a thing people said into their phones: "I can't tonight—Zeus has Thursdays." Across the world, scaffolds wrapped around long-quiet temples as if dressing old kings; concrete municipal roofs sprouted altars; office parks found room for shrines between loading bays. In basements and on rooftops, in stadiums and strip malls, the laurel wreath learned to live beside the fire exit.

Here, on the Acropolis, the center of it all, worship pooled like light.

Pilgrims queued in fresh-minted white—engineers, influencers, retirees in tour sneakers—each holding a sprig of olive or a phone or both. Bishops in gold breastplates kept the aisles clear without touching anyone, the way a knife clears butter. Priests moved like currents: Hera's in emerald; Athena's in dusk blue; Apollo's in white so bright the eye refused to land. The High Priests—named yesterday, crowned today—stood at the temple's thresholds like gatekeepers of weather.

The gods came late. They could afford to. Power was its own punctuality.

Zeus descended first, as if gravity belonged to him. He wore no crown because one would have been redundant. Lightning threaded his beard in lazy arcs; the air around him smelled faintly of rain on hot stone. He didn't walk so much as occupy. Every head lowered because kneeling felt, suddenly, like remembering how a knee worked.

Poseidon followed, taller than the surf, seaweed dark at the edges like the ocean had drawn him with charcoal. Hades emerged like the shadow of an idea people were trying not to have; his gold was old and dull and made other gold feel gauche. Hermes arrived last in a slipstream of applause, winged sandals whispering over marble, the grin of a man whose job was to know every secret and show none.

They took their places before the great wooden doors of the inner cella. The new High Priests flanked them—one for each godly "wing," a modern term Hermes had invented and Zeus had tolerated because brand architectures were concessions even kings had to make.

Zeus raised his palm and the sound fell out of the world.

"Mortals," he said, and the word did not carry disdain so much as ownership. "We return to you not as novelty, but as order. You have built towers and languages and crimes since we left. We have watched your wars and your weddings from beyond the last horizon. Now the walls of Tartarus crack. The Titans test their chains from within you. We will not allow the ruin of Earth."

He could have said anything. He said we.

On the periphery, Hades shifted his weight. Poseidon's mouth tightened in that way he had when storms rolled toward shore. Hermes's eyes slid along the edge of the crowd, counting, categorizing, calculating who had come with a question and who had come to belong.

Zeus spread his hands. Behind him, the Bishops—two from Rockaway flown in by chariot for the spectacle—stepped forward. Their gold plates gleamed newly minted; their faces wore expressions of people who hadn't practiced how to be statues yet.

"Yesterday you saw two," Zeus said. "Today, you see what faith deserves."

He swept his arm toward the assembled mortals beyond the rope lines. "From those who bring us news, who keep the laws, who guard the weak, who raise the good—heroes."

At his word, a line of supplicants approached the steps: a Nairobi teacher with her schoolchildren's petitions folded in a ribbon; a Manila paramedic still wearing his midnight shift; two municipal workers from Thessaloniki who had pushed a bus full of tourists out of floodwater; a young mother from São Paulo whose hands trembled as she carried the ashes of a brother the sirens had taken.

Zeus touched each forehead with two fingers. It looked like a benediction until you saw the way it took.

The teacher straightened as if a new vertebra had clicked into place; the paramedic's posture filled with a weight that wasn't muscle; the municipal workers' eyes brightened, then steadied. The mother simply exhaled—a shudder that became a stance. Their clothes were plain. Their presence no longer was.

"Heroes," Zeus said, and the word made the marble ring.

A cheer swept the Parthenon like a gust. People cried without meaning to. The new Heroes stood blinking, measuring their hands as if a hidden heaviness had finally admitted itself. A Bishop stepped to each, slid a gold band around an arm or a bracer over a wrist. The crowd surged closer, phones up, proof gathering for the rest of the world.

High above, a raven circled once, twice, then vanished into the glare. The city roared because the city had an appetite.

Poseidon leaned toward Zeus without looking at him. "This is how you grow storms on land," he said. "With noise."

Zeus smiled like a mountain smiles at a river. "This is how it felt," he murmured. "When we ruled the Earth and none denied it."

Hades made a soft sound in his throat. "You never ruled the Earth. You ruled those who wanted to be ruled."

Hermes's grin widened, not at what was said but at what it invited. "Language," he said lightly, as if he were ordering breakfast, "is a ladder. People climb up what we say."

Zeus didn't turn. "And you, messenger—are you climbing it, or setting it against a different wall?"

Hermes's head tilted almost imperceptibly. "I am ensuring we have walls at all."

For a fraction of a breath, silence grew fangs. Then Zeus lifted his hand again and the liturgy resumed, smooth as marble under oil.

The Mass—their word now, because it worked—continued with offerings and oaths. Around the world, copycat services followed by satellite and stream. At the Temple Mount, a portable altar under police guard drew more pilgrims than anyone would have admitted last week; in Rome, an old basilica's side chapel quietly exchanged a saint for a statue, and the confessional lines grew shorter; in Lagos, a football stadium booked for a revival served wine and olive branches to eighty thousand and called it Thursday Night.

Everywhere else dimmed.

Clergy with dwindling flocks turned to city councils for protection. Synagogues put up cameras and hired private security. Mosques added locks and took down banners to keep teenagers from spray-painting alphas and omegas on sacred brick. In Seoul, a megachurch lost power mid-sermon and came back with a livestream of Athena's emissary announcing a scholarship fund for girls in STEM.

The god of algorithms was indifferent and did its work. The trending bar calcified into a coronation.

Between steps of the service, Zeus sometimes looked out across the city, gaze skimming balconies and roofs and the lines of people still hiking up the hill in the heat. He saw a world with a vacuum in it and recognized the shape it wanted.

"High Priests," he said at last, turning to face the robed mortals he had picked like tools that felt good in the hand. "Each wing shall instruct and be instructed—as of today."

Hera's High Priestess—an auntie with a voice like a gavel—stepped forward and nodded at the couples in the front rows, telling them in three languages what fidelity would mean now that the gods watched again. Athena's High Priest spoke about civic duty and potholes in the same breath as strategy and stoicism, making bureaucracy sound like a kind of valor. Ares's man banged his chest, drew cheers from a corner of soldiers on leave, and promised protection without saying from whom. Hephaestus's crew rolled out a scaffold and raised it in sixteen seconds; the crowd clapped like they were at a magic show. Demeter's women promised nothing bad would happen to the wheat. Dionysus's priest promised wine enough for grief.

Apollo's High Priest waited until the cameras were hungry for him and said almost nothing—just enough syllables for the clips to lip-sync to later. Apollo watched him with the dispassion of sunlight. In him, vanity had hardened into principle; he believed in beauty the way bridges believe in weight.

When the talks finished and the chant resumed, Apollo stepped closer to Zeus's shoulder and spoke without moving his mouth.

"Let me go," he said.

Zeus barely turned. "To what?"

"To them," Apollo breathed. In the shadow of the column, a flare of golden annoyance crossed his face and disappeared, the way a reflection of a passing car disappears in a window. "The rumors. Fire in New Jersey. Air in the same breath. Their cameras see badly, but they have seen enough. I will prove what you have not proved: that we are better hunters than worshipped statues."

Zeus watched the crowd. The new Heroes were learning already: how to be looked at without flinching, how to stand without tiring, how to make a hand feel like leadership when you place it on another's shoulder. He liked the look of it. Authority suited the bones of humans.

"You will not prove yourself on mortals," he said. "You will show yourself to them. There is a difference."

"Then let me find the difference," Apollo said, and to his credit, he didn't look at Hermes.

Hermes had already looked at Apollo. He smiled like a man who had a secret and was trying out different shelves to put it on. "If Brother Sun insists on travel," he said aloud, voice bright enough for the front row to hear, "let him take my words with him. The All-Speak reaches where eyes cannot. Ask for the Titans in the language they can't avoid."

Hades shifted again. "Ask whom, precisely?"

Hermes's smile did not move. "Everyone."

Poseidon finally faced Zeus fully. "This—" He gestured with two fingers at the worshippers, the bristling Bishops, the High Priests finding their cues. "—this is a tide. It engulfs. It also recedes. You are pretending we do not remember that."

Zeus looked at his brother as if today were a story he'd told a thousand times. "When tides recede," he said, "they reveal what belongs to the sea. We will build where the sand shows stone."

Hades, who had his own sand and his own stones, did not nod.

The Mass ended the way it had begun: with a quieting of things. Offerings were catalogued by accountants whose fervor had moved from spreadsheets to sacrament without bothering to change fonts. The new Heroes were escorted inside to be told their duties, their geographies, and their passwords. The High Priests conferred about calendars and sponsorships and "wings" in the corporate sense—a word that made Athena vow to redesign it before Hermes trademarked it.

Behind the door, Zeus convened the smaller circle.

A long table of black wood, polished to a depth that suggested drowning. Around it: Hades, Poseidon, Hephaestus with his hammer across his lap; Ares because he would have kicked the door down otherwise; Hera with a ledger; Athena with a map no one else could read;

Hermes with a quill he had not dipped in ink and did not need to; Apollo still standing, too bright to sit.

Zeus's lightning collected lazily along the table's edge like spilled mercury. "Report," he said.

Athena placed a pin on New Jersey and then another, and lines spread out like cracks in ice. "Fire at a hospital. Air intervening. Witnesses unsure where one began and the other stopped. Cameras fried." Her finger moved. "Centaurs in Ringwood. Sirens at Lake Hopatcong. Harpies at High Point. Giants beside a pond in Sparta." She looked up. "Creatures come when power does."

Hephaestus's mouth curled. "And men come when there are tools to wear." He tapped his breastplate. "The Bishops behave. The Heroes will learn."

Hera's ledger clicked shut. "They will also fight among themselves. Make more, and they will build rivalries like they build cities—layered, loud, difficult to move."

"We will move them," Ares said. He had the look of a man who liked an answer you could hold. "Give me the names of the Titans. I will bring them back wearing their own bones."

"We have fragments," Athena said. "Air and fire waking close together suggests coordination, or at least recognition."

"Or coincidence," Hermes said. He had been doodling something that looked like a knot and wasn't. "Mortals trip over everything. Sometimes they trip into legend, sometimes into each other."

"Your cynicism is a costume," Hades said without looking at him.

"My costumes are cynicism," Hermes said, smiling.

Zeus let them be what they always were—arguments that could split the world and had. Then he said: "Tartarus."

The table went quiet enough to hear the olive trees breathe outside.

"The walls have shifted," Hades said eventually. He spoke like a man naming an illness in a child. "Not broken. Eroded. Someone worried the mortar, and the mortar remembered that time exists."

"Who?" Poseidon asked.

Hades's eyes were very dark. "Time."

Cronus's name did not need saying. It lived in the shape of their mouths when they said father and meant something else.

Zeus's jaw worked once. "We will know how. Ares."

Ares's grin bared teeth. "Finally."

"You go below," Zeus said. "You will not engage. You will observe. If a lock is rusted, you will oil it, not break it. If something has pried at our walls, you will pry at its name."

Ares looked like a blade that had been told it was a thermometer. He nodded anyway because he liked being chosen.

"I will take Hermes," he said. It was an attempt at practicality. Hermes could open a door that didn't know it was a door.

"You will not," Zeus said, not unkindly. "Hermes stays. His errands multiply."

Hermes bowed slightly, as if to say: the errands multiply because I multiply them.

"And I?" Apollo asked.

Zeus considered him—the pure assertion of person, the vanity that did not know it was vanity because it spoke the language of light. "You will go to the mortals," he said. "Take the All-Speak. Ask the questions I would ask if I wanted them to like me less: who saw the air move, who saw the fire that did not burn what it should. You will not hunt. You will host. Invite. See who refuses invitation."

Apollo did not smile. He inclined his head, a sunbeam accepting a mirror.

"Brother," Poseidon said softly to Zeus as the circle broke, "do not confuse applause with allegiance."

Zeus looked down at his hands, watched lightning lick the knuckles, thought of crowns and their weights and how men wore both. "I do not," he said. He looked toward the door where the Heroes waited. "I am building what allegiance needs when it forgets how to be itself."

Hades stood. "And if allegiance becomes empire?"

"Then I will remember how empires are kept," Zeus said, and there was nothing kind in it.

They left the room by different doors because gods liked symbolism even when they pretended not to. Outside, on the steps, a clutch of supplicants who had waited past the dismissal pressed forward with questions.

A woman whose husband had vanished at High Point cried out to Artemis's High Priest, "What do we do about the harpies?"

"Do not go to them," he said. "Do not sing to them. Do not listen when they speak. They are not yours."

A father whose boy had nearly drowned at Hopatcong begged, "Will you drive the sirens away?"

Poseidon looked at him long enough to count all the ways men had put boats into water. "You will learn your lake," he said. "You will live as if it is older than you and has earned the respect of your bones. Or you will not live."

A tourist asked, timidly, "And the centaurs?"

Athena answered that one. "Do not trespass. Do not tempt them. Remember that coexistence is not friendship."

Someone, braver or stupider than the rest, shouted, "Isn't that your job?"

Zeus smiled in a way that made good men rethink their posture.

141

"Our job," he said, "is to keep what sleeps from waking into war."
He extended his hand toward the new Heroes at his back. "Their job is to
lead you where you will not lead yourselves."

It wasn't mercy. It was policy.

By afternoon, five more parishes—no one had a better word yet—
announced their own Heroes: a logistics manager in Rotterdam whose
team already had a convoy plan for emergency evacuations; a U.S.
Marine in Camp Pendleton who took the oath with his jaw set; a Mumbai
sanitation supervisor who wept quietly and then told reporters the drains
would not clog next monsoon; a Brazilian favela organizer who refused
the bracer until Hera herself put it on; a Berlin nurse who asked if the
title came with childcare.

In Jerusalem, a rabbi locked his doors and turned off the lights while
his congregants argued in the courtyard. In Kansas, a pastor asked his
flock to fast and pray while his deacons asked for overtime. In Istanbul, a
muezzin gave the call with a voice that cracked and kept going.

At dusk, an image moved across phones: Hermes, alone on a narrow
street in Plaka, fingers to his lips, whistling a tune that wasn't music. In
its wake, posters curled off walls, stickers detached from poles, and a
thousand flyers promoting a thousand things fluttered in a little cyclone
around him.

When the papers settled, the walls were clean except for a single
fresh bill in a hundred languages, the ink still wet:

REPORT YOUR VISIONS.
REPORT YOUR MIRACLES.
REPORT THE ELEMENTS THAT OBEY YOU.
THE GODS WILL ANSWER.

Hermes tucked his quill behind his ear and strolled on, smiling to
himself as if he'd just laid a snare where the ground thought it was flat.

Night dropped on Athens like a velvet curtain. The Parthenon glowed
as if lit from beneath. Inside, the new Heroes slept in rooms that had not
existed this morning and dreamed the dreams the newly powerful have:

142

running without wasting breath, lifting without effort, being seen without fear.

Far below the hill, in a city apartment where no priest would visit, a woman lit a candle to a different god and frowned when the flame leaned toward her palm as if listening. In Rockaway, Bishops adjusted their patrol maps around a movie theater that used to be an altar to popcorn and now was an altar to war. In a hospital in New Jersey that still smelled faintly of melted vinyl, a nurse filled out a form that asked if anything unusual had occurred during her shift and laughed until she cried.

On the Acropolis, Zeus stood alone for a moment and let the applause he was still hearing fade from memory to echo.

"This is how it felt," he said to no one.

From somewhere behind a column, Hermes's voice floated, light as coin. "And how it fails."

Zeus did not turn. "Not this time."

Hermes smiled into the darkness because men lied to themselves and gods did, too, and he loved language enough to forgive it when it was beautiful.

In the morning, Ares would descend toward the cracks under the world. Apollo would cross a continent in three interviews without moving his feet. More Heroes would put on bracers and learn how to hold a crowd. More altars would be built in plazas where pigeons used to be the only worshippers. Other faiths would not vanish; they would shrink, as all rivers do when another draws their tributaries away.

The world was tipping, not because it had been pushed, but because gravity had remembered an older center.

And somewhere not on any map, a locked door listened to footsteps on the stairs and thought—without words—that rust tasted like freedom.

CHAPTER 16

Jack woke to the smell of toast and the sound of someone whispering, "We're late for crime."

He opened one eye. Chris stood in the doorway dressed like a normal Tuesday—khakis, blue button-down, an office-park lanyard with a plastic badge that read Assistant Regional Manager because of course it did. Ryan hovered behind him in a hoodie, hood up, face pale like he'd slept badly and the dream had followed him out.

Jack rubbed his face. "Wait. What are we doing?"

Chris checked his watch. "We're robbing a bank."

A beat.

"…okay then," Jack said, because sometimes the train's already moving and it's easier to decide you've always loved trains.

Down the hall, the house hummed with morning. His mom had left a note on the counter—Meatloaf for dinner. Don't ruin my pans. Love, Mom—and the Cape May postcard peeked from beneath a wedge of novelty magnets like it knew the schedule and didn't approve.

They ate in a hurry—eggs, toast, silence. Every time Jack looked at Ryan, he saw the hospital again. The heat. That moment the flames had listened and then stopped listening, like a dog that smelled something in the woods. The skin around Ryan's knuckles was chapped and hairline-cracked, as if the fire took moisture when it went. When his fingers flexed, a faint smell rode the motion—ozone and bleach, the after-taste of something the world had to correct.

Chris laid the plan on a napkin with the confidence of a man pitching an app.

"Timing," he said. "Friday, 12:40 PM, Hanover Ave., First Colonial. Manager does a cigarette-and-pretend-to-make-calls loop. Twenty-two minutes if he's feeling self-important; seventeen if he's trying to make a 1 p.m. Zoom. We go when he goes."

"And we're sure you can do him?" Jack asked.

Chris gave him a flat look. "I can do his posture, his gait, his coffee stain, and the way his left shoe squeaks every fourth step because he won't replace the heel cap. If he had a soul, I'd do that too."

No smile. Just data. Good.

"Inside," Chris continued, tapping napkin boxes—lobby, ATMs, back corridor, a rectangle for vault. "I go straight to the back office, knock the interior window, give them the 'courier's early in the rain, need the chamber open for transfer' line. It plays because I look like bureaucracy and bureaucracy hates questions. You"—he nodded at Ryan—"float near the ATM vestibule. If anything weird happens, you... flick the breaker."

"I don't have a breaker," Ryan said. His voice was tired. "I have a switch that gets stuck."

"Try not to flip it," Chris said. "But if we need a diversion, make it small. Smoke alarm. Trash can. We want people out, not running around on fire."

He looked at Jack. "You're air support. Literally. Don't show your face. Keep camera line-of-sight to a minimum. Sprinklers if we need them, doors if they jam, guards if they think they're action heroes. In and out. Fifteen minutes."

Jack stared at the napkin. His skull felt hollow and full at the same time—a bell ringing. Out of nowhere came the old, familiar jab of guilt: he was getting good at emergencies he created. His leg bounced under the table. The napkin started to slide, crawling in tiny jerks with every bounce.

"Hey," Chris said softly, catching it. "Breathe."

Jack did. The air obeyed like a dog that remembered heel. The napkin settled.

"Last thing," Chris added. "Second manager with Saturday authority. If he's on, we abort."

"We won't abort," Jack said. His voice came out like sheet metal. He hadn't meant it to.

Chris clocked the tone, nodded once, and didn't push. He stood, tossed the napkin, and the plan went with it like it lived in them now, not on paper.

They left by the side door. The day was hot without courage. On the street, the air had weight—news helicopters somewhere far off, the static throb of sirens a town over, the far glimmer in the sky that meant the New Temple was hosting another service and the city was answering yes. Lincoln Park had finally slid off the front page—"the man made of air" replaced by bishops and bracers—but forgetting and forgiving weren't the same thing.

Jack locked the door, then walked back to check it, then checked it again, only then following the other two out.

The car was already warmed up. Not their car—Chris's latest magic trick. He'd "borrowed" a silver Corolla from a gas station two towns over by becoming a flustered twenty-something with a vape who'd locked his keys in the pump bathroom, then becoming the manager with the spare key, then becoming no one at all. The plate was clean. The dash smelled like somebody else's pine tree.

They drove in silence. Chris kept it under the limit, two hands at ten and two, eyes flicking mirrors with a rhythm that looked less like paranoia and more like respect. He wasn't showy today. Just present. Professional. It calmed Jack in a way nothing else did.

Ryan sat in the back, hood up despite the heat. He pressed his palms together and then apart, together and apart, like testing the friction of his own skin. At a red light he cracked the back window an inch and let the world touch his face to confirm he was still here.

The bank rose out of low brick: two stories; white columns pretending to be important; glass doors pretending to be safe. The

147

parking lot was almost full. Friday crowd. People at ATMs with shoulders hunched like guilt.

At 12:39, the front doors opened and the manager came out.

Fiftyish. Thick in the middle. Bald at the crown. The assured-glum look of a man who'd survived a decade of audits and learned nothing could surprise him except everything. He checked his phone, checked the sky, checked no one, and took his little loop along the hedges. Cigarette. Call. Boredom.

Chris pulled into a space two aisles over. "Showtime," he said, and his face moved like time-lapse clay into the man's: jawline softened, brow lowered, eyes dulled. His shoulders slumped into that specific Lego-brick posture of an over-middle manager. He smelled faintly of stale coffee and copier toner because he'd decided to.

He glanced at Jack. "See you in twelve."

"To be clear," Jack said, "if I see you in twelve, we did something wrong."

Chris didn't smile. "We're already doing something wrong."

He got out and walked like the manager walked—like the floor owed him balance. He crossed the lane. He didn't look at the manager on his cigarette loop. He didn't need to. This was mirror work. He was good at mirrors.

Ryan exhaled once like stepping off a roof. "Okay," he said. "Okay."

"You can stay in the car," Jack offered. "We can do this without—"

"I've got it." He didn't sound brave. He sounded resigned. He pulled the hood tighter and got out.

Jack watched him cross to the ATM vestibule and take the spot where the cameras would only catch a profile and a hoodie. He watched Chris slide through the glass doors and nod to the guard like a man who signed paychecks. He watched the real manager stroll into the alley behind the building and lean into the shade to make his phone feel important.

148

"Twelve," Jack told himself, and the air under his skin came alive like an audience.

He pulled on a balaclava, tugged ski goggles down to his neck, and stepped out. Heat struck him. So did the noise of a day pretending to be normal. He moved along the sidewalk, head down, like any man with a podcast and a checking account, and drifted to the side door where couriers buzz for access.

A woman in a pencil skirt shouldered it open while juggling coffee. Jack followed in and she didn't see him because he wanted her not to. Air bent. Light stuttered. His outline became a heat mirage—something the eye wanted to correct and couldn't, so it gave up and looked elsewhere.

The lobby smelled like carpet cleaner and hope. A tired chandelier buzzed. The line inched. The guard watched everything and nothing, the way guards do when nothing happens until it does.

Jack stood by the brochure rack about home equity lines. Renovate your life, said the glossy, and he wanted to laugh. He watched the inner door to the corridor that led to offices and vault. He waited for the nod that meant we're in.

It came at 12:44. A quick flicker of the overhead—one, two, three—and then steady. To everyone else, nothing. To them, code. He slipped into the corridor like a draft and became a shadow in the corner, nowhere at all.

Inside, Chris was already the boss. He had the posture and the clipped tone, the voice pitched to the middle register authority uses when it wants to say I'm not the villain, the policy is. He signed a sheet with a signature that wasn't his and would fool anyone anyway; the eye often prefers to be fooled if it gets to stop working.

"Courier's early," he told the vault officer, a woman with hair too neatly pinned to belong to a good morning. "We need the secure chamber open and counted. I'll supervise."

She hesitated. People who live near vaults grow extra spleens for suspicion. But familiar exuded off him. The badge, the shoes, the squeak on the fourth step. The camera in the corner wanted to be bored. The camera stayed bored.

She keyed her code. He keyed his, which wasn't, and was perfect anyway. The heavy door rolled. Cold metallic air breathed out—dry, coin-clean.

Jack drifted past security, letting the air thicken between lenses and the world. Not enough to show, just enough to soften faces into suggestion, timestamps into mush. Each camera itched on his skin; he scratched them with static until they yawned.

From the vestibule came the faint click of the ATM door. Ryan had positioned himself exactly where they'd agreed—back to the street, eyes on the corridor, a human boulder. He chewed his lip like it owed him money. Close up, the chapped cracks on his knuckles carried that bleach-and-ozone tang again, like a storm learning to breathe indoors.

Inside the vault, Chris moved through the checklist. He let the officer talk—people talking can't watch. He softened vowels when she stiffened. He tapped a clipboard when she faltered and found the right line for her with a helpful smile that made him forgettable and, paradoxically, in charge.

"Pull four deposit bags," he said casually, choosing numbers that matched the afternoon's courier schedule. "Two for tri-count, two upstairs."

She did it. Doing her job felt like doing her job. He stacked the bags near the mouth of the vault—close enough for speed, far enough to respect the motion sensor's temper.

At 12:51, the real manager, on his second cigarette, checked his watch, crushed the butt into brick with the exact gesture Chris had practiced, and turned back toward the doors, annoyed at his own life.

Everything tilted.

The guard's face changed from a Friday face to a Tuesday face. The teller at window two glanced toward the corridor like a dog hearing a whistle. The vault officer looked up at the pane above her desk and watched a shadow move differently than the shadow she thought she knew.

And Ryan—hood up by the ATMs—caught the real manager's outline in the glass and went still the way prey goes still. He looked at the corridor. Thought about the plan. Thought about doors closing, time running, names being said out loud.

Heat twitched awake behind his sternum like a muscle impatient to sprint.

"Don't," he whispered to himself.

It didn't care.

Warmth crept up his throat into his cheeks. The air around his hands shimmered—not flame yet, but the suggestion of it. He clenched his fists. The smell arrived before color—ozone with a bleach bite. The sprinkler cage above the vestibule caught in the corner of his eye. He pictured it bursting. He pictured a small scare.

He opened his hand.

A fist-sized bulb of white heat popped—colorless until it met air— and then bent light wrong, the world hurrying to correct the error with orange. It struck the trash can; the liner went to vapor before it had time to ignite.

Half the lobby turned at the sound. A woman shrieked. The guard's hand flew toward his radio.

"Damn it," Jack hissed. The air jumped like a dog.

He sent a palm-wide blast into the sprinkler manifold above the vestibule. The casing cracked, the pin dropped, and the system burped to life. Water coughed from scour lines, then sheeted down in a steady, blessed roar. The temperature snapped twenty degrees—instant cold fog that bit the skin and made breath steam.

Screams inverted into that specific crowd sound that means someone else is in charge now. The guard shouted for evacuation. Tellers ducked behind the counter and popped the panic gate. Someone yanked the fire alarm; the building said what Jack wanted it to say: leave.

Down the corridor, the vault officer eyed the wall's blinking ALERT and frowned at the timing. Chris, halfway out of the vault mouth with two bags in hand, put on the universal expression of managers pretending they planned for this scenario.

"Alarm test," he said lazily. "Keep counting."

Suspicion pushed back. "I'm calling Rick."

He let a sliver of managerial irritation in. "He's on lunch. You want to keep a vault open until he wanders back?"

That did it. She returned to counting, angry in the precise way he needed—anger makes tasks finish faster.

Jack flowed down the corridor like AC. He found the second camera; turned its eye to milk. He breathed into the hinge of the glowing red crash bar on the back door and told it to stick—later. He skimmed the guard's holster and unseated the tiny retention strap so any yank would snag. He sent a thin slap of air into the real manager's chest as the man rounded the corner, trimming rage into confusion so he had to help someone up and be human first.

In the vestibule, Ryan hunched under sprinkler rain. He stared at his hands like they'd betrayed him. A lick of heat kissed his sleeve and died with a hiss; the odor left behind was hospital-familiar. He swallowed hard.

"Out," Jack said softly, stepping into his blind spot—a ripple, a presence. "You're good. Out."

Ryan nodded without looking and went with the stream, face down like any soaked guy trying not to swear.

And then the day tried to reassert control.

The guard, drenched and annoyed, decided it was his moment. He planted at the mouth of the corridor, radio squawking, hand near the gun like the concept of gun. "Sir!" he barked at Chris, who was stepping out of the vault with the bags like he'd been told to move them by God. "Sir, you can't—"

Chris met him with careful mildness—TSA-line voice. "Sprinklers popped in the vestibule. Relocating high-value bags to the upstairs dry room until all-clear. Copy?"

The guard's eyes narrowed. The fourth-step squeak wasn't where it should be—wet shoes, wrong cadence. He reached for his pistol. The retention strap snagged. The weapon stayed. He swore like betrayed by a friend. The vault officer took three quick steps and slapped the emergency, and the door began to roll shut with the slow certainty of consequence.

Chris didn't panic. His face smoothed into the scared-but-compliant version of the manager—the one that had gotten the real guy out of two audits and a DUI stop. He raised his hands. "Okay, okay—"

"Ryan," Jack said, and didn't have time to finish.

Panic is contagious.

The heat in Ryan's chest spiked, like a rheostat spun too fast. He tried to swallow it. It climbed anyway. His body wanted an outlet or it would choose one.

He lifted his hand, intending a little white-hot ping into the metal trash can—noise, smoke—and his palm opened.

The room gaped. The air at his reach puckered, vacuumed, and then rushed; the surge made a new flame where none had been. Not a ball. Not a beam. A hunger that ate oxygen first and remembered fire second.

A poster by customer service turned to ash in the shape of itself. A ficus exhaled weeks of hoarded breath and became a torch for one indrawn second before cold weight smothered it. Ozone knifed the nose. Bleach rode the back of the throat.

People screamed. Someone fell. The sprinklers coughed, then doubled; the lobby became weather.

Jack moved.

153

Air compacted around his hands like clay. He clapped once—soft—and a tight thud of pressure folded into the guard's chest, enough to sit him down without breaking anything he'd need. Two fingers flicked—glass above the next row of heads cracked; false rain multiplied; heat died quicker than it could live. He exhaled through his teeth; smoke obediently flattened and slid along the ceiling toward vents. He palmed the vault door and shaved a breath off its close; not enough to stop, enough to keep it from trapping a hand.

"Go," he told Chris.

Chris went. Two bags, posture now nobody. He slid into the stairwell. Jack slipped behind him, a ripple following a ripple, guiding the crash bar with a breath so it didn't slam.

They burst into the alley. The world cooled instantly. Wet heat poured from the back door like a body exhale. The sky above was white and indifferent. Across the asphalt a dumpster offered anonymity and smell.

"Car," Chris said. "North exit."

"Where's—" Jack began.

"Behind us," Chris said. "Lane meet."

They ran. The bags thumped against Chris's thighs; he carried them like weight he'd earned. Jack floated a half-inch without meaning to and set himself down again because cameras existed and he couldn't live like a dream all the time.

At the corner the alley opened to a side street. The silver Corolla idled at the curb, facing out, good boy ready to run. Ryan jogged from the kiosk line, soaked through, hood down now, face set in that wounded way of a man who did what he had to and hated that he had to.

Then the street did the thing streets do when the world notices them.

Sirens—not near, but vectoring. A long wail that makes people look up. Tires somewhere. A bus driver laying on a horn not for traffic but for history. Doors slamming two blocks away—the cops who had been waiting to be heroes again.

"In," Chris said, and Jack didn't argue.

They piled. Chris behind the wheel. Jack passenger with a bag under his feet. Ryan in back with the other, hands pressed flat to his knees like prayer.

Chris pulled out calm, then punched the gas like calm had rented the car.

The bags weren't sealed well—drawstrings tied by tired hands that believed in procedure. Rear windows were down to vent smoke stink and hot, wet air. Bills turned into birds—first a couple, then a handful, then a storm of green rectangles hurricane-ing the cabin. Sunlight glanced off the money blizzard in sharp, ridiculous flashes, turning the inside of the Corolla into a snow globe that had opinions.

"Close the—" Jack started.

"Working on it," Ryan said. He cranked the window. It stuck halfway. The car became cash weather.

"You two good?" Chris asked, voice steady as a level.

"Define good," Jack said.

"Conscious, capable, not on fire."

"We're two for three," Jack muttered, tugging the seatbelt across Ryan's shoulder because the idea of him pinballing in this tin can felt like an experiment in sadness.

They hit Hanover and traffic parted the way it parts for cars that look like they belong more than other cars. Chris threaded the Friday slowness with the same face he'd worn in the bank—average, forgettable, already gone.

Left. Right. Mirror. A cop car slid onto the avenue two blocks back and whooped its siren once like a knock. The whoop felt like a question: Easy way?

"Plan?" Jack asked, eyes mapping side streets like traps.

"Bloomfield split," Chris said. "Lose them clean. No stunts."

155

"Copy," Jack said, meaning it, intending for once to behave.

They reached the rotary and luck winked; green held. Chris didn't gun it so much as choose momentum and let the city be helpful.

"Left ahead," Jack said, reading the way air braided around cars. He felt traffic like tide.

Chris nodded, hands still at ten and two. He was best like this—clean, minimal, talent not in the show but in the edit.

"Hey," Ryan said suddenly, voice hoarse and small, eyes on his palms. "I'm sorry."

Jack glanced back. Ryan stared at the backs of his hands like they were out of warranty.

"It's fine," Jack said. "We're out."

"It's not," Ryan said. "When it starts, I can't... aim it. It's not fire. It's... taking. Like I open my hand and the air forgets what it is for a second and then remembers by burning."

Jack swallowed. "We'll figure it out."

Ryan nodded but didn't agree.

Sirens grew closer. Not one—two. The sound forked the air. Chris took the split, cut behind a bus, slipped around a delivery van parked like a hippo. He didn't breathe harder. He didn't talk. He drove.

Jack thickened the air around them just enough to weight their presence in other drivers' eyes—a nudge to attention, not physics. Cars glanced and looked away. The world did that thing it sometimes did around gods: chose to be cooperative.

They crossed the river. Cities change across water—different brick, different patience, different cops. Sirens dopplered and slid behind a line of trucks trying to make an impossible light.

"We might actually—" Jack began, and the car moved sideways.

Not fishtailed. Not tapped. Moved. As if a hand had swatted it out of its lane.

Chris corrected before Jack found the right shape for fear. The Corolla skittered back where tires paid for it to be. Bags lurched. Bills exploded—snow in summer. The belt dug into Jack's chest like it remembered it was a leash.

He could feel it before he could see it—the air deciding to belong to someone else.

CHAPTER 17

Apollo didn't land. He arrived, mid-stride, mid-air, as if the road had lifted to meet him and regretted the effort.

He was beautiful the way a blade is: form obeying function until function is all that's left to admire. No smile, no snarl. The expression of a man about to state a fact.

Chris swore once—simple, old—and wrenched the wheel. The Corolla angled. Apollo stepped into the angle like a dancer cutting off a partner's line. He placed one palm on the front quarter panel with insulting care and shoved.

The world tilted. Tires screamed. Sky replaced street in Jack's side window, the horizon briefly deciding it preferred vertical. The car hopped—light, absurd—and then thundered as it re-met the ground wrong.

"Hold it," Jack barked, and the wind bit the chassis like teeth, trying to keep them on their rails.

Chris grunted, jaw set, hands welded to ten and two. The Corolla skidded, straightened, skidded again.

In the back seat the bags tore open fully. Hundreds of bills spun into a cyclone, pinning themselves to the headliner, the glass, Ryan's hoodie. Inside the car it became a snow globe that had opinions.

Honks detonated from the shoulder. Pedestrians on the median yelled, "It's him! It's the air guy!" Phones came up like a field of metal flowers turning to light.

Apollo moved alongside—parallel, patient, inevitable. He didn't look winded because the sun doesn't. He rapped his knuckles on the roof as if knocking on wood to keep it honest.

Jack clocked the cop cars swinging onto the avenue; the crowd on the sidewalk filming because history pays better than work; Chris finding gaps that shouldn't exist and making them. In the back, Ryan curled away from the sunlight like it hurt, jaw locked, hands clenched—a boy trying not to break the toy he never asked for.

"Jack," Chris said—nothing in it but trust and a question.

"I've got it," Jack said, whether or not he did.

Apollo blurred; sunlight telescoped; their rear quarter panel crumpled inward with a metallic animal's scream.

The car spun—half a circle, then three-quarters. Jack threw his hand out; the street shoved back, trying to decide them upright. Air poured into the cabin through every seam like it wanted to help and couldn't pick a side. A billboard lawyer smiled past, upside down. Sirens braided victory behind them.

"Brace!" Chris shouted.

Ryan's eyes flashed—not bright, not holy, just too open—and his fingers opened a fraction. Heat kissed the roof liner and left a smoking thumbprint.

Apollo lined up for the finishing nudge, calm as geometry. He lifted his hand. "Yield," he said—gentle as a commandment.

Jack saw the palm. He saw the seam where you either become the person who stops a god or the person who doesn't.

He didn't choose. The wind did.

It tore up from storm drains, alley mouths, and a thousand air conditioners, shouldered the Corolla sideways, and slapped them into the oncoming lane. They missed a bakery truck by the width of a prayer someone else must've said. The money storm ripped loose and whirlpooled—a blizzard, a fog, a chorus. Bills wedged themselves like green insulation into every crack around the doors. A twenty smacked Jack's goggles and stuck; Jack stared at him like he'd been miscast.

Apollo smiled for the first time. Not kind. Not unkind. The smile of a man tasting the word finally.

He dropped—straight down like a comet—and hit them square on the hood.

White. Then noise.

The hood crumpled like a soda can. Chris held the wheel in a death grip and rode the skid with loose hips, eyes flint. Ryan slammed shoulder-first into the door, both hands clamped shut as if he could lock the warmth inside his bones by refusing it a way out.

Air came back to Jack first. Sound flooded in behind it: whoop-whoop-whoop from half a fleet; rotor slap chewing the afternoon to pieces; civilians yelling on the shoulder, "Oh my God—move, move!"; horns turning fear into punctuation.

Apollo walked up the hood, casual as a man mounting steps, each stride denting steel like damp clay. He laid his palm on the windshield; cracks spidered outward like frost in reverse.

Jack reached for air and got it. Too much. It arrived overeager, the way a dog tries to help and knocks the table over. He hauled it through vents and seams and shoved back against the windshield from the inside. Glass bowed, shivered, held.

Apollo's hand punched through anyway.

Fingers like noon-light through rebar drove past the safety film, seized Jack's jacket, and yanked. His seatbelt caught his ribs and socked the breath from him. He thumbed the buckle with a gasp and Apollo finished the pull. Jack tore through the torn windshield, hit the roof on his shoulder, rolled, and came up crouched, boots skating on a rattling steel drum of a roof while the car was still very much moving.

Wind bellowed in his ears. Lanes streaked under them like lit fuses. Cars veered wide as a god rode their hood and a man rode their roof like problems stacked on problems.

Apollo rose from the hood with magnetized purpose. Up close he looked less like a statue and more like a verdict—features clean, eyes the color of reflected noon. He stepped onto the roof; the Corolla shook as if checking its insurance.

Jack swung first. He didn't punch like Jack. He punched like air wanted an excuse. Wind knotted tight around his fist. He drove it into Apollo's jaw with a thunderclap the sky hadn't co-signed.

Apollo's head ticked a fraction—no more than a nod to the attempt. He answered with an economical hook to the ribs. Pain blew Jack's lungs through his teeth; the roof dented under his boot.

Don't hit him too hard, Jack thought absurdly, ribs stinging. He's still a god.

"Get off my car," he rasped, and swept his palm. A glassy shearwall of wind slid between them.

Apollo walked into it like a man into a strong fan. He kept coming. He caught Jack's forearm—no flourish, no waste—and twisted. The world tilted around that twist. Jack's elbow shrieked; his knuckles scraped paint. Apollo's other hand rose for the finishing strike—a clean, downward thing that would put Jack through windshield, hood, or history.

"*Hey!*" Chris yelled, voice breaking into delighted panic. "*Ohhh, shit—I did it!*"

Two arms shot out of the Corolla's side windows—arms that were not arms, slate-dark and too long, skin patterned like river stone. They unspooled from inside the car like a nightmare deciding to be useful— thick as bridge cables, jointed in all the wrong places. The suckers weren't suckers; they were tight, flexing coins of muscle that gripped without needing friction.

They snapped around Apollo's biceps and held.

The punch stopped mid-fall. Apollo's knee dipped under the check. For the first time since he'd appeared, his expression changed—slightly, a crease passing over stone. He told himself this was invitation, not punishment. Host, not hunter. The lie wore sunlight well.

Chris was laughing, half unbelieving, half nine. "Arms out the windows, baby! Calamari Special!"

The tentacular things cinched, muscles rolling like live ropes. They dragged Apollo down to a knee on the moving roof. The Corolla fishtailed, corrected, and kept arguing with physics. Chris kept driving. Of course he kept driving.

Jack didn't think. He planted and gathered wind from every ribbed groove of highway, every screaming mirror, every hot breath of every cop bearing down—and threw.

His fist landed, but the real hit was the decision in the air—pressure folding the space Apollo occupied into a smaller, meaner shape and expulsing that shape away. For a heartbeat there was no god on the roof —only absence peeling backward in a bright parabola.

Apollo went—twenty yards, thirty—his body a streak that made the light scatter like dust in a gust. He caught himself mid-spin, the way a cat remembers ground, and hovered above the fast lane, stunned and perfect.

"Go!" Jack barked, though Chris was already floorboarding it.

Above, the news chopper dove for the money shot—literally, cash still confetti-ing from the windows. Rotor wash stamped Jack's earlier windwork flat. The pilot's voice cracked over a loudhailer—indistinct words, very distinct excitement.

"Not today," Jack said, raising both hands.

He didn't blast the helicopter. He stole the air beneath its rotor disk —punched a rolling pocket of nothing into the column it depended on. Lift misbehaved. The machine lurched; the tail yawed; the pilot reacted like a pro.

"Mayday—losing laminar—taking it out!" the voice came fierce and focused.

The chopper crabbed sideways, climbed free of the dead pocket, and peeled off downrange, choosing dignity and fuel over hero points.

"Thank you," Jack muttered to the sky, hands shaking.

"We still got cops," Chris warned, serene and sweating. Sirens bound themselves into rope, a dozen cars deep, lights strobing the world into red-blue, red-blue stutter frames. Lanes closed behind them by default—brakes, gawks, uploads. The city was a stage; they were the idiots.

"Ryan!" Chris shouted, eyes never leaving the road. "Tail-off, buddy!"

Ryan had sunk low, face knotted, terrified of his own switch. He met Jack's eyes through the shattered sunroof, unsteady and ashamed. "If I start—"

"We'll steer it," Jack said, loud over wind. "Just one. Out the back. Away from people."

Chris cut across two lanes with elegant disrespect, lining them up with a green exit board looming ahead—NORTH / LOCAL TRAFFIC—bolted to a gantry that straddled the lanes like a goalpost.

"Make it the sign," Chris said. "Cleanest mess."

Ryan nodded once—agreement to jump. He shoved to his knees, squared to the open sunroof, and took a breath the way a diver takes the last one.

When he opened his hand, fire didn't come first. Thirst did—the air around his palm collapsing toward his skin, pressure bowing, heat choosing a shape. Light distorted, shimmering hard as if the afternoon had a fever. Then the world colored it orange to comfort itself.

The bolt leapt up, silent and hungry, and kissed the underside of the sign.

Metal didn't burn; it softened from the inside out—the retroreflective green blistering and curling, bolts groaning and then shrieking as tempered certainty failed. The sign folded like a hardback forgetting its page.

"Down!" Jack shouted, shoving a fat, rude palm-print of air downward over the gantry.

The whole assembly lurched, snapped a hinge; one side dropped, the other stuck, then tore with a sound every driver felt in their molars.

Behind them the green slab scythed into lanes, punching hoods, popping airbags, turning the first wave of cruisers into synchronized, glittering, deeply inconvenient pinwheels. A box truck locked up and sat on its haunches like commerce had changed its mind.

In two heartbeats the highway became a parking lot.

"Go go go!" Jack yelled—redundant. Chris was already threading a letter-slot gap between two braking sedans, the Corolla slipping through like mail.

In the mirror, Apollo blurred—a bright, furious line drawing a ruler-straight path. He hit the falling sign not with his body but with will, shouldered it just enough to keep anyone from dying, then cut through the chaos he hadn't caused and absolutely owned. He lifted his gaze, found them the way sunlight finds a shadow, and came on.

"Ramp!" Chris called. "Hold tight!"

They screamed up the exit. Local lanes peeled away like a blessing. Jack dropped through the sunroof into the passenger seat and yanked the belt across his chest with hands that didn't want to be hands.

Cash still swirled, desperate to be important. Ryan sagged back, palms smoking faintly where the air had kissed too hard. Sick. Twelve. He closed his hands like locking a dangerous animal in a small cage and whispered, "Stop."

The heat obeyed. It died against his skin like apology.

Behind, the main lanes were a charmed disaster—cruisers accordioning, civilians blocking, the chopper already gone to nurse its pride. Apollo vaulted a wreck in a contemptuous arc and landed on the ramp lip like stepping onto a porch.

"Left," Jack said, because the air ahead felt looser, and Chris took it without looking.

They dove under a rail bridge, tires singing, concrete roaring. For three blessed seconds the windshield was nothing but shadow and pillars and rust.

They burst into daylight and the residential grid opened like a hand. Chris picked a finger—tree-tunneled street, mailboxes pretending everything was fine—and gunned it.

Jack looked once in the cracked rearview. Apollo stood on the bridge, haloed by his own inevitability, watching them vanish into ordinary. He raised his hand, palm open, like a promise.

"Okay," Chris said, voice shaking now that shaking had permission. "Okay."

Ryan bent forward, elbows on knees, breathing like he was relearning it. "Did we—are we—"

"Not safe," Jack said. "Just... not caught."

Somewhere far off, a siren dopplered its confusion across someone else's map. The money settled by inches. A single twenty fluttered down into Jack's lap like a tired bird.

Chris snorted—half laugh, half sob. "If anyone asks," he said, "this was your plan."

"If anyone asks," Jack said, hands still trembling, "we weren't here."

For now, they weren't. The city swallowed them, the way it swallows everything, even gods—for a while.

Somewhere above, daylight circled back for another look.

CHAPTER 18

The Parthenon was no longer stone and ruin—it was power reimagined.

Marble veins pulsed with interior light, a low electrical hum running through columns like a heartbeat under polished skin. Drone rotors ticked in the hazy dusk; camera shutters clicked like rain; incense smoke braided with helicopter exhaust and the salt-bitter breath off the Saronic Gulf. A thousand throats chanted, some in harmony, most not, and still it sounded like a single word: more.

Bishops in mirrored gold breastplates kept the rope lines straight without touching anyone, faces unreadable in the reflections of a hundred phones. Beyond them, priests moved like currents—emerald for Hera, dusk-blue for Athena, blinding white for Apollo's wing—while news crawls on livestream rigs flickered with lag and wrong spellings. The hill had become a stage; Olympus, again, chose to make its entrance above it.

Inside the new throne hall—half temple, half boardroom, all weather —the doors slammed like thunder trapped in stone.

Apollo stumbled through—soot-streaked, bleeding, his right shoulder low, the usual gold on him guttering like a candle in a draft. His bow was gone. His breath came in clean, clipped measures, the way professionals manage pain.

Every god turned.

Zeus rose—not in concern, but fury; lightning threaded faintly through the floor, pulsing in the marble like nerves remembering their job. "My son," he said, voice calm the way a cliff is calm. "You return… alone."

Apollo's jaw worked. "I found them. Three. Fire. Air. And one who can change his face."

"Titans?" Athena asked, curiosity sharpened to a point.

"Or something worse," Apollo said. "They move like mortals. They bleed like mortals. But when they fight..." He hesitated, the admission tasting odd in his mouth. "When they fight, the world bends."
(They were only mortals. Why do I still hear them breathing?)

From the shadow of a column, Hermes tipped his head, lazy as a coin on a thumb. "And you came back for dinner after losing to mortals?"

Apollo ignored him. "They are not fully Titan yet. Their essence... leaks through. But they are becoming."

Zeus descended the dais. With each step he seemed larger—or the room remembered who owned it. "So you went alone," he said softly. "Without command. Without counsel. Without victory."

"It was an opportunity," Apollo ground out. "You wanted initiative. I showed it."

"You showed arrogance." The word cracked the air; a torch nearby popped in a little flower of gold.

Apollo went to one knee—half respect, half the weight of his father's mood. "I failed. But they're gathering. The air one protected the others. They fought together."

Athena and Poseidon traded a look: strategy and storm doing the same math. "If three have joined," Athena said, "more will follow. That implies leadership."

"Titans do not lead," Zeus said, dismissing the category. "They break."

"Things learn in the dark," Poseidon murmured, fingers drumming the trident's haft. "Even chains."

Zeus turned toward the great window over Athens. He stood in a rectangle of late sun, a god-shaped absence cut out of the horizon. "Then they will learn fear again."

Side doors opened. Translator earbuds chirped feedback; a badge lanyard snagged on a hinge.

"Lord Zeus?" A mortal voice, small but firm.

168

A handful of uniformed officials stepped in—local police, a UN liaison in a navy suit with a wrinkle that had lost a war, two aides with tablets already recording, and a Bishop escort on either flank. The lead—a forty-something captain with the posture of someone whose name earns yes—cleared his throat. "We represent the UN joint task force. Governments need... clarity. Your followers, the gatherings, public safety—"

"Clarity," Zeus repeated, turning slowly. "You request clarity."

"Yes, Your Majesty," the captain said, the title tripping out of him like a memory he didn't know he had.

The storm outside rolled in on cue. "Here is clarity," Zeus said. "We are not your guests. We are your gods."

A blue arc skittered across the marble, teasing the captain's boots. Ozone burned the nose; incense tried and failed to sweeten it.

"You serve law," Zeus said, stepping closer, "and we authored it. Obedience, not inquiry."

Athena's eyes narrowed—not disapproval, not assent, a note in the margin. Hermes watched the mortals as if measuring fear in grams.

Zeus lifted his hand; lightning fluttered in his palm, an impatient bird. "You wish for order? Then you will have it." He looked past them. "Bring forth the chosen."

From behind the throne, ten mortals stepped out—armor the color of wet sunrise, bracers catching torchlight. Their eyes had changed: human irises overlaid with a faint god-spark, like a reflection that wouldn't blink. The Bishops—divine enforcers, mirrored and unbending—shifted to make room, the distinction clear: Bishops are Olympus's mailed fist; Heroes are its human hand.

"These," Zeus said, presenting them the way kings present new borders, "are my Heroes. Blessed by Olympus, sworn to the Wings. They will be bridge and sword."

The lead Hero, a woman with a pale scar under her left eye and heat shimmer haloing her breath, bowed. "Lord Zeus. We are ready."

169

"You will hunt the Titans," Zeus said. "Find their vessels. Crush any who harbor them. When mortals question you"—he glanced at the captain—"remind them that Olympus rules again."

The captain's hand twitched toward his holster before training, or common sense, froze it. An aide's phone buzzed; another snapped a furtive selfie and thought better of it when a Bishop's mirrored visor reflected his shame back at him.

Athena stepped from her seat, voice cool. "The Bishops maintain sanctuaries. The Heroes extend reach. We will publish strictures."

Zeus nodded without looking at her. The mortals retreated, murmuring into radios, reports compressing into euphemism as they crossed the threshold.

"The Titans move," Zeus said when the doors sealed, the outside thunder thinning to a felt pressure. "The Heroes will answer. The world will remember obedience."

"Mortals' loyalty is a tide," Poseidon said carefully. "It comes. It goes."

"Then we will command the moon," Zeus said, and the temperature dropped a degree.

Hermes rolled his quill between finger and thumb. "Give mortals our strength, they will look for thunder of their own."

Zeus's gaze slid to him. "You question my will?"

"Never," Hermes said lightly. "I admire it from a safe distance."

Silence balanced on a knife. Then Zeus flicked two fingers. "Worship patterns. No nation untouched. Make the algorithm kneel."

Hermes bowed. The air did not entirely trust him to leave cleanly, but it let him go.

The council thinned. Apollo lingered at the edge of the dais, light pooling faint around his heels, diminished but still not human.

"You shouldn't have gone alone," Athena said, plain as a blade's back.

"No one else was going," he said.

"You're not the only one questioning Father," she murmured. "You're only the one doing it out loud."

He laughed without amusement. "So I'm the example."

"Exactly that," Zeus said, already close. He was quieter now—worse. "You disobeyed command. You revealed yourself. You failed."

"I fought three," Apollo said, lifting his chin. "I lived."

"Do not mistake survival for victory."

Zeus gestured. Two Heroes—new-made, reverent, disturbingly efficient—stepped in and took Apollo by the arms.

"Father—" Athena snapped, the word more warning than plea.

"You will remain within Olympus," Zeus said, not looking at her. "Cool your flame. Remember what burns it."

Lightning stitched the window; Apollo vanished in a brief glare, dragged toward confinement. For a heartbeat after, his breath still seemed to echo in the hall.

"This is how it starts," Athena said to the quiet.

The doors banged again. Hermes stumbled in, dust on his hem, translator earpiece still chirping a ghost of Greek.

"You are late," Zeus said, irritation already shaped.

"I was among the people," Hermes said, smoothing nothing into place. "Brand care. They adore you. A woman sells pendants of your face; a senator bought three. Capitalism thrives under divinity."

"You mock me?"

"Never," Hermes said, bowing with a grin that didn't reach his eyes. "Merely… reporting. Mortals need to believe you care."

"Do you?" Athena asked.

For once, Hermes's answer lagged. Too long for comfort, too short for confession. "Sometimes," he said, and then: "You ever wonder if we're the villains yet?"—soft, meant only for her.

Zeus cut across it. "Enough riddles. You will join the Heroes. Find the Titans. Root out those who shelter them."

"As you wish," Hermes said, and the wish did not sound like his.

He turned. Athena caught his look: not accusation, understanding. Hermes's mouth tightened—guilt's smallest shape—and then he was gone again, leaving the faintest jingle of coin and wing.

The chamber emptied by degrees. Priests outside rehearsed tomorrow's schedule in three languages; a helicopter thudded off toward the islands; the chant below rose and fell on a delay as livestreams buffered faith.

Zeus stood alone at the glass. Lightning webbed faintly through his reflection, a crown he didn't have to wear. Below, at the base of the mount, people knelt—sweat, perfume, cheap sunscreen, incense, hope. The sound of them pleased him more than thunder.

He closed his eyes and inhaled it and smiled. This was the real power —the part that doesn't crackle or stain; the kind you hear.

Behind him, Athena watched. Apollo in a gilded cell. Hermes swallowing jokes. Mortals with borrowed light hunting their own. Bishops glossed to a mirror shine. Heroes fitted for bracers and orders.

Outside, thunder pawed at the hills. In the glass, lightning flickered, showing a god already trapped by his own storm.

Athena wondered—not for the first time—if Olympus had ever truly been a home for gods... or only the prettiest cage ever built.

CHAPTER 19

Jack's garage loft always smelled like cut lumber and old summers—sawdust lodged in the joists, sunscreen ghosts in the couch cushions, warm car below breathing metal and oil.

Tonight it smelled like wet money and fear drying out. The dorm fridge under the workbench added its own anxious hum, a little motor trying not to be noticed.

They'd jammed the roll-up door half-open to bleed the heat. Out by the fence, the silver Corolla idled in memory only; they'd swapped it for his dad's beige Camry fifteen minutes after they cleared the ramp. The Camry now sat obediently under them—square, innocent—as if shielding the house from the curse of a god's handprint.

Up in the loft, they moved like people who'd sprinted a mile and only then remembered how lungs worked.

Chris had claimed the workbench and turned it into a counting station. He'd been quiet since they parked—focused quiet, not sulking—like a chef in the weeds. Cash ran through his hands in jittering green rivers. Every few minutes, without looking up, he tested something: eyes flicking wider, pupils splitting for a blink into four black coins; a ripple down his forearms that pebbled the skin then smoothed—river rock under light. Finally, with a sound like coaxing a stubborn zipper, he rolled his shoulders and—no ceremony—sprouted more shoulders.

Not full arms. Not at first. More like the permission for arms. Then the muscles answered. Two slick, slate-colored limbs unspooled from behind his lats, then two more—shorter than the things that had yanked Apollo, still too long for comfort. They braced stacks, ripped tape, reached for a Sharpie. His regular hands never stopped.

"Okay," he said to no one, delighted and weirdly gentle. "Okay… this is a thing."

"Please don't drip on the twenties," Jack said.

"I'm not dripping," Chris said, offended. "I'm immaculate."

On the old pullout sofa, Ryan sat with both hands pressed between his knees, head down. Hood off. The hair at his temples had crisped into tiny white semicircles where heat had kissed it. He stared at a dark scuff on the concrete like it might answer if he stared hard enough.

Jack opened the fridge and pretended to look for something to drink. Mostly he needed the door between him and the room for a second. His phone buzzed in his palm, screen full of the same clip in a dozen reposts: aerial footage, the Corolla threading a gap, a god landing on the hood like a lion on a moving jeep. Somebody had put EDM under it. Somebody else had overlaid WASTED in GTA font when the sign came down and the cruisers pinwheeled. He muted it all.

A still frame from one broadcast froze and zoomed their roof too long. Under the ruined sunroof, his face was a watery smear, heat above asphalt. Unknown suspect, possibly using technology to distort identity, the chyron guessed. Good. Let them chase the wrong god.

He shut the fridge without taking anything. His hands shook. He kept them on the handle until they remembered how to stop.

"Anybody hurt?" he asked. He'd asked it twice in the car. He needed it again.

"No," Chris said, still counting, still four-armed. "Not us. The pileup's a paperwork day, but the sign went long, most people braked. Apollo... deflected enough. You saw. He's a jerk, not a killer."

"He's a god," Ryan said dully. "We stole money and a god tried to pull you through a car."

Jack rubbed the bridge of his nose. "We stole money from a bank," he said. "Insured to the teeth. And we didn't set out to fight Apollo."

"You planned for it," Ryan said.

"I planned for something to go wrong because things go wrong," Jack said—sharper than he meant. "And because you—because we—are

174

still figuring out how not to light the world on fire when our blood spikes."

Ryan flinched like the words had heat. "I didn't mean—"

"I know," Jack said immediately, guilt biting. He crossed the room and sat at the other end of the couch, giving space but not distance. "I know you didn't. I'm not… I'm not mad at you."

"Little mad," Chris said, not unkind, tallying a rubber-banded stack. "At the fire. At the lobby becoming soup."

Jack shot him a look. Chris nodded: fair. One extra arm peeled tape from a roll without looking. Another coaxed the old printer into not jamming, because Chris refused to live in a world where printers won.

Silence followed—the leftover-adrenaline kind, crowded with words still choosing shapes. Outside, a car rolled by slow, then faster, a neighbor deciding the garage kids weren't building anything worth seeing. Far off, a helicopter chopped the evening thinner.

On the high-school TV, the all-news channel ran a banner: ROCKAWAY HEIST: GOD INTERVENES. Blazers took turns guessing things. One called Apollo a "public safety partner." One called him "an occupying force." One said vigilantes with a little grin, tasting ratings. Nobody said children. Nobody said we don't understand what we live with anymore and we're scared.

Jack clicked it off. The sudden quiet made the ballast buzz loud.

"Okay," he said, and heard it—like a meeting, like leadership. He hated that and did it anyway. "We have to talk about what this is."

Chris didn't look up. "Cash-based group therapy?"

"Not jokey," Jack said. "Please."

Chris's four hands paused, then two kept moving and two folded with the grace of a truce. "Not jokey," he said. "Shoot."

"We're not criminals," Jack started—and felt hypocrisy stack up like traffic cones. He pushed through. "I know what we just did. I know how it looks. But if we keep giving in to…" He searched for something not

175

the good feeling, because that would make him sound like a PSA and a liar. "...the pull. The bike-downhill, no-hands pull. We're going to make worse choices."

Chris's mouth twitched—almost a crack, then mercy. He let the sentence live.

"Today," Jack said, softer. "You—" he nodded at Ryan—"tried to make a little mess. We got a big one. I... I only meant sprinklers, doors, bones intact. Then I'm punching a god on the roof of my dad's least favorite car." He exhaled. "That's not a slope. That's a cliff. And—" he swallowed the honesty because it deserved its own air—"and I liked winning. I did. A lot. That's the part that scares me."

Ryan nodded, throat thick. "It's like... taking the cap off a bottle. The air wants it. My hand is the cap."

Jack felt that in his bones. The air loved him. It wanted to move because he told it a story about where it should be and it believed him. That love could ruin things.

"We are not villains," he said, and the words tasted weird because his mouth remembered the thrill of a sign folding like paper and the helicopter wobbling away. "I don't want to be the reason some kid grows up scared of the sky. We're not built for that."

Chris set a stack down, pushed his stool back with a squeak, and stood. The extra arms folded into him like he was shrugging out of a coat. When he met Jack's eyes, the mischief was gone. Something steadier remained.

"I like the score," he said, plain. "I like that we won a round. I like... that you didn't die. I like that I can be a calamari nightmare with fine motor control." A breath. "But you're right. I don't want to be a chyron for what the Heroes do to people. I don't want your mom watching that."

Ryan huffed a surprised laugh at "calamari nightmare," then pressed his palms together until his knuckles blanched. "I don't want to be anything," he said. "I want to finish school. I want to show my mom my diploma and not have her Google my name and get a burning bank."

A slice of evening light made the dust look like snow.

"Then be that," Jack said. "Take your cut. Walk. No one's chaining you here."

Ryan's shoulders dropped. "You're not mad?"

"I'll be happy if you never have to open your hand again near me," Jack said, then, quickly—"I mean that in the good way. I'll drive you. I'll fly you. Tonight."

A beat. Then Ryan nodded. "Yeah. Tonight."

"You'll keep this quiet?" he asked.

"If I'm caught, you're caught. If you're caught, I'm caught," Jack said. "Our parents would kill us before the Heroes could. So yes. Quiet."

They managed weak smiles. Jack's phone buzzed again. Police Seek Tips on 'Wind Suspect' in Bank Heist; Olympus Praises 'Heroic Intervention'. A towel-wrapped manager shaking his head like someone had told him dogs could vote. The roof scuffle, blurred. The traffic snarl under the fallen sign. No faces clean enough to harm—unless the internet became itself.

He killed the screen. The decision arrived whole.

"Okay," he said, softer. "We lay low. For real, not pretend. No flying for fun. No powers in public. No practicing in parks. We disappear for a beat."

"Motion to disappear in place," Chris said, hand up. "I've got a shift tomorrow pretending to manage a Verizon store I absolutely do not work at. Would be a shame to waste the nametag."

"Disappear in place," Jack said—because the joke mattered: normalize. "Also—my parents."

He pictured his mom's face watching the chase—the way she'd looked at the TV, then him, then the TV again, trying to reconcile two equations with the same numbers and different rules. I bet they aren't bad people, she'd said. They could have done worse. She had no idea she was absolving her son.

"They need out," he said. "A week. Somewhere without gods. Somewhere nobody cares who Zeus is."

"Disney?" Chris said, reflex.

"That's the capital of gods," Jack said. "West. Big sky."

He woke the laptop under the printer. Newark to Bozeman, earliest tomorrow, return open. He paid with a card that would be dead by Tuesday but worked tonight. The printer made a swallowing sound and produced confirmations. He counted out a thousand in crisp hundreds, slid them into an envelope stamped ROOFING WARRANTY.

Down in the kitchen, his parents were doing what parents do when the news shows the end of the world: boiling water and reorganizing coupons. The kettle whistled; the TV flickered with the sound off.

His mom looked up. "You look pale."

"It's the bulb," he said, and set the envelope down like a dog laying a catch. "Happy early anniversary."

She frowned, opened it, blinked. "Montana?"

"Mountains," he said. "No temples. No oceans for Poseidon to be dramatic about. You've wanted it since the cowboy movie phase. Go. Please."

His dad peered over her shoulder, then at Jack. "We can't just—"

"You always say you want to," Jack said. "Now I want you to. Spend cash. Groceries, gas, nothing flashy. Don't post pictures. Pretend you're in witness protection for a week. I want the house quiet. For me. For… this." He gestured loosely at the world.

His mom's eyes softened, then sharpened. She gripped his wrist. "They could have done worse," she said quietly. "Whoever that was today."

"Yeah," he said.

"We'll pack," she said, efficient again. "We'll be out tonight. Don't ruin my pans."

He kissed her hair, hugged his dad, and left before he could wreck the scene by staying in it.

Back upstairs, Chris had bagged three equal shares in contractor trash bags lined with grocery bags—one for each. A shoebox held rent/food/slush. The rest would go places slowly, or not at all.

Chris—back to two arms, two eyes—tossed him a bag. "Your cut, Captain Not-Captain."

"Don't," Jack said.

"You don't want to be in charge," Chris said, "which is why you should be."

"I don't want to be a lot of things," Jack said. "Let's do as few of them as possible."

Ryan stood carefully, as if the floor might give. He slung his bag and almost toppled. Chris caught a strap. The weight wasn't heavy; the week was.

9:14 glowed from the cheap wall clock. The air by the window felt clean enough to touch again.

"I'll take him," Jack said. "Less seen, less stupid. You—eat everything Mom didn't hide, and do not shift into anything with a beak if the neighbor's Ring is pointed in here."

"No promises," Chris said, already starfished on the couch with a family-size bag of chips he had not paid for. He flicked the TV on mute, letting the chase crawl like a fish tank. When Jack wasn't looking, he fished a wallet from his pocket—the bank manager's, liberated in the confusion—slid it into the tool drawer, then shoved it farther, deciding to be better without applause.

"Text me when you're down," he added, catching himself and smiling at the stupidity. "Or, you know, blow a leaf."

Jack slid the loft window up, stepped onto the tar-paper roof, and pulled Ryan after him. Night air felt like mercy. The neighborhood smelled like cut grass, charcoal, a tang from the river. Dogs barked and forgot why. The sky wore humidity like a lid.

"You sure?" Jack asked.

"No," Ryan said. "But yes."

They lifted together—Jack first, the air cupping him; Ryan pinned in a two-handed carry because air didn't love him yet. They skimmed the roofs, silent, leaving the garage light a square on the ground. Low along the tree line, over the dark spine of the creek, over the backs of grocery stores where dumpsters lived and teenagers learned cigarettes. Route 3 was a sheen to the south; Lincoln Park a rumor behind them; the black chop of Ringwood forest beyond the ridge felt like tomorrow.

He set down two streets shy of Ryan's block. They walked the last bit, bags in hand, like two kids coming home from a bad party. At the corner, Ryan stopped.

"I don't know how to… not be this," he said. "If it turns on."

"Call me," Jack said. "I'll snuff you out."

A huff that was almost a laugh. "Thanks."

They hugged like guys who don't, then did. Ryan peeled off across the dark lawn toward the porch light he knew. The door opened; a rectangle of warm made him a person again.

On the way back, Jack didn't hurry. He let the air carry him like a mother forgiving a late curfew. Over the river, he drifted and let his brain do math: routes, faces, the ache in his ribs where Apollo had rung him like a bell. Being good didn't mean anything alone. It meant choosing. He liked winning. He could still choose right after.

He landed a block from home and walked to let his pulse remember human. In the loft, the TV flickered; Chris lay spread, chips on his chest, one hand quietly growing a little sucker-patch to peel the bag back noiselessly—the man had found a way to be lazy in evolution.

"Trash can's right there," Jack said.

"I'm saving the environment by not getting up," Chris said, eyes on a new angle of their chase. "Oh—news says the bank manager told cops he 'saw himself' stealing the money. Poor guy thinks he's in a Black Mirror episode. We're clear."

"Good," Jack said. Relief cracked something he hadn't noticed clenched.

He grabbed the last bag—the one not split into shares—and slung it over his shoulder.

"Where—" Chris started, then saw the look and nodded. "Right. Be quick."

Jack kept low, ghosted downtown, and set the bag in the police station's side lot under the security light. He folded a note between the drawstrings.

For the cruisers.
Sorry for the metalwork.
Stop aiming at the people who are trying not to hurt you.

No signature. The air lifted him before he could try to be clever.

Back through the window, the house had changed shape: suitcases in the hall; the kettle's second whistle; his dad humming while folding socks wrong. The world narrowed to something manageable: two parents, a friend with chips, another walking home trying not to spark, a kid on a roof deciding he could be a person again by choosing it. He shut the window. He shut off his phone.

He sat on the floor and let his spine touch plywood and gravity prove it still cared.

From the couch, Chris spoke without looking over. "We did bad," he said. "And then we did less bad. That count?"

"It's a start," Jack said.

A long minute. The TV played them in slow motion: god, roof, sign. The crawl crawled. Somewhere far away, a thunderhead made a promise to a mountain.

181

"Lay low," Jack said again, to make it real. "Tomorrow we're boring."

"Tomorrow I'm a boring calamari," Chris said, the grin finally timed right. "Eight arms. One brain cell. That kind of boring."

Jack laughed into his sleeve—because if he didn't, he might cry into it. Outside, nothing exploded. Inside, nobody burned.

For the first time since a god hit their hood, he let air out of his lungs all the way to the bottom and didn't grab for more. He didn't need to. Tonight, the wind could keep itself.

He'd ask again tomorrow.

CHAPTER 20

Jack's kitchen looked like a breakfast bomb had gone off.

Pancake batter freckled the backsplash. Eggshells cratered the counter like a moonscape. Bacon smoke did lazy laps near the ceiling fan, sweet and greasy—burnt sugar riding bacon fat, the house wearing a diner as cologne. Chris stood at the stove in boxers, a "WORLD'S OKAYEST COOK" apron Jack didn't know they owned, eyes bright with the jittery optimism of a man trying to bribe karma.

"Bro," Jack said, stepping in like a detective at a crime scene. "Did we… get robbed by brunch?"

"Apology breakfast!" Chris announced. "For, you know—" he mimed a tiny, tasteful explosion "—the whole fire-tornado, god-on-the-hood, life-flashing thing."

Jack opened the fridge and stared into the cold like patience might be next to the milk. "You made enough apology for the tri-state."

"I didn't know your egg vibe," Chris said, gesturing to carnage: fried, scrambled, soft-boiled, and one hard-boiled that had clearly seen some things. "Diversity."

They ate. Chris chewed like redemption was calorie-dependent. Jack stayed in sweatpants and silence, scrolling past the same looped clips of the chase: their mangled Corolla under a news chopper, Apollo stepping onto the hood like a man boarding a yacht. A talking head called divine intervention a "public-safety partnership." Another called it "an occupying force." Someone coined wind suspect. The chyron tried to name a ghost.

The faces blurred together after the third replay. Every slowed-down moment felt wrong, like time itself had been bent to make them look guiltier.

Without his usual glib armor, Chris slid his golf county ID card across the table. "Here."

"You trying to invoice me for eggs?" Jack asked.

"That's me. Before," Chris said. "Chris Towers. New Haven. Two sisters. One golden retriever. Mom who makes lasagna that will make you weep and then confess."

Behind the ID was a folded photo: Chris, his mom, a dog that looked like it could guard heaven.

"I lost my license recently so I just keep it so I don't forget," he said. "If I wake up with... eight eyes or a squid arm, I want to remember there's still this."

"You're still you," Jack said.

The words felt fragile in his mouth, like glass promises. He hoped saying them out loud might help them stick.

"Yeah," Chris said softly. "I just don't always feel like it."

The air around Jack gathered—his tells were getting louder. He breathed and let it slip back toward the window.

"We can't sit around forever," he said. "We need to understand what we are."

And what we've become, he didn't say. The thought sat heavy anyway.

"Philosophically or scientifically?"

"Both. Apollo asked, 'Where are the rest of you?' He thinks there are more. Hermes talked about centaurs back in Ringwood—honorable and vicious. They've been here. They weren't invited to Zeus's party. They might know what's going on."

If we don't move first, we won't be searching, Jack thought. *We'll be hunted.*

Chris squinted. "So we're... what? Going to interview half-horses in the woods?"

184

"You got a better lead?"

Chris looked at the bacon smoke haloing the fan, then at the apron he was wearing. "Depressingly, no."

Side yard. Morning wind came to him like a pet stretching awake. Jack didn't command it; he asked. The maples answered with a single rustle—permission granted—and the air wrapped him in invisible bands.

Beside him, hoodie up, Chris eyed the sky. "For a guy who said 'lay low,' you sure love doing the one thing that's 'high.'"

"Fastest way to travel," Jack said.

"Next time, I'm growing wings."

"Next time, I'm charging for airfare."

They rose—over cul-de-sac, over the dark seam of the creek, over rooftops with trampoline scars and above-ground pools. The river flashed a quicksilver grin. A hobby drone buzzed up from two streets over— some kid's curiosity on four props—tilting toward them like a snitch. Jack angled a soft crosswind that nudged it back to its backyard with just enough stubbornness to feel like a glitch.

Every second in the air felt like borrowed time. Exhilarating. Terrifying. Addictive.

Chris shouted something profane that turned to laughter when the sound tore away. Jack didn't answer aloud; he could feel the air knowing him now. Not alive—aware. It wanted to be where he pictured. Loyal dog logic. It remembered him.
He liked that.
He hated how much he liked that.

At first, the woods did normal: park signs, trail blazes, a bulletin board with a sun-bleached BE TICK AWARE poster. Picnic tables tattooed with forever-love and fake numbers. Deeper in, the green got too green, light thick as syrup. The temperature slipped a few degrees in a way weather apps didn't acknowledge. Branches whispered with a rhythm that belonged to no breeze Jack wasn't making.

Chris hit the ground from the last glide with his usual back-adjusting thump. "Every time you fly me, I earn a chiropractor punch card."

"You're welcome," Jack said.

"Ringwood State Park," Chris read from the sign. "This is where golden retrievers do their taxes. Not where we meet mythological arms dealers."

"Things have been sighted here," Jack said. "Hikers reported shadows that run like deer but sound like people."

"So we're hunting cryptids."

"Interviewing them," Jack said.

"You've officially lost your mind."

They walked. The morning had that swollen quiet before summer storms—the kind that makes you lower your voice out of respect. Every footstep felt too loud. The air skirted Jack's shoulders in thin ribbons and looped his ankles like a cautious scout.

"You get that faraway look when you're listening to it," Chris said. "Like you're talking to your imaginary friend."

"It's not imaginary."

"I'm aware," Chris said. "That's what's terrifying."

Another half mile and Jack stopped. Head tilted. The air pressed tighter for one heartbeat, then unspooled.

"We're not alone," he said.

"You're doing the ominous tone."

"Don't move."

The forest didn't explode so much as rearrange itself. Hooves, first—dull thuds muffled by leaf litter. Then breath, low and rhythmic, not human. Branches lifted and settled as if making way for something the trees respected.

The first centaur took the trail ten feet ahead. Massive. Bare chest inked with scars like a map drawn in blade. Equine body thick through the shoulder, flanks nicked and healed. Human hair braided with leaves and bone charms. Eyes dark and precise.

Others slid out of green one by one until the clearing held a practiced horseshoe of a dozen. Spears in callused hands; lamellar armor glistening with dew; the quiet confidence of creatures who knew how to fight on ground that loved them.

"You said 'honorable,'" Chris whispered.

"I did."

"We still banking on that?"

"We'll find out."

The leader stepped forward, chin lifted. "Human," he said. He made the word do both disdain and curiosity. His nostrils flared. "And something... else."

Jack kept his hands empty and his stance honest. The air hummed, ready and held. "We came to talk."

"Lies first, then honesty," the centaur said. "You carry thunder on your skin. Olympus stink." His gaze flicked to Jack's chest, then to the treeline behind them. "And smoke. New smoke."

"We're not with them," Jack said.

"Then you are against them."

"Or door number—" Chris started.

The leader raised a hand. Three flanking centaurs moved like one. Vines—braided green and brown, humming with sap—whistled through the air. Jack slipped the first loop by half an inch; Chris yelped as one ringed his forearm and bit.

"Wait!" Jack shouted, palms up. "We're not enemies!"

"Then you are prisoners," the centaur said.

The vines cinched with a dry, living hum—fibers tightening, resin creaking. The air around Jack pushed back on reflex, meeting pressure with pressure; the loop shivered against a sheath of wind and held anyway, clever with thorns tucked inward. Chris's rope tightened once in warning, making his fingers tingle. Leaves overhead agreed to stop moving.

Jack swallowed heat. He could blow the clearing wide, snap every vine, turn the ring of bodies to swirling dust and apologies. He could. He didn't.

Not yet. Not like this.

He looked the leader in the eye. "Fine," he said evenly. "Then take us to someone who talks before they burn."

CHAPTER 21

The forest reorganized itself.

Hoofbeats first—dull thuds swallowed by leaf mold—then shapes stepped out of shadow: tall, sure, wrong in the right way. The leader came first, human torso burnished and scarred, horse body the size of a small car, mane braided with leaf and bone. A bow rode one shoulder, a spear the other hand. His eyes were a field general's—assessing, unimpressed, awake. The air smelled of horse sweat and iron over the sweet rot of last year's leaves.

They weren't alone. A dozen more slid into view in an easy arc at bowshot, every gap a lie. Spears, slings, blades. Armor whose surface still remembered stone grain.

Chris put his hands up slowly. "Okay," he said. "We're here for the tour."

The big centaur didn't blink. When he spoke, it wasn't English—not really. Words came out like clean gravel, vowels running long, meaning hanging between syllables. Somehow Jack knew it, not with the spreadsheet brain but with whatever part measured a room by how the air sat in its corners.

"Humans," the centaur said—except the word carried history: softwalkers, bright-boned, quick to burn.

Jack lifted his hands a fraction. "We came to talk."

The leader's lip curled the smallest degree. He answered in the same old tongue, his voice a low bell in Jack's ribs. The meaning slid into place because Jack wanted it to.

"Talking is a kind of trespass."

Chris glanced sideways. "You get any of that?"

"Enough," Jack murmured. Then, louder, careful: "We ask for audience. Not to bargain. To learn."

The centaur's eyes flicked to Chris, to the treeline, to the sky. When he spoke again, it was faster, like a test.

Jack caught half, missed a third, felt the rest. He didn't answer. He tipped his chin at Chris. "Translate. Word for word. No improv. If you don't know a word, say you don't."

Chris's eyebrows crawled up. "Since when am I Duolingo for horse-Latin?"

"Since now. I hear pressure systems. You hear letters."

Chris frowned, listened. His mouth worked around sounds he didn't own yet. Then, cautious: "He says we wear 'storm-scent'... that we wield what isn't ours. He asks—twice—who we bow to."

"Tell him: no one."

Chris did, syllable by stubborn syllable. The leader listened, face unreadable. The line of centaurs adjusted by inches—bows angled, slings loosened. Not relaxing. Recalculating.

Then the ropes came.

Not ropes from a hardware aisle. Braids of vine and something older —root under bark, sap over nerve. They dropped clean from the canopy and were on wrists, elbows, ankles before move made it out of Jack's throat.

They tightened and hummed. Not a threat, not yet. A boundary.

Jack tested them. The wind curled at his skin, thin snakes along the cords. He felt fiber give and a hard knot of enchantment under it. He could break this. If he chose to rip instead of ask.

He didn't. He stilled the air and let it sit warm over his forearms like a hand saying I'm here.

Chris flexed and the vine at his ankle tugged warning-hard. "Ow. Rude."

A younger centaur—female, gaze like a thrown knife—stepped close enough that Jack could smell smoke in her hair. "You will come," she said in the old tongue, consonants clean. "If you fight, the roots will know."

"The what?" Chris asked, then yelped as the vine twitched like a living thing. "Cool. The roots have customer service."

They moved. The formation folded around them and walked, precise and practiced, each flank paced for maximum humiliation. The light went older. The air cooled half a degree. Smell shifted from pine heat to damp stone and coppery worked earth. Hooves made a low-frequency drum that got into the ribs.

Hermes had said: honorable, intelligent, and they'd gut you with a smile. Jack had heard the slander. Now, marching under clean choreography, he heard the part Hermes hadn't said out loud: they remember. When gods were taxes. What mortals do with fear.

He touched the air again—not to break, to map. Threads slid between fibers, sampling the knotwork. A guard heard the whisper and sank his spear butt into soil.

"No tricks, sky-child," he snapped. Even child sounded like history being cruel.

Chris bumped Jack's shoulder. "We good?"

"We're not dead," Jack said. "They don't want us dead."

"That's a low bar."

The "clearing" wasn't a clearing—more a decision. A camp sprawled like a city catching breath: bark-and-hide lean-tos; racks of spears propped like organ pipes; low fires smoldering to keep coals honest. Foals—actual foals—skittered in a ring well out of spear range. Adults glanced, then kept working the way pros do when strangers wander onto the job site.

At center stood a stone, a pickup-sized slab carved in spirals that made Jack's eyes blink and re-read. The leader pointed. Vines lifted. Jack and Chris rose an inch—just enough to make dignity a chore—and drifted to a post burnished by a hundred such conversations.

"Tie them," the leader said.

"Can we not?" Chris tried. "Feels hack."

"Silence," the young female said without looking his way.

The vines tightened—firm, not cruel. The hum got into Jack's bones, a note he could almost sing. He stood straight as they bound him. The air leaned against his spine like a dog at a knee.

The leader stopped close enough for Jack to see the white nicks on his knuckles. He spoke in the old tongue; this time the weight did more work than the words.

"You trespass. You wear their scent. You call what is not yours."

"You mean the air," Jack said, slow. Not defiant. Naming.

The nostrils flared. "Breath is Gaia's. She lends. She does not gift."

"If she lends it to me, there's a reason."

A ripple moved the guards like wind through wheat. The leader did not ripple. His eyes stayed on Jack. "Say you do not bear Olympus."

"We don't," Jack said. "If anything, they're hunting us too."

Not the claim, but its shape, eased the clearing a thumb-width. Chris felt it and took his shot.

"We're not here to bargain," he translated, careful. "We're here to learn. To keep our heads down and not die. And because the gods didn't invite centaurs to their new temple, and that screams 'you have opinions.'"

No one laughed. The leader's gaze slid to Chris and back. "You came seeking knowledge."

"Yes," Jack said. "And to offer one thing."

A head tilt—the smallest concession to a child who might surprise you. Silence. Permission.

"Humans are scared," Jack said. He kept his vowels simple so Chris could carry bones across. "Scared humans make bad choices. They'll hunt anything that doesn't fit the map. You don't want war with us; we don't want war with you. Olympus wants both—makes them look necessary."

A sound moved through the ring—hooves shifting, a slingstone ticking rim.

"So?" the leader asked.

"So ask for a line," Jack said. "A line we don't cross. Ask the governor and the Attorney General to call it a Reservation. Your woods. Your law under basic human law. No hunting. No trespass. No cameras without permission. Patrols stop at the trailhead and radio for consent. No god sets hoof here without your say-so. Make them put it in plain words. Make them sign it where everyone can see."

Chris didn't pretty the old vowels; he delivered them faithful, like bricks.

The camp breathed in. The leader's gaze sharpened to a point sharp enough to cut rope. "You presume to teach us borders."

"I presume to keep you alive," Jack said. "And keep us from becoming the excuse to burn your trees."

Somebody approved and swallowed it fast. The young female flicked an ear but said nothing.

Silence stretched. Yesterday, Jack would've babbled into it. Today he held. Maybe it was the rope's hum. Maybe the wind at his back, jaw set because he finally had.

The leader's stare changed—from what are you to how far will you go.

"Release them," he said.

The vines loosened.

Jack didn't move. The air put a palm between his shoulder blades: steady, now. He snapped his wrists and threw a short, clean pulse. The knots popped. Fibers parted. The braids fell like they'd decided to retire.

Spears dipped. Hooves scuffed. The young female's eyes lit—not respect so much as pleasure at a clean technique.

Jack planted his heel and drove it down. The wind answered with a low, circular shove that rolled dust and pressed every chest in the ring—firm, not breaking. The centaurs rocked back half a step. Just far enough to register that he could have made it worse and chose not to.

"Leader," Jack said, letting the air carry the word like a baton, "we need your elder. Now. We speak plain. He hears or not. But we're out of time."

The leader held his spear like a line he was tempted to cross. He glanced right.

The elder was already coming.

He moved like a hill that had traded lessons for patience. Hair the green-gray of lichen braided to his waist. Scars mapping his flank. He stopped with the authority of someone who could make archers blink just by choosing not to be impressed.

"Who taught you to ask for borders?" he said.

Chris inhaled, ready to translate. Jack raised a finger. "I've got it," he murmured. The old words came if he leaned into them, if he let the air show them to his ribs first and brain second.

"Nobody," Jack said. "We just like staying alive."

The elder studied his face like a carving done by a nervous apprentice. He switched to English without ceremony. "You propose a line."

"A truce," Jack said. "Call it a Reservation. Your woods. Your law. Human law at the edges—no hunting, no trespass, no drones, no tours. If anyone crosses, they ask. And the gods don't enter at all without your say-so."

"You think your governor will grant this."

"I think he likes cameras," Jack said. "Give him a podium and a pen and a chance to look like he's preventing a war? He'll sprint."

A snort from the young female. The elder didn't look. He watched Jack, then shifted to Chris. "You speak our words."

"Badly," Chris said. "He told me not to improvise."

"Wise," the elder said, which Jack chose to hear as shared credit.

"We're not Olympus," Jack said. "Not their priests. We don't even know what we are yet."

"Titans," someone breathed—shaped like a wound.

Jack let it sit. "Something woke when the sky ripped. We don't know why. We don't want war with you. Not with them either. We just don't want the world to burn." He wished, fiercely and for a beat, that Ryan was here to hear this.

"It burns already," the elder said. "Hospitals. Roads. Your people run with guns at shadows they do not understand."

"And yours grab ropes," Chris said, then lifted both palms when Jack cut him a look. "Word for word. He said 'burns.' I supplied 'hospitals' because… it does."

The elder's eyes slid toward the trees. "You saved one of ours," he said. "At the road of iron chariots. You made sky where there was none. You broke the trap and did not break the men."

"I wasn't trying to make a point," Jack said. "He was hurt. It was wrong."

The elder inclined his head a fraction. "We remember debts."

A rustle in the shade to the right. Two figures stepped in not on hooves: human. A man late thirties, mechanic's forearms, a face that knew long drives; a girl nearly fourteen with her hair braided back and eyes like wet mercury. The man's palm rested light on her shoulder. He wore grief the way working people wore wedding bands—part of him now, not going anywhere.

"We vouch," the man said, Jersey edges sanded by miles. "They're the ones. The air and the hawk."

Jack's stomach turned once. The RV behind the fence. The statues. The father and daughter who hadn't asked for any of it.

"You're the builder," Jack said.

The man's mouth tugged sideways. "Mike Donnelly," he said. "I make what I can imagine out of what's around." He flicked two fingers. A curl of dull clay shivered, stood, and walked off as a stubby-legged dog. "But I'm batting okay."

The girl's attention belonged elsewhere. A shallow pen beyond the stone held three creatures the size of motorcycles—lion bodies, eagle heads, wings tucked neat as knives. Griffins, no plaque required. Muscle and breath and the side-eye of a raptor deciding if you were food.

She lifted a hand. Light gathered between her fingers—not a beam, not heat, more like a pressure change deciding to be brightness. The nearest griffin leaned, purring with a tiger's engine. The girl dialed it down, then rolled her fingers and the brightness inverted—coin-sized absence, no color, no shadow, a tiny wound in the air. She let it pop with a soft glass-kiss and grinned; checked her dad's face for a speed limit.

Mike's jaw tightened. He didn't scold. He didn't have to. "She doesn't burn anything," he said, as if he'd heard Jack's fear before Jack had. "It's not heat. It's persuasion. Light listens to her. Hides when she says quiet."

The girl glanced at Jack, then at Chris. He wiggled fingers and let his face ripple—just a blink of a hawk beak, then back. She giggled. "Do me," she blurted, then flushed. "Not— You know."

"Kid," Chris said, hand to chest. "Boundaries."

"I'm Tessa," she said.

"Jack," he answered. "This is Chris."

196

"Sky and change," the elder said, as if setting pieces on a board from a war he knew too well. "And the fire-boy?"

"Safe," Jack said. "For now." He wanted it to be true so hard it almost qualified.

"We don't want in your war," Mike said. "I got one job and she's it." He jerked his chin at Tessa, then at the pen. "We help here. Fix things. Keep heads down. If you're smart, you'll do the same."

"We're trying," Jack said. "Lines buy time."

"You're asking how you reach me," Mike said, reading silence.

Jack huffed. "Kind of."

Mike ducked into the dented Class C RV with the faded swoosh and came back with a pair of scuffed Powerbeats. "You like these?"

"They're fine," Jack said. "If you need headphones, I can—"

"Watch." The cups softened in his hands, remembering ore and oil and sap. The band split and thinned into two identical single ear hooks, each with a tiny disc where a speaker had been.

He gave one to Jack. It was tool-warm, as if it had chosen him. "No power. No tower. Think and it listens. If I don't answer, I'm busy keeping her alive."

The air nosed the thing like a curious dog. Friend? it seemed to ask.

"Maybe," Jack thought, and felt it settle in his palm like we'll allow it.

"Thank you," he said.

Mike shrugged like a man who's learned not to refuse good sense. "I saw you by the road," he said. "Not many make the right move when no one's keeping score."

"We're not keeping score," Jack said. "We just... don't want to be the excuse."

"Good," the elder said. He shifted his weight. The camp mirrored him without thinking. "We will send word. We will choose place and hour. If your governor lies, if his law-man lies, the line will be drawn with hooves."

"We'll be there," Jack said.

"Also," the elder added, as if naming weather, "the gods are not merciful. Do not let the bright one find you alone."

"Apollo," Jack said, throat tight.

The elder didn't dignify the name. "The sun thinks it is owed sight."

The wind flinched—just a hair. Jack tasted the ghost of burnt metal from a Corolla hood.

They stayed while shadows lengthened and the clearing shifted temperature the way a room does when a door opens you can't see. The elder told history like a veteran telling what he wouldn't: when gods stopped playing king and Rome turned worship into parade routes; how Tartarus's walls had thinned like spring ice; how not all Titans were alike —some thought, some stone, some weather, some want—and how ground mattered. Root fully and you became what you had been. Or—if the flesh learned to drive—maybe not.

"Maybe," the elder said, letting the coin-word hang. "Maybe is a thin shield."

He showed clan marks cut into edge-trees—spirals, antlers, riverlines —boundaries agreed to in ritual. "Each spring we meet," he said. "Each clan sends one. We fight until one stands. For one year that clan speaks for all. Then we meet again. Blood remembers. So do rules."

"Smart," Jack said. "Keeps knives pointed the right way."

"Knives point where we agree," the elder said. "Until someone lies."

Jack's phone buzzed, insistent with the world. He didn't look.

When they turned to go, the young female stepped in with the knife that had opinions. She measured him like lumber. "If you come again," she said, "call the wind before you land. Let it ask first."

198

He nodded. "It already did."

A twitch at her mouth. Not a smile. A receipt.

"Good?" Jack asked Chris.

"Next time I fly myself," Chris said.

"Please don't."

He meant it as a joke; it came out worry. Chris caught it and didn't poke. "Copy that, Guy-Who-Yells-When-I-Deserve-It."

They lifted. Jack first, slow enough not to spook anyone. The air came up patient, an old friend obeying house rules. Beside him, Chris blurred and tightened into something sky-true—a falcon first, then more, wings widening until he was almost too big for the clearing, an albatross remembering it had once been a missile. Two pumps and he was gone.

The canopy fell away to the gravel lot like a curtain drop. Not one ranger truck now but three—and a white news van angled for drama, satellite dish craned like a metal sunflower. A cameraman in cargo shorts had a rig shouldered. A reporter in a blazer practiced her what we're seeing behind me voice to nobody.

Jack could have angled off. He almost did. The wind pressed his ribs —a question.

"Yeah," he said, and felt it brace.

He dropped hard enough to rattle the van. Gravel jumped. The cameraman swore and swung the lens. The reporter's sentence died and came back as, "Oh my God—oh my God—are you seeing this—"

Jack let the air ladder up his legs, a waist-high column lifting him an inch so he didn't have to pretend he wasn't floating. It tugged his hoodie and made his voice larger than his chest.

"Record," he said, and the wind carried the word into their headphones, the dish, the open sky. "Tell Trenton. Tell D.C. Ringwood is closed. Effective now."

The cameraman's eyes were saucers. The reporter found her mic like a life preserver. "Who—who are you?"

"Doesn't matter," Jack said. The air hummed at his calves, obedient engine. "The centaurs aren't leaving. They don't want a war. They want a line. A Reservation. You keep people out, people live. You break that line, a lot of folks don't go home."

"Are you—" the reporter's voice shook, then steadied as muscle memory kicked in. "Are you speaking for the creatures in the forest?"

"I'm speaking to whoever makes the calls," Jack said. "Governor. Attorney General. You want peace? Put it in writing. Cameras on. Plain words. No gods in their woods without permission. No hunters. No tours. No drones. No hero cosplay. Do that, and nobody has to die."

A gust tugged his hood like a reminder. He looked into the lens. "This is your only warning."

Her next question was already forming when the wind decided patience was over. It wrapped him and lifted. He let it.

The van shrank. The lot became a postage stamp. Chris arrowed in from the right as an albatross, massive and ridiculous, wingtips knifing air like a zipper. He leveled with Jack for a heartbeat—one bright eye saying you went full PR on live TV, huh?

Jack didn't answer out loud. The air did what it always did: steadied his edges and made him honest. The thrill was there—hot and stupid. The guilt was there, quieter, a knot in wood you keep sanding and can't erase.

"Fastest way to travel," he told the wind, because it felt less like talking to himself when he said it that way.

It pressed his ribs in what might have been agreement.

Behind them, the reporter's voice climbed toward live. The dish slewed skyward. Far off, thunder answered—faint, but listening.

Ahead, the forest broke into miles of August blue, and the world—gods, Titans, cops, cameras, rules—waited like a storm you smell long before the first flash.

CHAPTER 22

Mount Olympus—formerly the AMC at Rockaway—sounded like a foundry learning opera.

Marble ribs groaned as new galleries shouldered into existence. Bronze doors sang when they shut. Hephaestus' hammers kept time somewhere in the bowels, beating a rhythm old as sparks. Outside, the plaza swarmed: pilgrims in white, gawkers in denim, cops with ringed eyes trying to look like a plan. Drones circled until a priest pointed and the air itself refused them.

Zeus stood beneath the grand oculus where stadium light poured in like sacrament. Lightning walked his shoulders as if he were the hill it loved most. He'd had statues. He'd had hymns. But adoration then was a tide. This was an ocean, warm and close and his.

Athena approached, helmet tucked under an arm like a judge's book. "No leads," she said. "The air-wielder and the fire-thrower are ghosts. The shapeshifter—harder still. Surveillance fails near them. Audio decays."

"Decays?" Zeus' voice cracked the oculus with hairline fractures only Hephaestus would see. "My eye does not decay."

"That's not what I said." Athena didn't step back. She never did. "We are being… denied. Either by design or by accident. Sympathetic phenomena around nascent—"

"Say their name in my hall again," Zeus said, "and I'll teach you what sympathy feels like on the wrong end of a bolt."

Up in the galleries, priests murmured and hushed themselves, learning quickly when not to breathe. Hera watched from a balustrade, a perfect pillar carved in patience. She did not intervene. You didn't haul a wildfire off the couch while it was still deciding which wall it hated.

Hermes leaned on a column and smiled like a bartender watching a bad couple pick a fight in public. "We could tell the people," he said lightly, "that the hunt is going well. It usually is, until it isn't."

Zeus turned his head. Lightning lit his teeth. "Tell them what I tell you, messenger."

"Always," Hermes said. "Eventually."

***

At the far end of the nave, a knot of supplicants jostled at a cordon. Two stood taller than the rest—literally. Shoulders bulked under fresh-gilded plates; forearms looked poured rather than grown. Today they were Heroes; yesterday, clerks. Zeus liked that about mortals: you could make them into anything if you promised their name outlived them.

He beckoned with two fingers. They trotted forward, eager as dogs.

"You two," Zeus said. "Names."

"Ethan, my—lord," said the first, stumbling between old and new etiquette.

"Marisol," said the other, eyes bright and hard and already drunk on the weight she could lift.

"Hands," Zeus said.

They held them out. He set his palms across theirs. The charge leapt clean. Bones thickened; tendons braided; skin lacquered with a sheen that wasn't sweat. It went to the brain last—always last—so they could witness the remaking and call it gift.

Ethan's breath caught. He looked at his fists with a laugh he strangled into a sob. "I could— I could throw a car."

Marisol flexed. Her voice shook. "You just gave my father his last good day back."

Zeus nodded as if he had meant that. "Bring me rumors, sightings, whispers. Bring me anyone who praises Titans with breath unbroken by fear. Bring them bowed or bring their names nailed to our doors."

They knelt. People cheered. Phones lifted. When the two rose again, taller by an inch and heavier by a lifetime, they glowed—the kind of glow human eyes invent around power when they want to believe it has a color.

"Next," Zeus said.

Priests ushered four more—broad-chested, tearful, ready. He worked through them with the method of a butcher who has decided names make meat tender. By noon he had made ten new Heroes. By one, twenty. Each left with a chest plate that fit like a decision and greaves etched with a lightning motif subtle as a billboard. They formed in ranks along the steps, a living answer to the question nobody asked out loud:

What happens when gods run out of patience?

***

Outside, the plaza's noise shifted—a wave rolling across the crowd the way weather does. A priest trotted in, breathless. "News," he panted. "Ringwood State Park—closed. Order came down an hour ago. The Governor—on the steps with the Attorney General. They said—"

He faltered. Two days had taught him how to edit for Zeus.

"Say it," Zeus said.

"They said, 'We've heard the call for peace. We'll formalize a Centaur Reservation. We ask Olympus to respect the line. We'll protect both sides from escalation.'"

Lightning crackled off Zeus' jaw in a geometry you didn't see in nature. "Protect both sides."

Hera's fingers tightened on stone. Hermes' smile sharpened a millimeter.

"The air-boy," Athena said quietly. "He did that. Or started it." Not praise—indexing. "He is becoming a symbol. Symbols outrun swords."

"Then break the legs of his symbol," Zeus snarled. "Smash his name so fine it becomes dust and feeds my storms."

He stepped off the dais. Marble under his soles learned it might learn pain. He stalked past a cluster of newly minted Heroes. One—barely twenty—stood a hair too close to the storm's path and looked up with the terrified joy of a parishioner sure the sermon is for him.

Zeus' backhand came with almost no windup. Not rage—reflex: the sun swatting a gnat inside its own corona. His palm met the boy's chest with a sound like kitchen knives shaken in a drawer. The young Hero left the floor, struck a pillar, armor ringing, spine complaining aloud. He slid down, conscious, dented where men aren't.

Phones recorded. Somewhere, a livestream chat bloomed: what the hell / is that allowed / he just hit his own guy.

Hera made a small motion. Attendants hurried to collect the boy—gentle, like broken glass. Zeus did not look after him. Lightning crawled his shoulders and ate itself.

***

—High Point State Park, 2:41 PM. Eagles knifed through ridge thermals. A family picnic froze as a shadow slid across plastic cups. A girl in a Mets tee said, "Mom, look," and filmed myth with jelly fingers.

—The Parkway, Exit 135. Harpies rode the exhaust columns like switchblades. Commuters said dude and no way and then said nothing.

—Jersey City rooftop. A drone operator lined up Olympus against sunset. A priest on the plaza pointed. The air reached up and turned the

206

drone into an obedient rock. He caught it on reflex and pretended he meant to.

—Ringwood gatehouse. Rangers chained the lot, faces set to historic. A reporter in a blazer practiced, "What we're seeing behind me—" until the wind landed a sentence in her lap. She said it live.

"Send the eagles," Zeus said. "All of them. High. Low. The old ones who remember the taste of Titan air. Rake the state from Greenwood Lake to the ocean. Anything that looks like a symbol, tear it."

A bronze whistle appeared in Hermes' hand. He didn't blow. He didn't need to. The roofline darkened as if a storm had changed its mind and become feathers. Eagles—dozens, then hundreds—took wing from ledges cleverly disguised as architecture. They spiraled up past the oculus, banked, arrowed out toward forest and river and the hot flat line of the Parkway.

"Artemis," Zeus barked.

She was already moving, tall and severe, every inch a hunt. She vaulted onto a massive horse the color of storm driftwood and thundered down the grand stairs, bow unstrung because symbols mattered until they didn't. Five of her ride followed, hooves drumming a rhythm that said we don't get lost in a language older than asphalt.

"Aphrodite," he snapped, pointing like a general tired of pretending he wasn't a king. "Charm the mouths that doubt. Remind cameras how beautiful obedience looks."

Aphrodite smiled with the kind of patience reserved for men confident in things they haven't earned. She swung onto a white destrier and went. You didn't argue when Zeus handed you a stage.

"Apollo," Zeus said.

Sunlight's favorite son unfolded from shadow near a high column like an apology. Handsome as noon, eyes more tired than vanity allowed.

"You," Zeus said, voice flat, "do not move."

"My—"

"Do not," Zeus repeated. The word rang off the round room with the finality of a door that had learned how to slam. "You went eager and came back empty. The wind-boy breathes because you forgot we do not ask the sun to try. We ask it to be. Sit. Look penitent. Practice shame."

Apollo's jaw flexed. He sat at the base of a column, carefully—like a man who knew standing without permission would add a sin to the tally.

Hermes peeled off his column and drifted over. He didn't crouch. He leaned—coworker at an office who understood both politics and printer. "Rough morning," he said.

"He flew like a lie that thinks it's true," Apollo murmured.

"Air always had ideas above its station," Hermes said. "Mortals, lately, too."

"Zeus humiliates me before the bishops."

"Heroes," Hermes corrected, pleasant as weather. "But yes. He does that now. He calls it leadership. The crowd calls it thunder."

"He struck one," Apollo said.

"He did." Hermes' tone stayed silk. "It will edit poorly. It will also remind the faithful that faith is dangerous, which—between us—keeps them honest."

"When were you last night," Apollo asked, "when the wind-boy climbed his soapbox and the Governor found a pen?"

"Among the people," Hermes said. "Maintaining our image."

"Which image."

"The one that wins." He patted Apollo's shoulder with warmth so expertly fake it should've had a watermark. "Stay bright. They still love you. Even when you fall."

***

208

On the steps, a priest in flawless drape assured the BBC worship times had expanded: morning mass seven days a week; Thursdays and Saturdays added evenings; two on Sundays "to accommodate demand." He said mass because it tested well.

On the sidewalk, cardboard sermons went up: NO GODS, NO MASTERS; LINES, NOT LIGHTNING; RINGWOOD ISN'T FOR SALE; HUMANS AREN'T HOUNDS. Across the plaza, a counter-chorus chanted: ZEUS PROTECTS; HUNT THE TITANS; SAFER WITH THEM. Between them, a thin blue line of police did baton math: how many seconds do we let people talk before we become the story.

In a Newark electronics store window, every TV replayed the same clip under a chyron that grew bolder each hour: STATE FORMALIZES CENTAUR RESERVATION; OLYMPUS SILENT. A kid in a soccer kit pointed—"That's the guy"—and his mother tugged him along. You didn't point at symbols in public anymore. Not if you had errands.

Hephaestus raised a half-circle of seats opposite the altar—an amphitheater-in-miniature where Zeus could assemble enforcers and talk to them like a coach with bad news. The floor sweated heat. The walls learned to carry sound.

"Keystone," he grunted without looking, and a keystone considered its loyalties and obeyed. Sparks fell like orange snow. A junior priest, finally given a task that wasn't waving incense at phones, held a bucket and tried to look useful.

"Careful," Hera said mildly from the peristyle, "or you'll train them to love you only when you're winning."

"I am always winning," Zeus said.

"Of course," Hera said, and her of course cut smoother than lightning.

Ethan stumbled back into the hall at 3:06 PM, helmet dented, lip split. He knelt. "We found a nest," he panted. "Something like a nest. In the Pines. Not Titans. Something else."

"Bring me Titans," Zeus said. "Or bring me a new face. That one bores me."

Ethan flinched like a dog that had learned the slipper. Marisol, behind him, set a hand to his shoulder and squared without letting her face betray a thing. Zeus watched loyalty and misread it as choice.

(Under a cranberry bog's lip, a thing of reed and wire blinked a lens made of mica. It had learned the shape of men who came in boots. It had learned the whistle of arrows. It had not learned mercy. It would.)

***

Hermes drifted toward the middle distance reporters love and mapped the edit in his head: bully versus guardian; thunder versus breeze. Make the two sentences comfortable together, and you owned the hour.

Above, eagles returned in messy V's, each with a report in the language of heights. Feathers on marble told a story of empty barns, moving shadows, and a boy who bent air around himself like it was born wanting to be a friend.

Hermes pocketed the phrasing. Born wanting to be a friend. Words were weapons when well-fed.

He sauntered back to Apollo, who watched the floor like he wished it would open and swallow him with craft services. "Chin up," Hermes said, voice low. "When Zeus finally misses, the crowd will be starving for a different kind of light."

Apollo didn't answer. The thought had started; Hermes had made sure of it. Seeds didn't sprout in sunlight alone. Sometimes you planted them in shame and watered them with spite.

Aphrodite did three interviews in twenty minutes, unannounced. Safety is a kind of love, she said softly, and every producer leaned forward like plants toward a window. She blessed a toddler with a kiss that made the kid stop crying; a camera caught it; the clip looped into evening.

Artemis lifted three poachers out of Wharton State Forest by their collars and left them gently on a sheriff's hood with a note pinned in boar bristle: PAY YOUR FINES. BRING FRUIT. NOT BLOOD. The sheriff held the note up for the press and pretended he hadn't thought for half a second of keeping it.

"Hours of worship," priests painted on fresh signs. "Donation boxes here; Hero intake there." A pop-up table sold laurel wreaths that would wilt by bedtime. A QR code under a bust of Zeus channeled offerings to "Storm Relief."

In a back corridor, two High Priests coached three newer ones on phrases that tested well: partnership, stewardship, order. They took obedience off the list before cameras found it, then put it back on for internal memos.

Zeus set a foot on the low step and leaned into the crowd like a storm into a coastline. "Hear me," he said, and the air of the hall stiffened like attention come to heel. "I made you. I make you still. I gave you teeth that will not break on bone. Find me my quarry. Tear praise from Titan mouths. Drag me the boy who speaks to wind so I can teach him the difference between weather and will."

The Heroes roared because roaring plugs the hole where fear tries to climb. Cameras drank it in. Somewhere, a producer smiled and cut the cheer against Jack's Ringwood clip to make a neat arc you could sell between commercials.

Athena's voice didn't lift. "Artemis will narrow the map. Aphrodite will soften edges. Time helps."

"Time is a noose," Zeus said.

"For whom?" Hera murmured, so softly you could pretend she hadn't.

He turned his head as if the word not had insulted his mother.

211

In the cool near-dark where the gallery made shade like a promise, the young Hero Zeus had backhanded earlier sat propped against a pillar, rib strap fresh, eyes open, learning the lesson mortals always learned eventually: gods didn't have tempers. Gods were tempers.

Outside, a chant rose from the rope line, weak at first, then finding itself: "Lines, not lightning! Lines, not lightning!"

Zeus' head snapped toward the sound. Hermes smiled at absolutely nothing.

And weather changes.

CHAPTER 23

Jack woke to the kind of silence that only happens after something loud.

The air in his room still hummed—soft, guilty—like it remembered last night's argument between trees and wind and hadn't decided whose side it was on. Dream scraps clung to him: hoofbeats in rain, words made of breath and dirt. Morning light cut a scalpel line across his face.

He sat, swayed. The floorboards answered with a long, slow stretch.

"Chris?" he called.

No answer. Then: a blender, and a man absolutely butchering "Eye of the Tiger."

"False alarm," Jack muttered. "Just chaos."

He dragged on a hoodie and headed downstairs.

The kitchen was a war crime. Eggshells in the sink, batter on the cabinets, a chalky outline of flour like a raccoon had died dramatically. The table sagged under eggs, bacon, waffles, and a smoothie that had given up on liquidity.

Chris stood center stage, phone to ear, spatula in hand, wearing an apron Jack did not authorize: WORLD'S OKAYEST COOK.

"—yeah, Zen Gardens," Chris was saying. "Do you have any openings this week? No, I'm not depressed, I'm… untethered. Tuesday works. Do you validate parking?"

He clocked Jack and grinned. "Morning, sunshine. I made breakfast! And lunch. And possibly dinner, depending on your bravery."

Jack rubbed his temple. "Was that you making the floor shake at three a.m.?"

"Me?" Chris flipped a pancake like it owed him money. "Nah. That was Mother Nature reminding us she's single and angry."

"No—seriously. It felt like a quake. Whole house rattled."

"Dude, this is Jersey. If the ground shakes, the Turnpike ate dairy."

Jack sat, eyeing carnage. "For a man who doesn't eat half this, you cook like you're feeding a football team."

"Coping mechanism," Chris said, piling a mountain. "Either I process trauma, or I make twelve pounds of bacon. Guess which one wins."

"You're complicated."

"Therapists love me. Or will, if they can wedge me in before Wednesday."

The house gave a subtle, rolling shudder. Plates rattled. The blinds jittered.

Jack's breath hitched. The air went still around his ears—as if every molecule held itself polite.

"Okay," he said. "You felt that."

Chris frowned, listening. "Yeah. That's new."

Another tremor. Stronger. The pantry door ticked against its frame.

"That's not seismic," Jack said. "That's footsteps."

"Footsteps?"

"Big ones."

The crash that followed had opinions. The walls flexed. Somewhere outside, something screamed at a size no street was zoned for.

They ran for the door.

Rockaway looked like the apocalypse had stopped for coffee. Driveways heaved. Streetlights folded. A sinkhole yawned where the intersection had promised to be. Through dust and heat-shimmer, something moved.

At first: a landslide wearing a shape. Then it stood up.

Shoulders like ridgelines. Arms flexing like molten metal cooling. A head haloed in heat. Eyes—twin furnaces taking inventory.

Typhon.

Every myth had undersold it. He was walking chaos—lava and storm given body. His laugh was thunder deciding to be personal. Each step cracked the street like glass.

"Is that—" Chris started.

"Typhon," Jack said. "Destroyer of Olympus. Storm that ends worlds."

"Cool," Chris said. "Cool, cool, cool. I hate this."

Typhon scooped a car and pitched it fastball. It vaporized a garage. Screams rippled.

"That is close enough to my house," Chris said. "I'm calling the HOA."

Jack's pulse hammered. "We lead him out. Away from houses."

"Define we."

"You get Aaron," Jack said, already moving. "Warehouse job. The welder."

"The metal guy?"

"He's one of us. Get him."

"That's—like—ten miles."

"Then fly." Jack shoved a folded address into his palm.

"If I die, I'm haunting your smart fridge," Chris said, sprinting back inside.

215

Jack stepped into the yard. The air came to him like a friend laying hands on your shoulders.

"Alright," he told it. "Work."

He launched. The wind wrapped him in invisible braces. The updraft popped shingles on the eave. Below, Typhon turned his furnace eyes upward.

Jack didn't wait. He twisted air into a sling and hurled a parked sedan. It hit Typhon square and folded like a soda can.

The thing barely blinked. Then looked up. Their eyes met.

"Good," Jack whispered. "We have his attention."

Typhon roared. Windows gave up across the block.

He dragged a molten hand along pavement. The asphalt smoked and glassed.

Jack climbed. "Come on, barbecue."

Typhon followed, plowing through houses like cardboard displays. Heat rolled off him in waves; every swing threw tiles and mailboxes and street signs into ugly parabolas.

Jack wove through wreckage, steering the airflow, trying to herd Typhon's rage toward space. He needed open ground.

Behind him, laughter like thunder unbuttoning. "Run, little wind. Show me where you've hidden."

"Right here," Jack said between his teeth.

He cut low, then snapped up again, baiting the monster east. Suburbs started thinning—the industrial fringe, then the old quarry—raw, open, loud-proof.

Perfect.

Inside, Chris hit the hallway at a dead sprint, thumbed his phone. "Henley, Paterson—yep." Ping. "Fourteen miles southwest." He grabbed a jacket, shouldered through the door, flung the phone onto the lawn.

"I'll send a postcard!"

Bones flexed. Feathers erupted. The man inverted himself into a bird in a handful of violent seconds—falcon first, then bigger, wingspan spilling shadow across the street.

He kicked, tore air, and launched—power lines humming at the insult of his wake. Smoke coiled behind him where Typhon's footsteps had scorched the macadam. He banked south, bronze eyes narrowing to a single line of intent.

Below, Jack and the monster wrote bad music into the sky. Each Typhon swing left shockwaves that split clouds; each gust Jack threw hit molten hide and got swallowed, turned into brightness.

"Okay, big guy," Jack muttered, lungs burning, balance razor-thin. "Let's take this somewhere less residential."

Typhon ripped a slab of street and pitched it. Heat grazed Jack's shoulder. He ducked, cut a line toward the quarry.

"Good," Typhon rumbled, all teeth. "Don't die yet."

The last rooftops fell away. Open ground yawned. Exposed stone waited like an arena that had been patient too long.

Jack looked back. Fire bloomed in Typhon's chest. Something like wings—no, anti-wings, planes of heat—unfurled.

Typhon leapt.

The sky cracked. Pressure hit like a fist the size of a city. The wind screamed, trying to hold Jack steady.

Below, the shadow rose—massive, winged, impossible.

Jack twisted for the quarry and poured everything into speed. "Alright, mountain of anger," he said. "We finish this out there."

Typhon's laughter followed him into cloud.

And the chase began.

CHAPTER 24

The sky wasn't blue anymore.
It was on fire.

Jack had a sudden, stupid flash of the weather app on his phone —sunny, high of eighty-two—as if any of that had ever meant anything.

Jack tore through smoke where neighborhoods used to be. Below, a claw had raked the world—streets unzipped, trees peeled, roofs folded like bad origami. Every step Typhon took carved a hotter, deeper wound. Debris spiraled off him in a wake that didn't believe in physics.
Every crushed roof was somebody's kitchen table, somebody's baby photos, somebody's whole boring beautiful life, and Typhon was chewing through it like scenery.

Jack's shoulders burned. Vision feathered at the edges. Breathing felt like dragging wind through broken glass. He didn't stop.
If he stopped, the only thing between that thing and the rest of North Jersey was prayer and infrastructure, and neither had a great track record. The air held him up—angry, loyal—pressing its palms into his back like: keep moving.

"Come on," he rasped. "With me."

The wind tightened around him in reply and snapped toward the molten colossus.

Typhon leapt again, heat-wings unfurling. The noise split the sky. Lightning spidered through the smoke. The monster grinned through all of it—a storm wearing a face.
Jack had never felt smaller; all his borrowed power barely added up to a particularly annoying breeze against a walking extinction event.

"Run, little wind," he thundered. "Let the world see how fast it breaks."

Jack didn't answer. He dove.

He scissored through the smoke trail and skimmed the rooftops, dragging a pressure wake that kicked shingles. He carved a narrow corridor of calm through chaos, hunting open ground—field, quarry, anywhere without families.

Typhon didn't care about open ground. He wanted witnesses. He wanted ruin.
Gods wanted worship; this thing wanted headlines and casualty counts.

Jack cut left—barely cleared a water tower as Typhon's hand came down and atomized it. Steam took the street in a rushing white wall.

The taste of burned metal hit. He gagged, climbed, scanned: the highway a mile off, a bead-necklace of abandoned cars, some burning, some just stopped. People running—mother and kid, a man waving, the asphalt under him fracturing like thin ice.

Typhon's shadow covered them.

"NO!"

Jack snapped around and slammed both hands down. The shockwave hit like a concussive halo, shouldering civilians sideways and out of the kill zone. Typhon's foot came down where they had been. Pavement shattered.
The kid's scream dopplered in his ears even after the wind had already moved them, like his brain insisted on replaying the almost.

The roar rattled Jack's skull.

"You save them," Typhon growled, gravel swallowing lava. "I break them again."

His arm scythed. A tail of molten rock followed, clean and obscene. It hit Jack mid-chest.

The world flipped.

The wind screamed but didn't catch him in time. He pinwheeled into a half-collapsed apartment block. Dust and glass erupted.

He lay there, gasping copper.

The ceiling cracked in a long, thoughtful line. Outside, Typhon's laughter rolled like bad weather changing its mind.

Get up, the air whispered, thin.

He tried. The air pushed—bandaging him with pressure—muscles misfired, and he dropped to a knee.
For the first time since this started, he felt the edge of what the wind could do for him—like a friend bracing a door that was already splintering.

The floor jumped. Not a tremor. Something deeper—an old hinge turning.

Dust lifted. The air stopped shaking and began to listen.

"…what is that?" Jack croaked.

Typhon paused mid-prowl. His furnace-chest flickered.

The street split.

Thunder underwater. Asphalt peeled like paper; concrete buckled; the ground took a breath.

Then—BOOM.

A geyser of earth exploded. Something enormous rose from the wound—slow, deliberate, inevitable. Human in outline, made of rock and clay and root, moss veining the shoulders like old maps. Amber eyes glowed steady, unpanicked.

Typhon's grin hiccuped.

Jack's heart pinged his ribs. "No way…"
Some buried, half-drunk part of him had always hoped the others were theoretical.

The giant looked up. "Enough."

The voice was tectonic plates doing grammar.

Typhon bared too many teeth. "Another crawls out of dirt."

The newcomer stepped fully into light. Every movement was a mountain deciding yes.

"You burn the world," he said, measured. "I build it again."

Typhon laughed. "Then die with it."

He lunged.

They met halfway.

The shockwave pancaked porches, turned cars into punctuation, sent birds rioting out of trees miles away. Jack bounced off rubble again and almost checked out.

Through smoke: stone fist to furnace jaw; molten claws raking granite chest; dust plumes colliding with firebursts. Two natural disasters arguing.
Jack had grown up watching disaster movies on cable; none of them had prepared him for feeling the argument in his fillings.

Typhon struck fast and wild; the earth covered titan answered with good engineering—redirect, absorb, return. For every mountain raised, a valley collapsed. For every clean shot, Typhon paid with flame.

Jack dragged himself upright. The air shouldered under his arms, steadying.

"Okay," he whispered. "I'm here."

He reached. The air obeyed—spiraling up from the ruined streets, skinning heat off molten rivers, condensing ash into clumps. He knifed a focused gust into Typhon's flank—just enough to tilt the monster—two massive earth spires followed, double-hammering ribs.

The sound cracked horizon.

Typhon screamed. "You think you stand against me? You are dirt and whispers."

"And yet Gabriel holds," he said in the third person, calm.

They worked in stuttered unison: Jack threading gusts between Gabriel's strikes, stealing oxygen from flame fronts, starving heat a breath at a time. It was working—barely.

He wasn't giving commands; he was guessing, reacting, trusting that whatever woke up in them in Mahwah had synced their instincts without asking permission.

Typhon's fury freshened. "Three ages ago, I buried mountains for less insolence."

He clapped. Air detonated between his palms.

The shockfront erased Jack's balance. He cartwheeled, blind, the wind clawing him and just—just—finding purchase.

A sound cut through the thunder. Not god. Human.

Down-slope: the evacuation wasn't done. People still trapped; cars on their backs; a porch on a family; fire licking new edges.

The choice hit like a fist. Help them, or help the line.
Either way, people died; the only variable he controlled was which faces he'd see when he tried to sleep.

Decide, the air said, not unkind.

He dove.

He moved like triage made kinetic: gusts to douse, vacuums to starve flame, pressure to lift beams without turning them into bullets. The wind carried kids to clear asphalt, tucked debris away, threw up a curtain of grit to blind sparks. Screams turned to coughing. Coughing turned to breath.

He spun back. Gabriel was losing ground.

Typhon had him by the throat, molten claws carving shoulders. Stone glowed, glassing.

Jack threw both hands, poured everything. A tight tornado corkscrewed around Typhon's torso—not enough to throw, enough to slow.

Gabriel broke the grip and buried an elbow in furnace ribs. "Hold him."

"I'm trying," Jack yelled. "He's—pulling air from me—"

Typhon flexed and the vortex shattered.

"Air. Earth," he sneered. "Where is your Fire?"

The sky brightened at the rim. A streak—orange, shaky, stubborn.

For a heartbeat, Jack thought dawn was early. Then it landed.

Ryan—trembling, jaw set—stood on shattered asphalt. Flame leaked from his palms like embers remembering how.
Fear rode his shoulders, but he'd shown up anyway, and in Jack's new, messed-up scale that counted for more than most miracles.

"I said I was done," he called, voice a wire. "Guess I lied."

Jack grinned blood. "Glad you did."

Fire listened.

Ryan raised his hands. "Let's see how you like three-on-one."

Typhon laughed—and missed a beat.

They moved without a plan and exactly together:
—Gabriel heaved slabs like shields, then like boulders;
—Ryan laced them in running flame, turning each into a molten hammer;
—Jack drove from above, shaving air into steering vanes, knifing shots into chest, eyes, knees.

The world held its breath.

Typhon staggered. Dropped to one knee. His chest-cage glowed in cracked geometry.

"This," he hissed smoke, "changes nothing."

"Changes enough," Jack said.

The arrow sang past his shoulder so fast the air didn't have time to scream. Pain lit under his ribs—ice-burn where it grazed.

Another arrow shattered against Gabriel's chest in brilliant, divine shards.

"Step away from the monster," said a voice smooth and silver.

They turned.

Artemis stood along the rim, bow drawn, moonlight in her eyes. The driftwood war-horse stamped, eager for verbs.

Typhon laughed—a wet, delighted wreck. "You bring gods now?"

Artemis ignored him. Her gaze measured Jack like distance on a range. "The Titans will not rise again."

She loosed. Ryan rolled up a wall of flame. The arrow went through it hissing and burned cold anyway. Gabriel stepped in, shouldering the shot, stone flaring where divinity kissed it.

"Behind me," the Earth Titan rumbled.

Artemis nocked with surgical calm. "You should have stayed buried."

Typhon pushed to his feet behind her, grinning like a cliff learning to smile. "Let them kill each other."

Jack rose, dizzy. The air around him trembled—out of sync with his pulse. He could feel the overlap now: fire making room for wind; wind respecting stone; stone absorbing hurt and returning weight. He lifted his palms—open.

"You already missed," he said, breath ragged.

Artemis' eyes narrowed—offended more by the sentence than the dodge.

The air exploded between them.

Not a blast outward, a hard birth of pressure—a wall that ate the next arrow and pulled dust into a single, ugly curtain. Fire smeared. Shouts blurred.

When it cleared, Jack was gone—slingshot skyward, the wind cradling him like contraband.

Typhon roared and launched after, hurling himself back into cloud.

225

The chase relit the sky.

Artemis lowered the bow and watched the streak of windlight fade north—head cocked, expression changing shape.

"Found you," she murmured to the air, which carried the words away like gossip.

Down in the quarry, Gabriel exhaled a sound like relief refusing to be obvious. Ryan's hands shook; he pressed them together until the embers listened. Sirens found courage and moved in. Somewhere in the city, a hundred screens replayed Jack's hover over a news van with a new chyron: QUARRY BATTLE: TITANS VS. MONSTER VS. GOD.

High above, Typhon closed, laughter raw. "I smelled you, wind-boy. Sun-brother brought me your rag—the one he tore. Sweat, blood, cheap soap. A perfect thread."

Jack's stomach turned. Apollo—on the hood, on the highway— fingers like daylight, yanking him through the windshield—the hoodie ripping under his grip. He saw the torn edge. He remembered not caring. He cared now.

Typhon's grin widened. "And the one who opened my door sent him. Tell the sky thank you when you fall."

Jack didn't ask who. He couldn't afford the truth yet.
Part of him already knew exactly which god wore that betrayal, and he shoved the knowledge into a box labeled later and locked it with pure denial.

He let the wind harden around his chest instead and pointed himself at the cold blue that promised space.

"Come take it," he said, and the air answered with a wordless, loyal shove.

The storm chased the boy who talked to weather, and every camera in the state went hunting for sky.

CHAPTER 25

Typhon's roar collapsed into a grind—less triumph now, more machinery overheating. The bowl had become a throat, the quarry a mouth that wanted what they were shoving toward it. Heat bled off him in thick sheets—less wing, more wounded engine.

Jack Callahan felt the air vibrate through his bones, not as sound but as pressure, as if the atmosphere itself were bracing for whatever came next. Every breath tasted of iron and scorched stone. Fear tried to root in his chest and found no soil to hold.

"Again," Jack said, because simple words hold better under pressure. The wind liked simple. It braced his back like hands on a kid's bike, carried him when his legs went to static, nudged his ribs when he forgot which way gravity had agreed to point for this second.

Aaron Whitlock's river—hijacked hydrants, burst mains, quarry seep pulled from cracked seams—narrowed to wire and knifed into every opening Gabriel made. Artemis's bow sketched facts. Chris ping-ponged between bravado and good decisions like the human embodiment of a coin flip that kept landing on edge.

Aaron's jaw was locked tight, teeth grinding as if pain were something he could chew through. Water obeyed him now, but it still remembered being heavy, remembered drowning before it learned how to carve.

"Push," Artemis called, not quite an order now. "Hard."

They did. Stone surged, water seized, air slammed; an arrow turned into a decision; and Typhon's heels kissed the cracked lip. The draft from below tugged at Jack's hair, at the hem of his torn hoodie, at whatever part of him believed in lowest points.

The monster backpedaled once, twice—then set himself stubbornly at the brink, holes in him glowing where Gabriel and Aaron had argued the light out. Steam screamed where Aaron's cuts met heat; the plume flashed white, then vanished as Typhon drank it for anger.

"Down," Jack whispered to the wind—not pleading, telling. The wind loved being told. It gathered in a column thin as cable and rammed under Typhon's jaw.

For a half-breath, gravity remembered whose side it was on.

A streak cut the lip. Gold. White. Intent. Apollo arrived like a conclusion.

Jack felt the temperature change before he saw the light—felt the air recoil, felt the wind tighten like a living thing recognizing a predator it had learned to fear.

He wasn't even supposed to be here. Zeus had leashed him. Gods chew leashes.

He dropped in at an angle that would shoulder a mountain, palm full of boiled sunlight, bored expression bending toward satisfied. Artemis's head snapped his direction in a way that had sibling carved under every syllable of her name.

"Apollo—" she warned.

Typhon swung. Clumsy for a god-monster; catastrophic for anything made of meat and rules. The molten forearm caught Artemis's horse at a perfect wrong moment and hurled it. The goddess kicked free in midair and landed in a three-point crouch on the rim, a bright slash across her hip where heat had kissed too long.

Jack felt the impact in his teeth. He'd never watched a god bleed before. He hated how mortal it looked.

Apollo didn't break stride. He aimed to finish—to add the flourish gods like to pretend isn't for the crowd. Gabriel aimed too—lower, meaner, where stone could matter most.

The spear the earth titan dragged out of nothing wasn't elegant. It was bedrock and shale, anger and leverage. He drove it with both arms, whole body behind it, and it hit true—through heat-soft armor into the banked glow under Typhon's ribs. The pit inhaled.

The spear took Typhon. It also shaved Apollo.

Light came away like blood.

Everything happened on top of everything else. Typhon howled, flung backward, finally—inches tipping into feet tipping into the old geometry that eats arrogance. Apollo twisted, surprise cracking clean across the face he wore when the sun pretended it never set. Artemis drew and fired at something Jack didn't even see, because he was busy not falling into the pit with the rest of his plan.

The quarry gulped. Typhon went down in a single obscene syllable of heat. The draft stuttered. The mouth shut. The world tried, briefly, to remember quiet.

Jack hung there, chest hitching, wind under him like a friend who refuses to admit you're heavy. His vision haloed black at the edges and then came back smaller. Chris sagged on the rim, two arms not sure where to go, the other two remembering they were mantis clubs and then thinking better of it. Aaron's hands shook; his river trembled around his fingers like a muscle post-cramp, a lace of water still threading the air before it lost its orders and fell. Gabriel took half a step like a house settling after a storm, the spear still an ugly thought in his hands.

Jack felt the weight of what they'd done press in after the adrenaline receded. The silence wasn't relief—it was shock catching up.

Apollo floated where momentum left him—twenty feet out, a hand to his ribs where light leaked not in blood but in resentment. He hadn't fallen. Gods don't, not where anybody can point.

Artemis straightened slowly; unstrung stillness slid back into her spine. The slash across her hip pulsed like a bad star. She clocked it, filed it under "later," ignored it.

Jack didn't have room for more data. His brain wanted to catalogue and justify; his body wanted to curl up in the silence and pretend it was over.

He said, because not saying something felt like letting the monster crawl back, "We're done."

"Leave," Gabriel added, a rock deciding the argument. He turned toward the slope, already subtracting himself from this sky.

Chris looked between Jack and the pit and Apollo and did the thing he does when there are too many options: he swore quietly, reverently, like a man in a church he didn't choose. "Yeah," he said. "We're done."

They weren't.

A helicopter nosed in, cautious and greedy. The camera under its belly blinked live in a language that didn't need text. Along the rim, people who should've been three zip codes away climbed trucks and roofs and the wrong side of barricades, phones held high like electric offerings. Sirens braided the horizon. The smell of cooked pavement made lies easier to believe.

Jack felt the eyes before he saw the lenses. The weight of being seen pressed heavier than any gravity had all day.

Apollo's mouth recovered first. Not a smile—something worse. The line men wear when they're about to rename a thing in public and dare you to correct them. He tried on expressions like suits; the one that fit had a sermon stitched in.

Artemis crossed to him in three unshowy steps and lifted her free hand. "Hold," she said—low, to the only person on earth that command might still work on as a concept.

He looked at her hand, then at the scuff Gabriel had left. Heat had the indecency to flicker along the cut like it was entertaining. He looked past her at Jack and Aaron and Chris and the empty space where a stone man had been, and in that glance Jack saw a story aligning behind the god's teeth.

Jack felt it too—the shift from battle to narrative, from consequence to control.

She touched his forearm the way she had in older wars, when pulling him back meant keeping villages alive. It startled him; gods aren't used to being handled as if their bodies are parts, not metaphors. "Don't," she said. Soft. Sharp.

Her mouth thinned. The wound pulsed again. Minutes or faith. She picked faith.

She turned from Apollo and faced Jack, not closing distance, just bridging attention. "Eleven," she said.

"Still not following," Jack admitted—brain down to three shelves, all full of wind.

"Twelve pillars," she said. "Always. One lost—Zeus's lesson. You're at least three and a half." Her gaze skated over Chris, over Aaron, lingered on the empty place in the dirt. "Find the rest faster than they find you."

"We were eating pancakes," Jack said stupidly, like chronology was a defense.

"Yes," she said. A sound that might have grown up to be a laugh didn't. "You are very mortal about it."

Jack felt suddenly, violently mortal.

Air shoved Jack's jaw—go, anxious. He nodded—to the wind, to the reality where he wasn't in charge of any of this except his own ankles.

He slid an arm around Aaron's chest. "We're out."

Aaron nodded, a short, exhausted hinge. The river sagged from his fingers and puddled, confused without orders.

Chris gathered himself. "I'll make sure nobody follows," he offered —which could mean he'd turn into a hawk and scream at reporters or a rhinoceros and spook a news van. With Chris, you accepted vibe as strategy.

Gabriel was already leaving properly. He walked to a place in the floor that agreed with him and stepped in. Stone met shin, knee, thigh, hip—swallowed him with all the ceremony of a tide erasing footprints. You don't wave when you're a continent receding from a shoreline.

Jack and Aaron lifted. The wind took them with that eager strain that always felt like it wanted to do more than physics allowed. Chris sprinted, feathers ripping out of his shoulders in a hurry, and punched sky as a falcon ragged from bad decisions and better timing.

They'd made it fifteen yards when Artemis flinched.

It wasn't theatrical. It wasn't goddess-dramatic. It was small, cellular —a body saying "no" to a bright, terrible exposure. She put a hand to her side and blood—divine in the disappointing way that still looks like blood—darkened her fingers.

Jack stalled midair without meaning to. The wind protested—move —but he hung for one unwise heartbeat to see if a god needed help from a man who was barely a plan with elbows.

Apollo saw the flinch. Saw the extra bend in her knees. The imagined fact assembled itself quickly and cleanly: *They did this to you. They will do worse. I will fix the narrative.*

He turned his palm. Light bloomed—tidy weapon of a man who likes his killing elegant.

Artemis moved faster than the light. She stepped inside his reach and pressed her hand—blood and all—flat to his chest. "Listen," she said, and the word landed like a commandment in the ribs. "You will tell Zeus this ends. The mortals we fought with are not monsters. They held. They steered the doom away from children. End your crusade."

Apollo's jaw flexed like it wanted to object on principle. She didn't give him the opening.

"Jack said Typhon hunted him," she continued, barely above a whisper—no arrow of voice now, just a thin, true blade. "Do your geometry, brother. For the monster to fix on one scent, it had to be given that scent." Jack saw highway glass; Apollo's hand in his hoodie; the rip —his shirt torn clean in the roof fight—becoming a thread. "You went to Tartarus. You put your hands on the bells. They never sang." Her eyes, fever-bright and ice-cold, cut small. "Why?"

Jack didn't breathe. Aaron's grip found his forearm and tested bones. Chris flared above and banked—instincts torn between get out and *this seems like crucial tea.*

Apollo's face did something Jack had never seen it do: it broke and then fixed without the glue of shame. "I—"

A shadow of Typhon lingered on the lip—broken rib cage of lava glass and cooled fury. Jagged things protruded—teeth that had never belonged to anything living.

Apollo reached without looking. Fingers closed around a shard of cooled light, one of the claws the monster had planted in the world. He lifted it as if fate had left him a handle.

Artemis saw the thought before he finished thinking it. "Don't," she said again, not command, not threat—plea.

He drove the shard in.

It wasn't a god-killing blow; that's not how gods die. It was the end of a conversation. The point slid under her ribs at the angle a physician would choose if the prescription were silence. Her eyes widened once—surprise, not fear. She looked at him the way only someone who knows you back to your first story can: clearly, without mercy.

"Coward," she said, almost gently.

Her body loosened in a way that made human sense, then came apart in a way no coffin understands. Light unstitched from skin. Form thinned. The steed she'd ridden dissolved into a smear of cold brightness and then into nothing. Where a goddess had been was a lifting of air, a taste of iron and sap, a pressure drop that made Jack's ears pop like weather turning wrong.

A man on the rim saw everything.

He shouldn't have been there. Bandage around his head. Hardware-store hammer on a leather loop. The look of someone who'd come to help after and arrived into *during.* Blood dried in a fan across one cheek. Phone broken in his pocket. He held the hammer like maybe he could fix the street with it.

He made a small sound when the goddess came apart.

The helicopter dipped and breathed dust across the rim; the moment that mattered smeared into grit and heat-wobble.

Apollo's head turned. Not god-fast. Human-fast. The way you turn when a cat knocks something off a shelf in a quiet kitchen.

He stepped through settling dust—one, two, three precise strides—took the hammer from the man's limp hand with the courtesy of returning a loan, and put it across the witness's skull with a motion so economical it could've been instructional.

The man went down in a heap of wrong angles. Breathing stopped trying, then forgot to be offended.

Jack moved without asking his legs. The wind yanked him backward so hard his teeth clicked. It wasn't protecting him from the god; it was protecting him from the next bad sentence he was about to be in on camera.

The helicopter lowered a hair. The belly-cam found Jack, then Aaron, then the falcon's ragged line. Zoom. Focus. Archive. Headlines pre-writing themselves in fonts designed for outrage and relief.

"Faces," Aaron hissed, remembering for both of them. A last ribbon of water clung to his wrist like the saddest bracelet. "They've got our—"

"Go," Jack said, equal parts order and apology.

They went.

Gabriel was gone like cliffs are gone the day after a storm. Chris rode dirty thermals up past the chopper's appetite and dove to drag it wide in a hawk's ugly, brave game of chicken. It worked for three seconds—which is a lifetime on live TV.

Jack took Aaron by the ribs and let the wind do the lifting, because the wind loved doing—loved being the thing when he had no more left to be. The quarry fell away in a long exhale of heat. The rim shrank to a rumor. A god's voice rose through rotor chop and August: clear, cold, authored.

234

"People of this city," Apollo said.

Jack didn't look back. He didn't have to. The wind gossiped at his ear, a friend bringing news he didn't want.

"You have seen the Titan scourge," Apollo continued, every syllable a polished stone. "Masquerading as men. Bringing monsters. Bringing death. My sister—" a beat so precise it deserved a metronome "—has fallen in their chaos. This ends."

Chris flapped into their slipstream, feathers missing, eyes too bright. "Fun update," he said, almost calm. "We are officially the villains of the week."

"Shut up," Aaron said, not unkind.

Jack didn't speak. The air made decisions for him—right here, up there, over that fence—like a GPS very sure of the route when the driver was a cough with legs. He had the stupid impulse to thank it and did. Pride was a luxury. Oxygen wasn't.

Below, streets tried to remember their jobs. Fire trucks bullied intersections. A kid on a BMX stared up with his mouth open, forgetful of traffic. A woman on a porch cried into both hands without knowing exactly why yet. The town felt like the moment before an apology that hasn't decided who's giving it.

"Quiet," Jack said to the two beings who could hear him and the one that could only love him. "We go quiet. We find the others. We stop being available to the story he's telling."

"Copy," Aaron said. He kept his eyes on the horizon like it might let him take another step if he respected its line.

Chris huffed something that might be a laugh, might be a sob, and settled on neither. "Cool," he rasped. "I'll… not post about it."

Jack almost smiled and hated that he did. It hurt. He let it.

A line of roof peaks became a ribbon under them. The quarry's heat thinned to normal summer. The chopper peeled off, seduced by cleanup and blood. The wind pressed Jack's jaw, a nudge: left, then up. There. Trees. Shadows. Away.

He trusted it. The air hadn't lied to him yet—anyway not on purpose. He angled toward the dark stripe of woods where maps grow less sure of themselves.

Behind them, Apollo's last words chased the skyline.

"This is your warning," the god said. "The sun sees you."

Of course it does, Jack thought. The sun sees everything. It's what it misses on purpose that matters. Good. Then see everything.

He didn't say it out loud. He saved his breath for flying and for whatever waited under the trees, where the wind sounded less like applause and more like advice.

They slipped into shade. Heat loosened its grip. The air didn't relax; it tucked closer, possessive, as if to say: *mine*.

"Not leader," Jack reminded it—and himself and whoever else needed to hear a man argue with oxygen. "Just... trying not to be the reason people die."

The wind didn't understand the difference. It simply carried him, because that's what it loved, and because for the first time that day there was somewhere to go that wasn't straight into a god's sentence.

They vanished into the green. The quarry kept smoking. The news found angles. The story the sun preferred took shape in a hundred living rooms and a million mouths.

On a ruined rim that used to be a place where kids drank warm beer and told each other they were braver than they felt, a god stood over a cooling stain that had been a sister and a man. He stared at the hammer in his hand like it had told him a joke he did not enjoy.

He lifted his face to the helicopter. He didn't have to practice his expression. It had been waiting for him his whole life.

He opened his mouth and the world, hungry for certainty, ate whatever he gave it.

Far from that, wind pressed Jack's cheek with a dog's insistent touch.

Stay with me, it said without words.

"I'm not going anywhere," Jack answered, and wished it meant what he wanted it to mean.

CHAPTER 26

By morning, Olympus found a microphone. Night bled into sirens, the quarry still breathed heat through police tape, and a dozen "exclusive sources" had already rehearsed their grief.

On the Parthenon steps, flags learned to hold still for cameras; priests polished gold that didn't need polishing; a podium appeared as if marble grew lecterns. The gods didn't sleep. They staged. The whole scene felt less like faith and more like a press junket for the end of the world.

The chyron did what chyrons do: turned calamity into a crawl.
ZEUS: TITANS WALK AMONG YOU. TURN THEM IN.
ARTEMIS FALLS. OLYMPUS VOWS JUSTICE.

The anchor's voice was velvet over razors. The live shot wobbled, steadied, found the Parthenon steps—flags stiff, microphones bunched like flowers no one wanted to smell. Zeus stood at the podium and did not so much speak as occur. Even through the screen, even in living rooms that still smelled like coffee and panic, his presence pressed on lungs.

"Mortals," he said, and every camera mic fought not to distort. "You have welcomed back what we buried. You have given shelter to old crimes wearing your faces. Titans."

He tasted the word like a hunter tasting wind. The pause afterward invited every living room to fill in its own nightmare.

"They are not men. They wear men. Find them. Find them all. Bring them to me."

He didn't thank anyone. Thunder doesn't do closing statements. He pivoted and launched—out over the crowd, tearing the air into a white seam. Athena turned sharply and followed; Ares hot behind; Demeter a green weight among the gray. Hermes glanced once at the cameras with

239

his little cat-smile and vanished down a side corridor like a rumor. Apollo did not step out at all. Somewhere, someone at home rewound, squinting, counting which gods had shown up and which hadn't.

The anchor swallowed. The chyron got louder.

They flew home like a storm trying to beat itself to the horizon. The news cycle tried to keep up and mostly failed, tripping over words like unprecedented and historic until they tasted like cardboard.

Zeus took the sky in strides. He accelerated on principle. The others ate his wake and lied to their muscles about catching up. Clouds fattened under them and ripped on their shins. The world below tried not to look up and failed, because when gods move like that the ground remembers what fear is for. Dogs howled. Traffic slowed for no reason anyone could name.

Behind them, the quarry cooled—a new mouth in the world sucking heat, police tape a necklace for a throat too big to wear one. Helicopters orbited like eager flies. Every orbit carved a little deeper groove into the story people would tell each other later about where they were when the monster fell.

Mount Olympus—the new one, the one that made architecture magazines and infuriated zoning boards—reared from the city like a memory made arrogant. They hit the upper terrace so hard the marble asked for a union.

Zeus didn't land so much as crash into standing. He paced the colonnade like a caged animal that thinks the bars are a suggestion. The air around him popped and snapped—the sound electricity makes when it wants witnesses. Columns and priests both tried to stay out of his radius.

"Where were you?" he demanded of a question that didn't have a person to wear it. "Where were we?"

No one answered because some rhetorical questions have teeth. Even the eagles on their perches shifted, suddenly interested in the floor.

Ares planted his spear and leaned forward into violence like it was a friend. "Say the word," he said, almost tender. "We level the county. We plow the cities. We salt the fields. They'll hand us their monsters in baskets."

He sounded like a man offering to take out the trash.

"If you salt the fields," Athena said dryly, not bothering to sigh, "the mortals die and our worship drops precipitously. You can't draft a famine."

She spoke like she was reading off a spreadsheet, but her hand was tight on her spear, white at the knuckles.

"They killed Artemis," Zeus snapped.

"No," Athena said—careful. "Artemis died on their battlefield. The difference will matter if you want allies who can read."

"They killed Artemis," he repeated, louder—because volume is a kind of truth when you're a king.

His hands flexed; lightning licked his knuckles. He looked toward the shadowed arch that led deeper into the temple, as if expecting his daughter to stalk in with a fresh wound and a complaint about mortal incompetence. The emptiness held. That was the thing about immortals: when one of them wasn't where they belonged, the absence rang louder than any alarm.

"Enough," Zeus decided—a word that means: the consequences you feared are now chores. "We do not wait. We do not soothe. We do not reassure shopkeepers. We hunt."

He pointed—first at the Heroes standing along the wall like expensive statues that might suddenly decide to be useful. Men and women dragged out of crosswalks and boardrooms and gyms and offered god-adjacent power like a promotion you can't refuse. Gold at chest and greaves; eyes already unfocused the way zealots' eyes get: half-rapture, half-exhausted.

"Bring me fifty more," Zeus snarled. "A hundred. The strong. The devout. The ones who look good bleeding in front of cameras. Bless them with speed and strength and a voice that carries to microphones."

241

A priest flinched and bowed. "Lord, the blessings—"

"—are mine to give," Zeus said, and the priest's hair tried to stand up inside his hood. The smell of ozone turned every breath into a reminder of who owned the sky.

He turned on the older ones, the names with gravity. "Eagles," he snapped, and two enormous birds tore free of shadow as if shadow were a curtain pretending to be real. "Scour. Bring me the smell of air twisted wrong, water moving with will, earth that rises, fire that thinks."

Ares bared his teeth in what passes for a grin. "Good," he said. "At last."

"Aphrodite," Zeus said, not looking at her, because looking means weighing and he didn't want to weigh. "You ride. Smile at them when they bring us names. They break faster when beauty thanks them."

Her lips curved without warmth. "As you like." She was already rehearsing which version of pity played best on camera.

"Demeter, calm their granaries. Panics starve. We need them hungry for the right reasons." A flick toward Athena—one concession spat like a seed. "We'll make a list."

"I'll deliver a taxonomy of threat that won't make the senate throw up," Athena said. "And a script your Heroes can memorize."

"Make it short," he growled. "They're not known for paragraphs."

He whirled then—sudden, vicious—because movement keeps grief from finding men like him. His hand lashed out and backhanded the nearest Hero—a square-shouldered SWAT-captain type who'd made a midlife bargain.

The human flew—over a bench, into a column, armor singing the one note metal sings when it remembers it's softer than god. He slid to the floor in a gold clatter and stayed there.

Zeus' chest sawed. "Stay out of my radius," he said to everyone and no one. "Or I forget what you're for."

Ares liked that. Ares likes when "you" and "for" are neighbors.

Athena's mouth thinned. She didn't move. Her stillness said more than any argument would have survived.

"Go," Zeus snapped. "Find me the ones who wear Titans. Bring them alive." He paused long enough to pretend mercy. "If possible."

He launched again, punctuation by exit. Columns threw their shadows aside.

The hall remembered thunder for a long time after. Even after the sound faded, tension hung in the air like residual static.

Apollo still hadn't stepped into the white of the terrace. He lingered in the cool belly of Olympus, where old rituals feel like rules instead of theater. He stood in a side aisle with his palms flat to stone as if touch could cool the place inside him that light had burned. The stone didn't cool him, but it gave his shaking fingers something that wouldn't break.

Hermes' laugh arrived from nowhere and everywhere. "Press conferences not your color?" he asked, leaning in the doorway as if he'd grown there by accident.

"Not yours, either," Apollo murmured.

"On the contrary," Hermes said. "Every color is mine, if the lighting's good."

"Leave me."

"Of course," Hermes said, and left—air already busy convincing itself there had never been anyone in it at all.

The quiet had weight for one breath.

Then the quiet got colder.

"Apollo," said the voice that never raises itself and never needs to.

Hades isn't a silhouette; silhouettes suggest romance. He's the outline a candle throws just before it eats the wick. He stepped out of rafter shadow and the rafter felt relieved.

"Lord of Lies," Apollo said without heat.

"Please," Hades said. "That title belongs elsewhere in this house."

He looked at the sun-god the way a physician looks at fever, the way an accountant looks at a ledger with an interesting error. "You brought it back," he said.

"I contained it," Apollo said, reflex snapping the words into place. "We needed a crisis. We needed need."

"You wanted a stage," Hades said, almost kind.

"Do not belittle—"

"Never. I'm here to make you big."

Apollo's laugh was raw. "Now?"

"Especially now." Hades stepped close enough that Apollo could smell cold iron and wet stone—the honest scents of underground. "Your father is wind and temper. He will thrash. He will bless fools. He will spill human blood to build a throne he already sits on. When the crowds tire of thunder, they will want light." A beat. "Clean light."

"He must not know," Apollo said, the *he* heavy as a mountain. "If Zeus—"

"Zeus expects you to be a knife. He will scold you for being a scalpel. Let him. Meanwhile—" Hades tilted his head, kindly as a wolf. "You cut the wire to the bell. Tartarus stirred and no alarm sounded. You told it when to wake, and you told which monster where to find daylight."

Apollo's mouth tried denial and failed. Confession remembered it was strategy. "They weren't supposed to escape first."

"They?" Hades asked, so softly Apollo had to lean toward the quiet. "Or she?"

Apollo's gaze jerked—automatic—to the place where Artemis wasn't.

"Regret," Hades observed, almost interested. "That's new for you."

"She hesitated," Apollo said, too quickly, as if speed could make it a reason. "She thought."

"She thought," Hades agreed. "Which is why she was my favorite hunter." A gentle scalpel of truth: "You silenced a witness."

Apollo flinched like struck. "I—"

"You did," Hades said—simple truth, kinder than any excuse. "And now the story is yours. Tell it loudly. Constantly. Fill the sky with it. 'Titans killed Artemis.' Make it a song children can sing."

Apollo's hand found his ribs—the place a stone spike had tasted ichor. He pressed until it hurt like atonement. "And if I fail?"

"Then Zeus learns what you did," Hades said pleasantly. "And kills you, and I get you back." A courtly shrug. "There are no bad outcomes for me."

"Comforting."

"You want comfort? Ask Demeter. You want a plan?" He fanned invisible cards. "Here it is."

He laid it out in slices, each cut leaving Apollo lighter, hollowed, ready to be filled.

"At noon you go to the marble. You tell them you saw Titans lose control. You tell them they lured a monster to suburbia to test themselves. You tell them Artemis fell defending their children. You promise to carry her memory into the hunt. You do not cry; you crack. Once. Tastefully."

Apollo swallowed instruction and let it bed down with shame. "And the others?"

"Send your eagles. Let your father bless Heroes until their joints shatter. Show the world a frenzy. Be the cool center of it. When monsters show—because monsters love parades—arrive second and finish the shot." A final card: "When you need a door opened—"

"Tartarus," Apollo whispered.

"I will be where doors are," Hades said.

Their eyes met until both men had decided what they were after.

"Grieve for your sister," Hades added, turning back to absence, as if grief were a tool to pry open softer men. "It sells well."

When he was gone, the temperature found its way back to mortal winter from whatever season kingdoms keep in their bones.

Apollo exhaled a breath he hadn't told himself he was holding. He straightened his tunic, wiped nothing from his mouth with the back of his hand, and built his face for the noon broadcast—one muscle at a time, a craftsman at a wheel. Somewhere under the work, the guilt sat stubborn and bright.

He started toward the light.

On the mortal channel, the panel had multiplied—one general, one pastor, one pundit whose brand was being certain. They argued from the same script in different fonts while the lower third did cartwheels. Every sentence circled the same hole: who's to blame, and how loudly.

When the camera cut to the Parthenon again, Apollo stepped into frame as if the marble had been waiting for him to make sense of it. He put both hands on the lectern and made himself smaller, the way men do when they intend to be trusted. The sun gleamed off his shoulders like product placement.

"My sister," he said, and the microphones leaned forward because grief is good television. He didn't cry. He cracked, once, like Hades told him, and a million living rooms nodded as if they recognized the sound.

"They brought a monster to your homes," he said. "We will bring them to justice."

He didn't look up when the crowd shouted. He waited until silence returned to him like a favor, then left the podium without rushing, because rushing is for the guilty.

Behind him, Hermes crossed the terrace carrying a body that didn't cast a shadow because it was built out of light that had forgotten how.

Cameras zoomed. Headlines wrote themselves. A thousand viewers reached for tissues without knowing if they believed any of it.

***

Meanwhile, a TV glowed in Aaron Whitlock's living room, throwing god-pale squares across a couch where Jack tried to pretend his spine and the cushion were friends. He watched Apollo make promises and tried not to inventory the places his ribs throbbed in sync with the words. Every time the god said Titans, Jack felt like the screen was pointing at him.

Chris stuffed containers into a cooler like he was solving a puzzle about love and leftovers. "If no one's staying here," he said for the third time, softer now, embarrassed by how domestic apocalypse could be, "the food's going to go bad."

He needed something normal to hold, even if it was Tupperware.

Aaron paced; half a glass of water wound itself into a spiral every time he forgot to hold still. The water responded to his nerves before his mind did.

Jack pushed to sitting. The air did that loyal thing—hand under ribs, the I've got you, idiot of a friend that learned his weight by catching him too many times. He nodded at Aaron, at Chris with the cooler and the guilt.

"Thank you," he said. "We might've stopped something worse."

He didn't add: For now. He didn't have to. It was in the room with them.

The TV disagreed and took a poll.

Onscreen, Zeus' decree re-ran as B-roll: Find them. Find them all. Bring them to me. The city wore it like new weather: sirens braided with church bells, drones buzzing past police helicopters—competent locust cosplay. Text chains lit like Christmas: where did you see them last; was that a hawk or a guy named Chris; are we supposed to clap for the sun or hide from it.

***

For now, the camera kissed Apollo's face and the world decided—again, too quickly—what story it preferred to survive.

Olympus worked.

Priests trotted, arms full of shining. Ares' laughter haunted a far hall like a bad song you know by heart. Demeter's hands moved grain on maps the way weather crosses plains. Athena stabbed a stylus into a tablet, drafting structure out of fury. The whole mountain thrummed like a machine pretending to be holy.

Zeus stood alone at the balustrade and looked down on a city that had relearned his name. His fists clenched until the bones in his wrists felt like lightning rods. He told himself the tightness in his chest was rage trying to escape and not grief with nowhere to go. Admitting the latter would mean accepting something had been taken from him that he couldn't strike.

Soft footfalls. "Father," Apollo said, voice pitched to practical. "Orders?"

Zeus didn't turn. "Bring me the one who wears air," he said. "Bring me the water. Bring me the stone. We'll root the rest by their holes."

He might have said *Bring me the one who killed my daughter*, but the sentence broke its ankle on truth and fell.

Apollo bowed in a gesture so perfect it looked mirror-taught. "As you wish."

"And Apollo," Zeus said, finally turning, finally letting his eyes do the inventory they'd avoided—ribs, scorch, the place where a spike had said hello. He lifted a hand, not tender, not cruel; just enough to suggest something biological had made itself heard beneath the god. "Do not fail me again."

Apollo let the words enter him like nails through wood and made no sound at all. Inside, another voice—quieter, uglier—whispered that he already had.

When he was gone, Hermes drifted from a column's shade, all easy angles and the kind of smile that lets people tell on themselves.

"Your son looks… purposeful," he murmured.

"My son looks like a god," Zeus said, which is a very different sentence.

Hermes' eyes slid toward the corridors where cold lives. "Careful with him," he said too pleasantly. "Some animals kick hardest when you saddle them after a good run."

Zeus didn't answer. Hermes' sentences arrive with tripwire you discover with your shin. He leaned out over the city and imagined it already compliant, already chanting, already hunting on his behalf.

"Open season," he said quietly, to the weather, to himself, to a world that learned to mistake instruction for prophecy.

And the eagles leapt from the parapet like knives with wings, and the Heroes lifted their gold and practiced looking righteous, and the humans below opened browsers and doors and eyes, hungry for a name to hand to thunder. Parents pulled kids inside a little earlier than usual and pretended it was about homework.

Somewhere a falcon cut the sky in half and refused the camera.
Somewhere a river twitched because someone had woken thirsty and dangerous.
Somewhere the ground rolled its shoulders like a wrestler before the bell.

And above it all, the sun polished its expression for noon, while a shadow deeper than weather stood where doors keep the world honest and smiled, because every plan, eventually, comes home.

249

CHAPTER 27

A week had passed since the Olympus press conference.

Jack packed like a man trying not to look like a man leaving.

Jeans. Two hoodies (one sacrificial). The black compression shirt that made his ribs stop voting on every breath—the replacement for the one Apollo had torn open on the highway. Three pairs of socks that did not match and never would. The beat-up running shoes that had seen better sidewalks. Travel-sized toothpaste because he remained, against all evidence, civilized. The blue notebook with nothing but names and questions and arrows between the two. One photograph—him and his parents on a boardwalk, hair chaos, fries between them, the Atlantic pretending to be harmless behind them.

He hovered on each item a second longer than he meant to, as if putting it in the bag meant admitting there was a version of his life that didn't fit inside these walls anymore.

Everything went into the old rucksack he'd sworn he would replace three years ago. The zipper rasped—and held. Good enough.

On the kitchen table, his PTO request lay printed and signed like a permission slip for adulthood. Three weeks. Family. Colorado. The HR portal had replied *Enjoy!* with a stock gif of mountains that looked like default wallpaper on a computer he was currently too wanted to open.

Colorado was a lie that sounded like a postcard. That was the point. He'd text Aaron and Chris the truth. He'd tell his parents some of it and let the rest go unsaid, the way families do when loving is heavier than honest.

He rolled his shoulders. Everything hurt in ways he could list and ways he couldn't. When he exhaled, the air caught the weight under his ribs and held it the way it had started to: like a good dog refusing to let you fall just because you're acting proud. The sensation had become familiar enough that the idea of *not* having it there scared him more than the gods did.

"Stay with me," he said softly, felt ridiculous, didn't care.

The house felt smaller since helicopters learned the ZIP code. The TV was muted but still shouting—a panel of people who had never been chased by a god explaining what to do if you met one at a light. A red ticker promised DEVELOPING. A drone replayed the quarry as if reverence were a deprecated feature. The crater looked like someone had tried to punch a hole in New Jersey and only half-succeeded.

He signed the PTO form again, because ink felt like control, and set it beside the sedimentary mail: coupons, cable offers, a brochure for *Zen Gardens: Wellness That Fits Your Busy Life!*—funnier if he hadn't heard Chris try to book an appointment during breakfast yesterday.

The front door opened. His parents came in on the same breath.

"Jack?" his mother called, then stopped in the doorway and did a small inventory with her eyes that usually ended up more accurate than a lie deserved. "Going somewhere?"

He stood. "Three weeks of PTO. I've been hoarding it like a dragon. Figured I'd use it before HR turns it into a tote bag."

His mother set a tote on the table with the thump of someone determined to mother through catastrophe. Tupperware bulged. The whole bag smelled like oregano and hope. She put a palm on the form— not to stop him, just to feel it.

"That was you," she said, skipping the part where euphemisms waste everyone's time. She didn't say *the air guy.* She didn't need to. Eye contact did the specificity.

Jack's mouth failed to be helpful. The house was quiet except for the TV pretending to be civilized. A chair found the back of his knees and he sat with less grace than he wanted.

"I don't know what I am," he said, truth scraping on the way out. "But I know I'm not a bad guy."

Silence has shapes. This one had corners and a couch in it. It also had years of scraped knees, school pickup lines, and small forgiven screwups stacked in the corners like evidence.

His dad's jaw worked side to side like a bolt with the wrong socket. "You're our son," he said finally, as if filing the only paperwork that mattered. "Which generally means you're an idiot with a decent heart."

His mom didn't smile. She lifted her hand until it hovered over his head, decided he was too old to pat, and squeezed his shoulder instead. "Those boys on TV," she said, glancing at the screen and refusing its narrative with her whole posture, "the ones chasing you while the world burns—they don't know you. I do. Whoever returned the cash to the police station and told people to stop dying in a park? That sounds like you."

He let the air warm the back of his neck, steadying. "I'll keep it that way," he said.

"You better," she said, and only then straightened his hoodie like that could keep knives out. The gesture was pointless against gods, perfect against fear.

He hugged her. He hugged his dad. Hugged. Not nods, not back-claps, the real thing, because leaving without the real thing is a sin even atheists understand.

"I should—" he said, making the gesture people make when they have to leave and don't want to.

"Go," his dad said, nodding like a man who'd been practicing for a week. "Before your mother thinks of more sandwiches."

His mother swiped a handful of mail into a neat stack. Order is a religion when power is a rumor. A lighthouse postcard slid loose and skated toward the edge. Jack shifted; magnets clattered; a family photo dominoed into the sink.

"Jack, can I toss this?" his mom asked, pinching the postcard like a bill. "You know I hate clutter."

"Which one?"

"This. The lighthouse. It's been up here for weeks. Pretty, but—"

He rescued it. Cape May Lighthouse, dead-center in a blue that tried too hard. He'd seen it in a hundred beach stores and never once thought it might mean anything.

He flipped it, ready to roll his eyes at *Wish you were here.*

There was no wish. There was his name.

Jack, thanks for finding us.

No return address. The postmark was a gray kiss. Beneath the line: names—first names only—stacked in cramped, trying-to-be-casual script.

Aaron	Lena	Gabriel	Mike
Ryan	Tessa	Iris	Grace
Christina	Jude	~~Sarah~~	

…and *Jack* again, an arrow from the top line anchoring it to the sentence as if the writer wanted to point: this was your mess, but also your miracle.

The kitchen tilted. He steadied a hand on the table. The air leaned in like a friend at a rail.

His mother watched his face change and hovered her palm again. "What is it?"

"It's…" The postcard had been on their fridge while he negotiated with centaurs and lost arguments with gods. On their fridge while a monster turned suburbs into a cautionary tale. He remembered smudging the corner with ziti grease last week and never once flipping it, because lighthouses were for Instagram, not maps.

His eyes found the third name.

"Christina," he read, and barked a laugh that startled everyone including himself. "Oh, come on. His legal name is Christina. Of course it is. Of course."

He called Chris immediately. The lock screen was still the dumb hawk selfie because you either lean into ridiculousness or it leans on you. The line grabbed fast, eager.

"Yo," Chris said, no hello, just life—car interior hum and a half-remembered song under his breath. "If this is about the cooler, I left two lasagnas and a ziti. Don't politicize it."

"Christina," Jack said, and enjoyed the exact silence it earned.

A beat. Then wounded dignity: "In fairness, it's a family name. Also spelled like several saints, which feels on brand for me."

"Someone mailed a postcard to my house." Jack slid the card under the kitchen light. "These names," he said, keeping the edge mostly out of his voice. "This is a list."

"Gabriel," Jack said, touching the fourth name. "He… saved us."

"He saved us and terrified me," Chris said cheerfully. "So: probably one of ours."

"Ours? What is this, a reunion? Thanks for the trauma, see you at Applebee's?"

"Buddy," Chris said, pride slipping under the sarcasm, "you got us together without trying. Now we try on purpose."

Jack looked at his parents—faces doing impossible math: pride, fear, groceries. He turned the postcard back. The lighthouse looked less harmless now. A thing that pointed, not just posed.

"I need to go," he told Chris. "We need to go. Artemis said twelve pillars. One lost. That leaves eleven."

"Eleven," Chris echoed, low whistle. "That's a lot of group chats."

"Start small. Aaron first. Ryan, if he'll have us. Gabriel… if he wants to be found."

"Copy." A pause, then softer: "For the record? If anyone calls me Christina on the road, I will body-shift into their high school gym coach and make them do burpees."

"Your legal name is Christina," Jack said gently. "This is the hill I'm dying on."

"On brand for the Air guy," Chris said, then—quieter—"You good?"

Jack looked around because it was easier than looking in. The fridge grin of magnets. The lighthouse turned map. The tote of food as strategy. The PTO form trying to make a life into a plan. His parents watching him like watching could be protection.

"I don't know," he said—either bravest or laziest, depending on your angle. "But I'm going to do the right thing until I figure out what I am."

"Good plan," Chris said. "I'm ten minutes out."

"Of where?"

"Your house."

"You could have led with that."

"I wanted the postcard beat to land," Chris said, smug. "It's called theater."

"Of course it is," Jack said, and hung up before his mouth forgave him for liking this idiot so much.

He turned the card for his parents, let them read what destiny looked like in pen. His mother's eyes moved line to line. She touched his name and lifted her finger quickly, as if ink could smudge fate.

"Don't be a hero," she said, which in their house meant: be decent, pick your battles, come home.

"I'm not," he said. "We're just going to find the rest of us before Zeus does."

His dad huffed—laugh or surrender. "Take cash," he said, already fishing his wallet, because fathers bless with bills when gods are stingy with miracles. "And the emergency card. And the pepper spray, even if I'm not convinced it works on mythology."

His mom cupped his face. "Text me every morning. Don't make me hunt a god just to file a missing persons report."

256

He nodded and rested his forehead against hers for a breath. The house exhaled with them. For a second he wanted to shove the bag under the bed and pretend the world had no idea what his name was.

A horn beeped outside. Twice. Unsubtle. Chris.

Jack slung the pack. He slid the postcard into the notebook—a talisman with a ZIP code. He pinned the PTO form under a crab magnet with a smile that had seen things. He kissed his mother's cheek. He clapped his dad's shoulder and didn't pretend it was enough.

"I'll bring the Tupperware back," he said at the door.

"You better," his mother said, "or I'll join your little Titan road trip and embarrass you in front of your friends."

He grinned and stepped into weather.

Chris's car idled crooked in the driveway, trunk open to reveal what you find under a rock labeled *Bachelor in a Crisis*: blankets, protein bars, three shirts, a cooler, duct tape, and bolt cutters with opinions. Chris leaned against the fender in a hoodie that read WALLINGTON: IT'S A TOWN and sunglasses that cost either eight dollars or a midlife crisis.

He raised his arms. "Christina reporting for duty," he said, resigned, then laughed because it was funnier if he owned it.

"Don't make me get it embroidered," Jack said, climbing in.

"We could do jackets," Chris said. "Hawk on the sleeve. A wind emoji no one over thirty understands—"

"We are over thirty," Jack said.

"Depressing," Chris said, and pulled away.

The neighborhood had learned to pretend normal since the news trucks left for shinier panic. A kid on a scooter hadn't been told he was mortal. A woman jogged with a dog who had definitely seen more gods than he'd signed up for. A sprinkler ticked a fence, misaligned and committed to it.

Jack looked up. The sky was a clean sheet of afternoon, the kind of blue that made optimism feel almost reasonable. The air pressed the window like it didn't want to be left behind.

"I know," he murmured. "You're coming."

Chris glanced over. "Talking to your boyfriend again?"

"Don't be jealous," Jack said. "He carries me."

"Same," Chris said.

They turned the corner. The road offered itself like a long patient ribbon. Jack set the postcard on the dash, lighthouse forward for any curious cop. On the back, the names felt like coordinates he couldn't see yet.

He tapped them. "Aaron. Ryan. Gabriel."

"Iris," Chris added. "Lena. Tessa. Grace. Jude. Sarah. Mike. And Christina."

"Shut up."

They hit the Parkway and the world opened the way only highways do: promise disguised as asphalt. The radio stayed off. For a minute the only sound was tires and the small quiet between two people who no longer had to sell their friendship to themselves.

After a mile, Chris cleared his throat. "Game plan?"

"Start obvious," Jack said. "Aaron at home. Ryan at campus—if he hasn't bolted. The father and daughter by Ringwood if the centaurs tolerate visitors. Gabriel... we don't find him. He finds us. He seems like the earth type."

"Pun," Chris said, approving. Then, more serious than he sounded: "And after?"

Jack watched the horizon lean toward the west like a hint. "After we find the rest, we decide what we are."

"That sounds like work."

"It is." He put his palm to the dashboard and felt the air under the hood, over the hood, threading the vents, rushing the road. It pressed back, ready. "But it beats waiting to be hunted."

"Facts," Chris said. "Also, I brought snacks."

"Saint Christina provides," Jack said.

"You're never letting this go."

"Not even a little."

The city unspooled. The Meadowlands widened. Bridges held the car like a promise. Jack's phone nudged a news alert and he didn't look. Somewhere ahead, a hawk carved a clean line and then decided it didn't belong in metaphors and banked away.

Jack leaned his head back for one heartbeat. The cabin hummed. The wind on the car sounded like a drum skin pulled just right—tension that doesn't snap because it knows what it's for. For the first time in days, his chest expanded without feeling like an apology.

He opened his eyes. The postcard slid a little, stopped, pointing, as if it had chosen a compass.

"Okay," he said to Chris, to the names, to the day. "Let's go find our people."

"Copy," Chris said, fingers light on the wheel in a way that meant he could become ten different creatures before the next exit and none of them would be a coward. "West? South? Up?"

"Anywhere there's wind," Jack said, because he could finally hear the map that wasn't on paper. He cracked the window two inches. The air reached in like a friend leaning across a bar to tell a secret.

The road bent. The car took the curve. The names waited like a chorus that hadn't learned its harmony yet.

Behind them, Olympus polished its armor and sharpened its reasons. Ahead, a country full of lighthouses waited to be more than postcards.

The wind leaned forward like it knew the way.

ABOUT THE AUTHOR

Stories arrive when they're ready, and this one waited until Brian Bychek was too stubborn not to finish it.

Brian grew up in North Jersey and still calls it home with his wife and their three young children — an adventurous son and twin daughters who ensure the house is always loud, joyful, and slightly chaotic. Somewhere between diaper changes, midnight bottles, and stolen quiet hours, this book came to life.

Before all of that, Brian fought and beat testicular cancer that had spread through his abdomen and both lungs. Writing became therapy during chemo in 2019, when he finally picked up the notes he'd been sketching since 2015 — a story that once stretched from Canada to Argentina but eventually found its heart where his always has been: North Jersey.

Tartarus Falls started as a "what if" on the Atlantic coast… and became something personal — a story about power, belief, and the thin line between gods, monsters, and the people who stand up anyway.